The Scavengers and the Stray

Rae Ryan

Contents

To everyone who lost family and friends by being their authentic selves: may the family you find exceed your wildest dreams.

***

and to mom and dad

Chapter 1

Jump Scares are for the Bears

F loating untethered in the inky nothingness that was both time and space, its vastness expanding around her, Sierra had to remember that gargantuan explosions of light and matter created all this emptiness. From such great destruction, a universe was born to cradle new forms of life, including her own.

Staring at the desiccated remains of a world-builder, its black hull barely visible against the consuming darkness, except where it blocked the light of distant stars like an ominous shadow, Sierra struggled to imagine how such destruction could foster life. The lights from their ship snapped on, illuminating a pathetically small portion of the giant vessel. The ship's name was stenciled on the hull in bold, gleaming white letters: *The Hope of Trappist.* Sierra would never understand the ubiquitous and formulaic naming convention of *The (noun) of (destination)* favored by megacorporations like Omnia.

This one had been a long hauler, slow moving, its people in cryo for the glacial journey to another, better planet in a previously untraversed galaxy. The journey from its origin to a gate was only weeks, but once through the gate, it would have taken decades to travel to the inert planet they would have brought to life. After establishing the colony, they would have constructed a new gate, with the help of raw-metal printers on-board the ship, expanding the gate system and making travel to the nascent planet far faster.

Like a sleeping whale, the listing vessel had a blunted nose that coned outward to hold all the equipment needed to start a new colony. Sierra expected the pirates who'd disabled the ship had likely scrapped all the expensive assets—loaders, air reclaimers, batteries, bots, and 3D printers—and its passengers either sold or killed. Sometimes pirates left the people alive, but space was vast, and they'd run out of food, air, or power long before trash collectors like herself were sent to clean up the remains.

A large asteroid framed the *Hope of Trappist,* and its pumice-like body drew the ship in with its meager gravity for a slow but eventual collision. Sierra guessed that was where the pirates had lain in wait to disable and gut the *Hope.* She took in the wide gash along the dull black hull where the pirates had used a concentrated laser beam to slash through the engine, stopping the ship in its tracks and disabling its defenses. It likely destroyed the backup generators that powered the cryo containers in an emergency. She very much hoped she was wrong, and the hundreds of passengers aboard blissfully slept through the ship's disemboweling.

The gash had torn the Omnia Corp emblem in two. Like a crooked smile, the jagged edges folded in on themselves and revealed the decimated interior, vomiting bits of metal and equipment into space. Sierra watched a beat-up water reclaimer spin aimlessly outside the hull. It would fetch a good trade value if it was intact.

Everything was quiet. Space was eerie like that, trapping sounds into oblivion. The inside of her clunky mechanized suit was a different story; the humanoid machine she piloted felt more like working in a coat closet with a narrow porthole to space, if that coat closet smelled like the inside of a gym locker. A signal light beeped on her console, reminding her that air wasn't free, and she had three hours before she'd need to return to the tow ship for a refill or she'd be sucking on fumes and turning blue.

The mech was an absolute beater and a far cry from those Sierra had maintained and operated in her former life as a mech operator in the heart-hammering world of the Galactic Battle Mechs Federation. If she had her way, this purgatory of one dead-end job after another with crappy rented mechs would come to a close ASAP, and she'd return to the mech battle arena.

Until then, she'd lay into Hazel for giving her another piece of shit mech, if she survived long enough. For the price Hazel charged, the mechs should have a decent air cooler; instead, it was hot as balls in the tiny compartment, and the smell of her own sweat made Sierra want to gag when combined with the smell of ozone and fried electrical components. The mech wasn't advanced enough for a three-sixty view, limiting her information access to a console installed below the viewing bubble and her sleeve. The flexible screen of the sleeve wrapped around her forearm and currently displayed information on the external environment collected and transmitted from their ship.

"*What a waste,*" Tovi said over the crackling line.

His equally beat-up mech sidled up beside her. The suit was about three times the size of a person, with the cockpit inside the mech's chest as sleek and conforming as a refrigerator, typical of the cheap mechs used for trash removal.

"*I can barely move in this thing,*" Tovi said. "*Next time, we need to ask for an oversized suit.*"

"Sorry, buddy. I asked, but they were fresh out. As long as we make a profit on this job, we should have the credits to get Archy up and running, then no more rental mechs for us," Sierra said.

She didn't know how the lanky six-foot-five Praxian managed inside the tin can. His chest was strapped to the chair and bright yellow kinetic gloves covered the thick, roughened skin of his arms, an evolutionary trait meant to protect him from his home world's intense radiation and frequent sandstorms. According to Tovi, his reddish-brown skin was common of midlatitude Praxians. Sierra took his word for it, since he was one of the few Praxians she'd ever met.

Sierra had a pair of maroon gloves she'd picked up the last time they'd been on station. They'd both pored over the newest innovations in kinetic mech products, splurging a little too much and getting an earful from Cecil. They couldn't afford the battle mechs on display, no matter how much they daydreamed about joining the mech battle circuit, so they settled for the more affordable accessories. Their threadbare credit situation didn't stop them from flipping through the well-worn pages of Iz's scrapbook detailing their dream battle mech and its ideal accessories in a riotous montage of creatively clipped images and specification lists, accented by Iz's all caps comments and hand-drawn hearts.

"You think anyone is alive in there?" Tovi asked.

"According to the flight log, it had nearly a hundred and fifty people on board. The pirates hit the engine, but I can't see if they destroyed the backup." She pulled up the overhead display and turned on the thermal camera. It shuttered, then crapped out. "Goddammit," she said, thumping on the side of the camera hanging over her head. "This fucking piece of shit machine can kiss my ass."

"Is it just me or have these gotten worse lately?" Tovi asked.

"It's not just you. I don't think Hazel bothers to maintain these death traps." The camera flickered on, picking up the intense cold of the ship. "Nothing on the thermal. We'll have to get inside to see more."

"What's left on our shopping list?"

"We need another hydraulic for the left leg, any sensors we can find, and most importantly, an air reclaimer." Cecil's raspy voice piped through their mechs; he'd overheard their conversation from the safety of the flight deck.

"I wouldn't mind a better propulsion system. The one we have needs too much to get it working right," Tovi said.

"Fingers crossed they left us something to work with. Cecil, can you release the bots?" Sierra asked over the intercom.

"Sure thing."

She glanced back at their ship, the *Who Wants to Know*, a medium-sized tow vessel they'd cobbled together like Frankenstein's monster to make their precious baby. It didn't look like much to outsiders, but they'd put more than their fair share of blood into its conception. The central body was tubular-shaped, housing the flight deck to the front, then coning outward to encompass the twin two-story compartments on either side. The top level housed the sleeping chambers, galley, and medical, while the cargo bay and engine room were on the lower level. Winging to either side were two ion engines they'd salvaged from a more powerful ship that had suffered an electrical fire, putting it out of commission, but the engines were in good shape. Iz had wanted to give it a singular paint job, but in deference to the less than legal activity they dabbled in, it was better to remain anonymous. They went so far as consistently changing the ship's name to avoid unwanted attention from sentients with long memories.

A dozen bots detached from an external chamber Sierra had welded onto the ship, unfurling to the size of a large dog and then hovering next to the ship for a moment before lights flashed on and the bots booted up. The bots spread out, stretching a canopy big enough to enclose three mechs between them; ion engines propelled them forward in sync to sift all the bits and bobs of shredded metal and plastic floating around the hull and capturing it in the canopy.

Sierra moved her hands in front of her chest, and the gloves signaled the mech to move forward. After a bewildering pause, it jerked forward as its ion engine sputtered to life. Tovi followed as she made her way to the docking hatch, not willing to risk getting snagged on the hole the pirates had made on the side of the ship—not with the bucket of bolts they were working with. Once they'd forced the door and were inside the ship, Sierra could see the extensive damage. Wires hung from the ceiling and pieces of metal were pulled back with the surgical precision of a jackhammer, revealing where the pirates had taken out the reserve batteries. Sierra engaged the magnets on the mech's feet, and she jolted as the mech glommed onto the floor.

"*It was a smash and grab,*" Tovi said, assessing the damage. "*They cut everything of worth out of the ship. I'm going to release the peepers.*"

Sierra watched as a hatch opened on the back of Tovi's mech and two dozen finger-sized bots popped out, their tiny ion engines revving up and a single camera eye emitting light off the front. Iz, bored and with nothing else to paint at their fingertips, had given each one a unique paint design and a name like naval ships of Earth Before. One painted like a shark with comically large teeth whizzed by her on its way to investigate the rest of the ship.

"*Comms are coming through,*" Cecil said. "*Our peepers are peeping.*"

"Jeepers, creepers, where'd you get those peepers?" Sierra said in a low, menacing voice.

"That's creepy every time you do it," Tovi said.

She smiled to herself. "What are friends for?"

"You have a real twisted idea of friendship," Cecil said.

"Honestly, it's Iz's fault," Sierra said. Iz had been singing it the entire time they'd been painting the things, and now the song lived, rent free, in her brain.

"Don't blame me! I didn't sing it like I was about to skin someone alive. Plus, Tovi was the one who made me watch the movie," Iz's voice said over the line.

"We're headed to the cryo-center. See if anyone's alive. I'm not seeing any warm bodies on the cam," Sierra said. Even in the cold cryo-beds, Sierra should see the heat from the machines.

They moved through the hall into the command center. It was a large room and the center of ship activity. But more importantly, once the ship was in orbit around a barren moon or exoplanet, it acted as a space station until the terraforming was complete. Sierra counted ten stations ringing the circular room, all in disarray. Tovi picked through the command center until he came to a toppled metal beam blocking the way into the next chamber. He rotated the pincer arms of his mech, leaned down, and grabbed the beam, closing the pincers around it and moving it to the side.

"I'm going to strip the control station," Sierra said. "I'll be right behind you."

"Roger." Tovi disappeared out of the command center.

Sierra flicked a command to articulate fine rotating saw blades from each of her mech arms. The blades cut into the control panel on either end, and she maneuvered them to cut a large rectangle out of the control panel, then retracted the blades and used her pincers to remove the panel. Inside was a mess of wires and circuit boards. She switched out her arm attachments to finer hand controls, separated the panels from the wires, and stored them in a compartment near her chest.

Pirates tended to go for big-ticket items. They couldn't feasibly take everything of worth, and hardware was tough to move on the market, but components like motherboards and circuit boards were worth a lot to Omnia, the company who owned the ship and paid for its salvage. Sierra moved efficiently through the command room, cutting up the place like a butcher and stowing anything of value.

"Made it to the cryo-center. Lights out in here," Tovi said, his voice tight.

"Shit," Sierra said and let out a disappointed sigh. In the ten years they'd been doing this, they'd only found people alive twice. And yet, they couldn't help but get their hopes up every time.

"Going to seal it up."

"Bingo!" Cecil said over the line. *"Found us an air reclaimer, level four, block seven. In good shape from the looks of it."*

A shock of excitement ran through Sierra. "Finally. I'm on my way."

"I'll be there when I'm done with this," Tovi said, mirroring her excitement.

Sierra picked her way through the ship. After clearing the main areas, the ship almost appeared normal. The hallways were undisturbed, the only sound coming from her mech's magnetized feet clunking against the metal floor and reverberating into her mech. She could imagine the people who should have been walking these halls decades from now, settling down on a new planet, full of hope.

For her and her crew, hope took the form of scrap parts they smuggled off the ship and sold on the underground retail market, the only way they could pull a decent profit from these salvage jobs. She found the life support system in an auxiliary maintenance block the pirates must have missed. The room was small, housing a set of emergency equipment, likely for the head of maintenance in case of fire or pressure loss, and a floor-to-ceiling row of lockers.

"Jackpot," she said over the line. She deployed a bag from her on-board storage and maneuvered her mech to place everything she could in the bag. "Tovi, it's got everything we need to get the mech going." She was buzzing with excitement. They could finally get Archy up and running, and that meant no more rental mechs on the verge of spontaneous combustion.

Tovi's mech appeared in the doorframe, and he ducked inside. *"This is perfect,"* he said, then paused. She saw him staring down at his console through his equally small porthole. *"Hold on a minute, my sensor is showing movement in here."*

Sierra cinched up the bag, then returned her attention to her screen. "I don't see anything."

"Over there," he said, pointing to the bay of lockers, half flung open with personal items—clothes and bags—suspended inside and drifting around the room like dust motes. There was so much stuff, it was hard to focus on any one thing.

Then a locker door, up and to the left, swung open a little wider. Sierra's breath caught as she wondered if the pirates—or even the original occupants—had booby-trapped this room. Maybe that was why they hadn't come in here.

She swung up her arm, and using the controls on her glove, switched out her active instrument to a ballistic beanbag gun, then aimed at the locker.

"Any movement?" Sierra asked, her sensors showing fuck-all.

"It's very slow, almost cautious. It's not moving much."

"What does that?" Sierra asked, running through all the possibil-ities. Then she saw movement with her own eyes, a darting flash of black, and she jerked back.

"*Wait!*" Tovi yelled, his voice pitched down. Sierra stumbled back a few steps, trusting Tovi but wanting to put space between herself and whatever had darted out of the locker. She scanned the room, seeing nothing.

"*Don't move,*" Tovi said, now facing her, his gaze trained above her head and expression serious. His long, foxlike ears flattened in concentration.

"What is it?" she asked, her voice a low whisper. The hairs on the back of her neck raised. She absolutely hated not knowing what kind of threat she was facing, but she trusted Tovi with her life.

"*Just stay still.*" He moved with painful slowness, like he might spook whatever flesh-eating monster had attached itself to her mech. Tovi's face—humanoid in most respects, except for the double eyelids to protect from sand, the absence of a protruding nose, and the deep lines of his skin—was grave, his brows furrowed.

He reached up and fumbled at something that scraped with an ear-piercing screech on the metal of her mech, then brought his hands down, displaying a very black, very shiny cat.

"*It's a cat!*" he said, a ginormous smile covering his face, exposing his sharp teeth.

Sierra let out a ragged breath, adrenaline making her heartbeats thrum in her ears. "You might have told me, you ass."

"*Where's the fun in that?*" The smile on his face was like the sun blooming over a planet's edge, and with a big black cat held in his hand extensions, gazing up at her like the most innocent thing in the galaxy, she failed to be appreciably upset. It had large green eyes like kryptonite and little paws that kneaded at the air. The tips of its long, pointed ears were adorned with fanciful fluffs dusted white. Its little pink nose twitched inquisitively, then its mouth opened, and Sierra guessed it was meowing into the vacuum of space.

"Oh my God, is that an AIcat? How is it operational? It should have been wiped and combusted when the ship was compromised," Iz said over the comm. Peepers circled the cat, coming in for closer inspection. The cat took a swat at one and sent it sailing across the room to bump into a locker.

"It must be worth a fortune," Cecil said.

"We aren't selling it, Cecil," Iz said, voice raised in annoyance. Sierra imagined she could feel Iz's glare leveled at Cecil.

"How did the pirates miss this?" Sierra asked.

"Maybe it's not an AIcat and just a fancy compdroid," Tovi said, making doe eyes at the cat, which was transfixed by the peepers swirling around it.

"I thought all of Omnia's ships used AIcats as an extension of the main AI interface and as a backup. And they all appear identical," Sierra said.

Of the group, she was least acquainted with the megacorporation. It was an incredibly cute cat; its energetic tail, bifurcated probably more for style than sense, was swishing back and forth, no doubt designed that way to make it the most pleasant compdroid possible. Sure, it had its utilitarian uses, but companion droids largely provided emotional support to their owners in the rough and isolating space environment. AIcats were one-part compdroid, providing companionship to the occupants of the world-builder, and one part watchdog, keeping an eye on the ship, and no doubt its inhabitants as an extension of the central AI. Sierra felt her own compdroid shifting and weaving through her unruly electric blue hair.

"That's correct," Cecil said. *"Their AIcats vary in color, but all of them have the forked tails; it's a proprietary design. This is definitely an AIcat, and something must have gone very wrong for it to be functional when the main AI was destroyed."*

What iss that? Rupert said through their mindlink, slinking out of her hair and then rubbing his scaled head against her cheek.

"You heard, it's a cat."

It lookss... unintelligent.

Rich coming from him. He was a base model, all Sierra could afford when she'd wandered into a secondhand compdroid shop fifteen years ago, lonely and desperate for company and laying eyes on the cutest little snake, brick red with black diamonds down its back. She wouldn't trade him for all the mechs in The Endless Sea. Someday, she thought wistfully, she'd get him an upgrade.

"How are we going to get it back to the ship?" Tovi asked.

Sierra held up her bag with a raised eyebrow. She didn't love the idea, but she didn't have a better alternative, since they couldn't open their mechs in the vacuum of space.

"Oh, she's not going to like that." Tovi's frown told her he didn't much like the idea either.

"She's a she now?" Sierra asked. "We'll put her in yours. We don't want her tearing up the life support system."

The cat was distracted by the peepers circling around and didn't notice the bag Sierra had taken from Tovi's storage and held open until Tovi placed her inside. Sierra quickly cinched the bag and was grateful there was no noise in space as the cat thrashed and clawed at the bag.

"Poor kitty," Tovi said, sad eyes tracking the flailing bag, his ears flicking in concern. *"She's going to hate us now."*

"We can print some tuna. I'm sure you can bring her around in the end."

Sierra's console dinged, reminding her she needed to change out her air canisters. "Let's head back and let this cat out of the bag," she said and was satisfied by Iz's snort of laughter and Tovi's eye roll.

Chapter 2

Letting the Cat Out of the Bag

Iz was waiting for them as they cycled through the airlock and the inner door opened, bouncing on their toes in excitement.

"Kitty, kitty, kitty!" Iz said as they ran in to grab the jerking bag, their afro puffs bouncing in time. Sierra smiled at their retreating form. Iz was like a living mural, brightly painted and ever changing as their story unfolded, and an absolute joy of a human to behold. They were wearing a pair of sparkly pink overalls that were splashed with paint over a mesh green top. Blue paint dotted their brown skin like constellations; they must have been working on the mural in the cargo bay. Trailing behind them, using their eight legs to propel themselves through space, was Iz's compdroid, Pixie, a deep purple dumbo octopus the size of a human head and so cute, Sierra couldn't stand it. However, their cuteness was tempered by having the personality of a pissed-off honey badger. Iz had modified Pixie to move through any atmosphere like it was water, a genius bit of code and tinkering.

"Be careful, she's in a bit of a huff," Tovi said, regarding the cat currently trying to fight its way out of the bag.

Sierra opened the hatch to her mech and was greeted by the sound of a screeching cat.

"I can't tell you how happy I'll be once we're done with these rentals," Sierra said.

She kicked the leg of her mech and a metal plate fell to the ground with a clink. Sierra shook her head and followed the sounds of the cat. The airlock opened into the cargo bay, currently housing Archy, their work-in-progress mech, and the high-value items taken from the scrapped ship; they would tow the ship's mangled carcass behind them. She and Tovi took the stairs up into the galley, a room just big enough for a table, a small kitchen, and two couches that folded down from the walls. It was a tight fit, but it was where they spent most their time in flight. They found Iz in the galley, sitting on one of the couches and holding the bag like a baby, making soft shushing noises and rocking it back and forth.

Pixie was smart enough to keep their distance, their usual deep purple shading to magenta. *You do not need another companion. Plus, it is defective. Why isn't it transmitting?* Pixie chose to mindlink to everyone on the ship with implanted mind synthesizers, better known as mindsyncs, making their feelings broadly known.

"She's not defective," Tovi said, approaching the shrieking bag of indignant suffering. "I think she's only just activated. It takes some time to tune in to the right frequencies and make a connection."

Iz set the bag down and undid the cinch. Cautiously, the cat poked its little pink-and-black nose out of the bag and pushed her head through. Her eyes widened and Sierra followed her gaze to the very large, very furry brown bear standing in the mess door. This particular bear was wearing a black vest under a gun holster and a porkpie hat sitting jauntily on his head, and his name was Cecil. Cecil was a Nhethian, a bioengineered race of earth animals, and the crew's long-suffering business manager.

The cat made a mad dash out of the bag, jumping onto Iz's lap, then the table, slipping on Iz's coloring book pages and their colored pencils, knocking them to the floor as she launched herself across the galley and out of sight in a tripping zigzag pattern. Maybe she *was* defective.

"Don't get attached. An AIcat is worth a few hundred credits. We're better off selling it," Cecil said, walking farther into the room and adjusting his porkpie hat with a lacquered claw as dark as the void. If the hat didn't sit just right, it wouldn't translate his growls into Universal. It was an old design, but he refused a permanent mindsync implant. Like many Nhethians, he was distrustful of bodymods. Sierra had to plop down on the foldout couch to get out of Cecil's way, since he took up most of the room in the galley.

"Cecil, we are not selling a poor, orphaned kitty cat. Can you imagine how scared she must have been, all alone on that ship, when those pirates killed her family?" Iz said, folding their arms over their iridescent overalls.

"I don't think this particular AIcat has much going on upstairs. It's not broadcasting. It's definitely defective."

"Shows how much you know about androids, or anything at all, for that matter. Go manage something else." It was the closest Iz could come to telling someone to fuck off. Iz fixed broken compdroids in their free time, and their heart expanded to encompass everything from a broken pencil to a busted teapot.

"I'm managing our finances, and that cat could put us in the black. Plus, I'm allergic to cats."

"It's not a real cat, dumb-dumb. It doesn't have dander."

"I think this is one we'll have to put to a vote, don't you, Cecil?" Sierra asked.

Cecil didn't seem happy about it, but he wasn't sunshine and roses on his best days; a bear's face was difficult to interpret.

"All in favor of keeping the cat?" Sierra asked, already knowing the answer. Everyone but Cecil raised their hand, and Iz raised both their hands like they desperately had the answer to a teacher's question. "Everyone against keeping the cat."

Cecil raised his clawed paw, and Pixie swirled their little tentacles over their head in a frenzy. Cecil let out a huff of defeat. "I don't know why I keep working with y'all. We're supposed to be out here making money; instead, you just fritter it away, and you better be careful with that snake or the cat will eat it. Don't say I didn't tell you so. No one listens to anything I say," he said, taking his rant with him as he retreated to the flight deck and his own private office space. Iz stuck out their tongue at his retreating back.

"Cecil might be right about Rupert," Sierra said. Hearing his name, Rupert unwound himself from her blue hair and curled around her neck, covering the tattoo of his likeness, then brushed the side of his head against her cheek. "You hear that, Rupert? There's a new kitty in town, so be careful and don't attack her."

She's not too ssteady on her legss. I'm unconcerned. Rupert wasn't the jealous type, unlike Pixie, who appeared poised to commit compdrodicide the next time the cat walked near an airlock.

Rupert flicked his forked tongue against her cheek and rested on her shoulders. She scratched under his chin absentmindedly, enjoying the feel of his scales against the skin of her neck.

"What are we going to name her?" Tovi asked.

"You've decided she's a she, then?" Sierra asked, returning to her previous inquiry.

"Doesn't she remind you of Lulu?" he asked, his gaze lingering after the cat, his big green eyes soft and a little misty, like he'd been transported back in time.

Tovi seemed to have formed an immediate attachment to the fluff ball. Most social species had an android companion, Praxians being an exception because they rarely left their home planet. On the surface, Prax was an oasis of beaches and sandy dunes, an enticing prospect for foreigners, except for the intense radiation that would cook most carbon-based beings like an egg on the hood of a car in a heatwave, and that was the way Praxians liked it. Tovi had grown up off planet and had diverging, if warring, views on Praxian social norms.

Sierra was briefly puzzled, then she remembered the black cat from their Tapata days. She'd been compdroid feral, not belonging to any one person and reverting to the basics of her coding, but she was tolerably friendly on her own terms. She used to follow Tovi through the junkyard while they went scavenging for parts, catching rodents and fighting other cats that got too close. He'd missed her when she'd disappeared one day and never came back.

He used to make up stories about how she'd fallen in love with a cat across town and they'd gone off to have kittens together in an uptown junkyard, where the cars had air conditioning and leather seats. Sierra had disagreed and told him that Lulu was far too independent to get knocked up by a city slicker. No, she'd joined a cat gang, and they were out terrorizing the poodles on Ninth Street.

Tovi had loved that cat, and Sierra could see the resemblance. Lulu hadn't had the white markings, but they were similar in color and size. If Sierra were honest, it could've had scales and neon eyes and she'd have agreed with him. Who could say no to the hope in those big, pleading eyes?

"I like the name," Iz said. "She looks like a Lulu. I'm going to put out a blanket and bed, and crochet some cat toys. I can grow some catnip in the lab. Let me see what yarn I have. When we're back on station, I can grab some more yarn."

"Not sure Lana will be happy about more yarn," Tovi said.

"She will be when I show her the new cat. But don't tell her yet. I want it to be a surprise."

"You're taking her?" Tovi asked, his voice forlorn.

"Just while customs inspects the ship. I don't want her confiscated as Omnia property. One glimpse at her forked tail, and they'll seize her," Iz said.

Iz was the only crew member who had a place off-ship to stash Lulu while customs searched the ship, so it made sense, but Sierra could see the tension in Tovi's jaw. "Watch out, Tovi might run away with her," Sierra said.

Not everyone iss sso fickle. Your family will not leave you.

"I was being sarcastic, Rupert." Sierra was glad Rupert only spoke to her. She took in her crew's blank stares, letting them guess what Rupert had said, as it was usually of the violent variety.

Tovi raised a questioning eyebrow at Iz, who was notoriously bad at keeping a secret, especially when they were excited. "I doubt it will stay a secret for long."

"What? I'm totally going to keep this one a secret," they said, as innocent as a crocodile on land.

"Uh huh," Sierra said.

Iz crossed their arms. "I can keep a secret when I want to."

"We have four weeks' travel time to find out," Sierra said.

With a pissed-off cat, a grumpy admin, a frantic knitter, and a pensive Praxian electrician, it might be a long four weeks, but Sierra had the mech upgrades to work on, and that at least would keep her distracted—she might even get most of the work done. They'd finally have their own mech and not have to spend more than half their profits on rentals. With the extra money, they could afford the much-needed repairs to their ship and save for a second mech, one she could enter into mech battles and make some real money. All their hard work might actually pay dividends.

Chapter 3

Hope Springs Infernal

Tovi stared down at the wiring harness and rubbed his forehead. There was a fault somewhere in the system he'd been trying to isolate for the last hour, and every time he fixed something, another problem cropped up. He needed to take a break before he tore his hair out.

The mech was belly up in the cramped square of their machine shop, hydraulic arms and legs starfished in all directions, an absolute hodgepodge of parts across manufacturers, models, and versions. One arm was bare metal and the other flat black and blue. The legs were a garish safety yellow, taken from a loading mech that was outmoded a decade ago. Sierra was great at finding parts, combing through ads on the net and going on junkyard expeditions, finding shiny morsels and bringing them home like a dead mouse laid on his pillow. The talent was useful in theory, but the salvaged components required time-intensive reprogramming by him and Iz. Sierra was a top-notch mechanic but useless with anything involving programming.

Everything smelled of oil, grease, and dust. He couldn't tell if the smell was coming from the room or his once safety yellow coveralls, now gray streaked with grease. He was due for a new pair; no amount of soap would get the grease out of these, and the smell was overpowering. Sierra was in the belly of the beast, retrofitting the new life-support system they'd picked up in the salvage, and he could hear her cursing a blue streak. Occasionally, parts would go flying up and out of the cab. Iz found it difficult to be around Tovi and Sierra when they worked, unused to the general fog of anxiety and random outbursts that came with mechanical work, so they had made the medbay their tinkering room.

They had repurposed a section of the cargo bay for a machine shop. It was cheaper than renting storage and they could work on the mech in their free time, but with all their supplies mixed in with mech parts and salvage scrapes, he desperately wanted breathing room.

Luckily, Cecil was fastidious and had everything wrangled into its own rigidly delineated space. The high-value parts they'd pulled from the pirated vessel over the course of a few days were packed away in padded yellow shipping cubes stacked higher than he could reach along the starboard side. They removed the parts from the salvage so the shell of the ship could be easily gutted and decomposed for recycling when they returned to Octto Station. Next to the shipping cubes stood the two mechs they'd rented from Omnia's Impound—dented, scratched-up pieces of excrement that they were.

Sierra had rearranged them this morning in a striking pose with one humping the other. Yesterday, they were in a bear hug. Tovi was more convinced than ever that long space flights were detrimental to a sentient's mental health. Most Praxians would agree with him, throwing in a sidelong glance suggesting he go back to where he belonged instead of messing about in space with humans and other genetically modified sentient beings. He'd only lived on Prax until he was fourteen, long enough to remember his home world but not long enough to call it home.

The crew's personal supplies, like food, medical equipment, space suits, and all of Iz's art supplies, were secured in stationary lockers, decorated with an in-progress mural Iz was painting—and had been working on when they'd returned from their salvage. It was an abstract cubist-style depiction of their own ship flinging through space. Its bold colors and harsh lines did things to Tovi's brain, and he'd catch himself staring at it for long stretches of time, like mentally walking a labyrinth.

He jerked his attention from the painting when he felt something brush against his leg. Lulu, the newest member of their crew, was rubbing against him with a rumbling purr. The tow back to Octto Station was a four-week journey, and it had taken two weeks for Lulu to come out of hiding to occasionally scamper across the ship and disappear again. In the last two weeks, she'd grown more curious and friendly, investigating hard-to-reach areas and sniffing out the other inhabitants of her new home. It had become apparent that she was a bit off balance—something to do with her internal stabilizers—and she tended to weave more than walk. Watching her calculate a jump was like watching a drunk try to puzzle out stairs.

"Finally decide to join us?" Tovi asked, bending down to run a hand along her back. He got the sense she was trying to reach him through the mindsync, but all he got was the feeling of vastness and terrifying newness. "Don't worry, you'll get there. It takes time to form a link, but I'm sure it's isolating for you."

He sat on the floor, trying to coax her into his lap. She just stared at him and bumped her head into his knee.

"Too soon?" he asked.

Sierra popped up from within the mech, a spring sticking up from her hair. "Too soon for what?"

"I wasn't talking to you," he said, pointing to the cat.

Sierra blinked, then smiled before climbing out of the mech's chest. Sierra was chaos incarnate. She wore a bright orange coverall, equally grease- and food-stained on the front, and clashed terribly with her pale white skin with blue undertones. She'd wrangled her electric blue hair into a high bun, butterfly clips keeping the small pieces out of her face; the clips had been a gift from Iz, and she'd use them and lose them at every opportunity. And yet petulant curls managed to pop free in defiance of reason and gravity.

Rupert coiled around Sierra's neck like a choker, the safest place for the small snake when Sierra was working. With her sleeves rolled up, Tovi could see the montage of tattoos on her arms. Some glowed in the dark and others moved like a mirage. Any time they were somewhere new, she'd find a burgeoning tattoo artist and fill in any open spot she could find; she insisted they told a far more interesting story than anything she could come up with on her own.

"I can't figure out this short. Think I need a break," he said, rubbing at his eyes.

"Maybe a cat nap?" she said, laughing at her own joke, and Tovi smirked. She sat down next to him and ran her hand along Lulu's arching back. "You know, once we get this mech running, we don't have to only take salvage jobs anymore."

"We are not putting all this work into a mech to do battle royales. We can't afford the repairs."

"I didn't mean that. Someday, maybe. I meant private jobs doing transports or working docks," she said, and Tovi could hear a hint of disappointment in her tone.

They both wanted to fight in the mech competitions; it was how they'd bonded in the first place. They'd made a great team as teenagers in the junkyards, putting together battle bots and cleaning up on the bets to a cheering crowd of onlookers and bookies. They'd dreamed of one day fighting real mechs, like the matches they'd grown up seeing on the net.

Mech battles were fought in teams—one person manned the mech while the other remotely operated some of the mech's weapons and dictated strategy. Half the fun was watching teams work seamlessly or epically fall apart under pressure. Tovi and Sierra would switch off responsibilities, but they were most successful with Sierra as operator and Tovi on tactics. Their unofficial battlebot tournaments had a dedicated following until the day a fight got out of hand.

Since then, Sierra had spent some time in the mech battle circuit, paying off her debt, but Tovi knew she missed it, the thrill of the fight, the feeling that she was good at something and could kick ass. Just her, Tovi, and the machine. He craved the thrill as much as she did. It was part of their long-term plan, but they had to be smart if they didn't want to land in more debt.

"Have you heard anything about your conclave?" Sierra asked, averting her gaze to the mech.

"Some people have seen Praxians on Terrana, but it's a party aster-oid. It could have been people dressed up as Praxians for a lark," Tovi said. He'd created an algorithm to scrape the net for any mention of Praxians on forums and social media sites, hoping to catch a glimpse of his family. He hadn't seen them in seventeen years, since the ill-fated incident that separated him from his Praxian conclave and Sierra. Secretive by nature and necessity, tracking down Praxians was tough, but he hadn't given up hope he'd find them again.

"With the extra income, we could start working on a battle mech. The cash prizes are climbing even in the minor leagues," Tovi said to change the subject. He wanted more than anything to see Sierra smile, to give her hope. Hope wasn't something she was good at manufac-turing on her own.

Sierra's eyes lit up like Tovi had told her Freshies Gelateria was giving away free scoops. "You think so? I've had my eye on a mech body I saw buried in a junkyard over in Dumptown. It's not fancy, but its internals are in good shape."

Tovi's curiosity was piqued. "How's the wiring?"

Sierra typed on her sleeve. Tovi's sleeve dinged with an alert asking if he wanted to accept the photos she was sending. He accepted and two dozen photos popped up on his sleeve screen. He scrolled through, zooming in on the usual problem areas, checking the joints for corrosion and the state of the electrical components.

"It's missing an arm," Tovi said. "But we'd probably replace it anyway. Did you see the Five Points tournament yesterday? The Bee had a six-axis arm."

"I did see that. As a distraction technique, it worked fabulously. I couldn't tell if it was coming or going. Chopped the arm off Mad Mike before the end of the first round."

"We could use Iz's plans for a plasma torch. They have a few ideas for speeding up the mech, something about a three-access rolling base."

"That's a great idea," she said, before casting a scrutinizing eye over the dock. "We'll need more space."

While the rest of the cargo area was packed full, except the central area that needed to stay clear for the loading ramp, their machine area was chaos. Squeezing in another mech would be a magic trick.

"We need to clean this up before Cecil sees," Tovi said, noticing the ever-expanding mess.

"Too late," came Cecil's gruff voice.

They turned to the door leading into the heart of the ship to see Cecil standing there, arms folded over his hairy, barreled chest. Tovi could appreciate Cecil's grumpy disposition and exasperation with humans; he had more right than most to keep his distance from meddling homo sapiens.

Tovi had heard the lecture a hundred times, a cautionary tale. It was a foundational text in his conclave's ethos, always told with excessive sympathy for the humans who'd woken up one day to learn their planet had been repossessed by the Consortium of Planets. The Consortium had broadcasted a message across all communications devices. Truckers heard it on their radios, every phone dinged with a text, computers blanked out then looped the same short video. It all boiled down to the same message. Tovi had seen a copy of the video that had been recorded one hundred and seventy-two years ago. A clear voice with an inscrutable accent said, "The Consortium of Planets hereby repossesses Planet MW-2348 also known as Earth for violating Section 3 sub-section 12 of the Planetary Stewardship agreement. Habitable conditions have entered critical failure, endangering the majority occupants of the planet. The Consortium has identified the minority occupants as grossly culpable, and their influence must be removed to ensure the safety of the majority."

Everyone had thought it was a joke—until the ships appeared in the sky. Large and hovering impossibly in Earth's atmosphere, like upside-down trees with the roots exposed to space. Humans hadn't known other sentients existed let alone that there was a governing body. Indignant, puffed-up leaders tried raining nuclear weapons on the ships, ready to destroy the world if they couldn't have it for themselves.

The Consortium disintegrated the weapons, followed by any leader who protested their intervention. After such an impressive show of force, humanity succumbed to the inevitable.

They were carted off Earth to a new planet, free from other inhabitants and given a chance to prove humanity could do better.

Not only did humans fail on their new planet, they failed spectacularly. A genetic research company spearheaded a plan to create sentient Earth animals as a publicity stunt and to manufacture more realistic versions of compdroids. Turned out they couldn't control the new population like they could with androids, and they birthed a new race of sentient beings that called themselves Nhethians.

When the Consortium found out, the council decided humans couldn't be trusted after they'd squandered their second chance. Humans were redistributed across the universe with the hope that their destructive nature would be diluted. The planet was handed over to the new Nhethian population and humans were once again without a home, and this time for good. The Consortium created an embargo against any planet having a population of humans greater than fifty percent, turning humans into space nomads never to have a planet to call home again.

Cecil's grumpiness could be boiled down to the historical dynamics of Nhethian-human relations, but Tovi was certain Cecil was egalitarian in his belief that all sentients were idiots, as evidenced by his pointed glare at Tovi.

"Hey, Cecil, we were just going to take a break. Want a coffee?" Sierra asked with an innocent smile.

"What I want is for the pair of you to pick up after yourselves. Why are there wrenches on the ground? Why can't you put a tool away when you're done with it? It's not that hard. See, watch."

He waltzed over, his massive paws swinging at his sides, picked up the three wrenches Sierra had thrown out of the mech during an earlier rant about the absurdity of combining parts from four different manufacturers, all of whom used different tools for the same damnable job, and proceeded to put them back in whatever place he thought best.

"So that's how you do it. Can you show me how that works with metal shavings?" Sierra asked, batting her eyes.

Cecil glared at her. "You take a broom and a dustpan, and you sweep it up. I also noticed that you have machine shop material outside of the perimeter."

Cecil had taped out a square encompassing the back half of the cargo bay to within ten feet of the loading ramp in a bold yellow tape, the brightest color he could find. Sierra's welder was partially over the line, along with some of the discarded wiring Tovi had been working on.

Tovi gave him a sheepish smile. "Oops?"

"It's there for a reason; there are safety issues. What if the wiring blocked the loading ramp? It could crush something important." Cecil was a fantastic administrator, but he didn't have a blithering clue how anything actually functioned from a mechanical perspective. Tovi felt bad. He knew it bothered Cecil, and Tovi appreciated the work he did on the ship; however, it was far too much fun to poke the bear.

"I'm sorry, Cecil, I should have kept an eye on it," Tovi said.

"Not everything's your fault, Tovi," Cecil said. "It's mostly Sierra's bad influence."

"Hey! Just imagine how much worse I could be. We promise to be more careful, Cecil, we pinky promise," Sierra said, holding out a pinky.

Cecil blew out a gust of air through his nose and ignored her antics, but his disapproving gaze lingered.

"Was there another reason you came down here, Cecil?" Tovi asked, hoping to avoid a blazing row.

"We'll dock at Octto Station in about four hours. I suggest you clean this mess up and get ready. We don't need to give customs another reason to fine us," he said. "And get all the skimmings into the chamber."

"Thanks, Cecil, you're the best," Sierra said, patting him on his shoulder, which she had to stretch to reach. Cecil grumbled as he walked out of the loading bay, ducking under the door before it hissed shut behind him.

Tovi and Sierra stared at the mess of discarded wires, butchered electrical tape, sawed-off bolts, mangled metal plating, and smeared grease, then at the carefully labeled bins in Cecil's handwriting—with glittery embellishment courtesy of Iz—for each type of waste against the back wall, and got to work.

When they'd finished tossing all the junk into generally the correct containers, they double-checked the secret compartment Sierra had welded into the landing gear box. It was technically illegal to keep anything they salvaged, but *legality ain't no hill for a climber,* as Tovi's caregiver used to say. They never got a fair price for their salvages, and Omnia's Impound, who held the contract for this salvage, always found a way to pick away at their profit. He and Sierra checked everything they'd left off the claims form was crammed inside the housing and then sealed it with the welder.

Sierra flipped up the welding mask, revealing the shit-eating grin Tovi had come to know and love. "Let's get this show on the road! I'm ready to get paid and stretch my sea legs."

"You and me both," he said, snaking an arm around her shoulders and walking side by side to finish securing the cargo bay.

Chapter 4

Bad Dates Leave a Bad Taste

After mooring the carcass of the destroyed ship in the shipyard to be dismantled and recycled, the crew docked at Octto Station. With every intention of going out that night, they dressed in their best for dancing and cavorting in the cheap bars of Octto Station.

Tovi chose a fitted vest in maroon and gold paisley over a black-collared shirt with a slight sheen, maroon pants, black leather shoes, and a gold chain hanging from one ear. He assessed himself in the mirror hanging in the cargo bay, fixing his cuffs and then flattening his collar. Praxians favored thick, intricately designed robes that protected them from the stinging sand. Tovi, however, preferred interstellar styles with flashy details. He figured nothing would stop the stares from strangers, not even traditional Praxian wear, so why try.

Iz elbowed him. "You look good."

He fiddled with a stray strand of hair and tucked it behind his ear. "Thanks. Hazel just makes me nervous."

"That's because she's a raging asshole," Iz said. Their curly black hair was tied up in a puff, and they wore a color-blocked dress in primary colors with gold bangles on their wrists and hoops in their ears. Pixie glommed onto their head like they were sucking on their brains. Iz unzipped the gym bag slung across their body. "Isn't that right, Lulu-baby?" Lulu's pink nose pressed against the opening, and she let out a little meow. "Lulu agrees. I'm going to take her to meet Lana and get her reskinned so she won't be immediately identified as an AIcat. Don't worry, I'll bring her back."

Tovi nodded, pressing his lips together and trying to smother his anxiety. Sierra and Cecil were better at dealing with Hazel than he was. He just wanted to do his job and not fight for every credit they were owed. He was tired of fighting even for the small things, and this wasn't a small thing. He stuck a few fingers into Iz's bag and scratched Lulu under the chin. He'd become increasingly fond of little Lulu and was loath to have her leave the ship, but if the ship was searched by customs, they might seize Lulu as contraband. They would need to disguise her, and quickly.

They all stood on the loading ramp with the two rental mechs, and Tovi pressed the switch to lower the platform. The artificial light of the station was blinding and burned Tovi's eyes, even as his inner lids came down to protect his corneas. He was hit with the scent of gas and rubber, which made him want to abandon everything and run out of the docks like his hair was on fire. He craved the smell of fresh food and warm bodies and the sound of people talking, not the wind-tunnel noise that kept air circulating with a deafening whine. All his senses were heightened after nine weeks in space.

Octto Station wasn't the oldest ring station in the Zytoma system—not having the kind of credits or patronage for forced artificial gravity, it relied on ring gravity—but it wasn't the youngest either. It had a middling reputation, which made it a good place to get lost, but the independent station didn't draw too much attention from anyone who might be interested in a hostile takeover. Omnia's Impound occupied a dock front location; its four large garage doors grinned like yellowed teeth next to a storefront with metal bars on the doors and windows. Above the door, a beat-up pink neon sign read *Omnia* and blinked at odd, asymmetric intervals. For a company that could afford world-builders, it was a pathetic showing.

Two techs were waiting. They didn't acknowledge the crew's existence as they brushed past them, climbed into the mechs, and picked up the yellow crates housing the high-value items to be weighed and assessed. They took the crates through the open garage doors and disappeared inside. Sierra offered them a two-finger salute and headed for the front door, Cecil on her heels. Cecil wore a baby blue blazer over a chevron shirt. Nhethians were mixed on wearing clothes, most feeling it was a lingering tool of their oppressors, while others, like Cecil, disagreed. He enjoyed the personal expression and the way he cleaned up in a well-tailored suit.

"I don't want to wait around in case customs decides to do a search of the ship," Iz said, eyes shifting around the dock like the port authority goons might drop from the ceiling like ghoulish spiders at any moment, which wasn't out of the realm of possibility.

"I'm sure you want to go see Lana too," Tovi said.

Iz smiled at the mention of their partner. "Yeah, I miss her. I also have an appointment to get my hair braided. I'll be busy for most the cycle with that."

"I'll let you know where we end up."

Iz gave him one of their signature hugs that felt like being wrapped in a warm blanket before they hurried off.

Tovi wasn't in any hurry to join the others and face the inevitable altercation with Hazel, so he loitered outside, checking his sleeve for the most recent news and any messages he might have missed while he was away. Sentients were moving around the dock, loading up their ships with goods and sentients or disembarking into the station. The sound of repair work—metal hitting metal, welding torches, sentients shouting to each other—blurred into a hum of noise.

"Hey, Tovi!"

Tovi immediately regretted his choice to stay so exposed in the loading dock at the sound of Ryan's voice. "Ryan, what are you doing here?" Ryan was tall by human standards, but short by Praxian, coming to Tovi's chin. His long, pale white equine face was framed by manicured eyebrows that could cut ice. Conventionally attractive and a total jerk, he was the kind of guy Tovi routinely fell for.

"What? You don't sound happy to see me," Ryan said, his long legs bringing him close enough for Tovi to smell his peppermint spice aftershave.

"The last time I saw you, you made off with our salvage, so no, I'm not thrilled to see you."

"That was just business."

"You bugged my room to get that information." There were nights when he'd lain awake imagining what he would say to Ryan if they crossed paths again. It was going to be witty and cutting, and he'd keep his cool—none of which was happening now.

"But wasn't it worth it?" Ryan said with a suggestive smile. Tovi absolutely hated how Ryan's sultry voice had once sent a shiver down his spine; now it was a freezing chill.

"No, it wasn't, Ryan." It had put them in the red, they owed Hazel thousands of credits, and he'd let the crew down. He'd been—and still was—ashamed of himself. "If you don't make yourself scarce, I'll punch you in the nose again. And no amount of cosmetic surgery will make it right."

Ryan winced a little at that, but his smirk barely faltered, and he tucked loose blond hair that had fallen charmingly in front of his face behind his ear, something Tovi once found endearing. "I come with a peace offering."

"I don't want anything from you," Tovi spat back.

"Not even a chance for me to make things right?"

"That's not possible."

"Okay, better, then? I need help on a job, and I'm willing to cut your crew in on thirty percent to help me out."

"Thirty percent, how generous of you. You want to 'make it right' by offering to underpay us on a job. Who's helping whom here? You can take your job and shove it."

Ryan held up his hands in surrender. "Hey, I just thought you might need the work," he said, his eyes lingering over their ship, disdain written in the upturned angle of his nose.

Compared to the sleek, fully upgraded, patch-free ship Ryan captained, their secondhand, cobbled together ship was a shit stain in space, but it was their shit stain, and they'd worked hard for it.

Out of nowhere, a knee came crushing into Ryan's abdomen. Ryan let out a strangled yell and fell on his ass, wheezing for breath and rolling to his side. Sierra stood over his crumpled body, her face hard as titanium and consumed with a cold fury. Sierra was imposing in a white bandeau top, exposing the star tattoos covering her chest like freckles, under a cropped black blazer, matching slacks, and black boots. The montage of black bracelets covering her wrists and forearms jangled together. Her earrings and the stud in the side of her nose gleamed ominously in the harsh light.

"Fuck off, Ryan. Go find someone else to manipulate, then let down, just so you can feel superior for a brief moment before you remember you're just a fart in space," Sierra said, arms folded as she glared down at him. Ryan hissed and tried to take a breath.

Sierra cupped her ear and leaned down. "I can't hear you, Ryan. You need to speak up."

"Just leave him, Sierra, he's being an idiot," Tovi said as he walked away, ignoring the sentients who stopped to see what the commotion was about. He didn't want to deal with this right now, didn't want the reminder of his disastrous encounter with a man he'd actually liked. *Embarrassment* wasn't a big enough word to encompass the situation. Tovi wanted to get a few drinks in him, unwind, and have a good time with his friends. Why Ryan had to drag himself out of whatever pretentious hive of villainy he inhabited to rain on his parade, Tovi didn't know, and he didn't want to find out.

Sierra followed after him. "You okay?" she asked, jogging to keep up.

She meant well, but he didn't want her pity or her help dealing with Ryan. "Yeah, fine. How's it going with Hazel?"

She stared at him for a moment before answering, not believing him and no doubt weighing whether she should push the subject. "She should be done with the intake by now."

"Fine, let's get this done and get out of here." Tovi followed her into Omnia's Impound, relieved she'd let it go for the moment.

Chapter 5

Swoon to the Tune of a Mech's Croon

Six Months Earlier

"Stop pouting," Sierra said, shoving her arms into her bomber jacket and moving around the cramped room that resembled a war zone, picking up things at random: a half-used ChapStick, her tactical knife, and a battered chocolate-flavored nutrient bar.

"I'm not pouting," Tovi insisted, his arms crossed over his chest as he leaned against the doorjamb.

"Yes, you are. I'm not happy about it either. Don't you think I'd rather be going to a mech battle than doing a job? I can't turn down a call out," she said. Her gaze swept around the room, checking to see if she forgot something.

Tovi grabbed her work badge hanging on a hook on the back of the door and held it in front of her face. She grabbed it and hung it around her neck. "Thanks. It's not like you have problems making friends," she said.

"Not everyone is as nerdy about mechs as we are." Being pissy and not inclined to stop himself, he leaned into the whining.

"Won't argue with you there. I have to run. I'm already late. Have fun and take pictures so I can live vicariously through you." She stood on her tiptoes, and he obligingly leaned down so she could kiss his cheek, then she ran out the door and through the ship. She was always running late for something.

Iz was hanging out with Lana and her family, and who knew what Cecil got up to on station. Tovi didn't mind doing things on his own; he was good at mingling, but he couldn't talk tactics and geek out on the mechs with random strangers. He sighed melodramatically, miffed no one was there to witness his tragic circumstance. Determined to make the best of the situation, he pulled down on his red vest, smoothing his hands over the silky fabric to make sure the black buttons were straight. The black shirt he was wearing was equally silky, and he loved the feel on his skin.

Satisfied he was presentable for the Mech Open Day, he walked in Sierra's footsteps, exiting the ship and then securing it behind him. The Open Day was hosted by the Galactic Battle Mechs Federation and held at the Octto Fairgrounds, a faux grass lawn stretching a hundred yards and used for open air events, from soccer to festivals. When he reached the fairgrounds, he scanned his sleeve at the entrance, registering his ticket, then walked into the maze of vendor booths and swarms of avid mech enthusiasts. While the festival ran for two days, the demonstrations and fights were only held for a few hours on the second day of the festival. The whole crew had made the rounds the day before, perusing the new mech models on display by the various vendors. They'd wandered the wide lanes, soaking up everything mech—from advancements in arm attachments to new accessories.

He and Sierra had coveted the novelty operator gloves in bright colors. Today, Tovi meandered through the lanes, weaving around families staring up at the imposing mechs on display. His destination was the demonstration field, a wide swath of empty ground where he'd finally get to see the mechs in action. The plan was to get there early and snag a good seat, and when he arrived, there were only a few dozen sentients with the same idea. He grabbed a seat in the front row, just behind the empty box seats for highfliers and sponsors, a place he'd give his left arm to be.

Tovi played Asteroid Crush on his sleeve to pass the time. Sentients filled the stands, arms and tentacles full of popcorn, cotton candy, fizzle sticks, and base burgers. Energetic instrumental music trumpeted from the speakers, signaling the beginning of the entertainment. It was more propaganda than anything else, with each company putting on a show hoping to win lucrative contracts from local businesses. A hidden announcer settled the crowd to a low murmur and introduced each mech by company name, operator name, and title. Unsurprisingly, the operators were all high-ranking employees within their respective companies, taking the company mech out for a joyride.

The mechs walked out on the field when they were announced. They waved to the crowd, then performed a short demonstration of the mech's capabilities while the announcer enthusiastically read from a script, detailing its specifications and hyping the crowd.

Omnia was the last mech to make an appearance—with the Jag 356—and Tovi leaned forward in his seat. He'd spent more than his fair share of time in Omnia mechs, but the Asset Protection Division never received something as expensive or efficient as the commercial mechs. Military mechs were a different beast, clunky and utilitarian. The Jag 356 was sleek, gleaming white like a swan with dark blue detailing on the shoulders, head, and feet. Its decorative winged ears gave it sophistication and a daring allure. It was so damn beautiful. Tovi's chest ached with want.

The Jag 356 flew onto the field and swept up, then slowed its descent with one leg bent and the other straight, like a freaking angel, pulling a sword from a holster on its back and then pointing it upward. How could an inanimate object be so pretty? It landed gracefully and sheathed the sword. Intellectually, Tovi knew this kind of mech was a plaything for the rich, a status symbol meant to make people like him drop their panties, and it was working. There was no practical use for a mech too beautiful to scuff up with hard labor or battle. If Sierra were here, she'd scoff at the ridiculousness of the thing and the waste of resources. Tovi was a sucker for all things shiny and luxurious, despite the fact—or perhaps because—he'd never been privy to such luxuries.

He was practically drooling as the hatch opened on the mech's chest, unfurling lazily and to the greatest effect. Out stepped a man made diminutive by the beast he stood upon, but Tovi recognized him nonetheless as the Regional Controller of the Zytoma system for Omnia Enterprises. Omnia liked to keep it in the family, employing entire bloodlines without batting an eyelash at accusations of nepotism. Ryan Randolf was the son of Dahn Randolf, the President of Marketing and Communications at Omnia. Dahn's father, before his death, was the CFO. Tovi found the gossip about rivalry between Ryan and his siblings far more titillating than Randolf ancestry. Tovi had heard tale that Dahn kept an extensive and complicated spreadsheet delineating a points and ranking system for every Randolf. What they were fighting for was anyone's guess, and guess they did; they also gambled on the eventual payout. Tovi had his money on a private dwarf planet.

He'd never seen Ryan in person, and much to his chagrin, he was incredibly handsome. His flowing blond hair reminded Tovi of a horse he'd seen in an old western, majestic and otherworldly. He had a decided urge to pet the man, and wouldn't Sierra be aghast?

She'd call Ryan preppy, no doubt. And he was, Tovi couldn't deny the obvious. He wore a complicated maroon suit that gave airs of royalty, with draping fabric and high shoulders that contrasted his pale skin.

Ryan waved at the cheering crowd, flashing perfect white teeth and a slightly lopsided grin that softened the harsh lines of his face. When the crowd died down, Ryan stepped on a hover platform, joining the rest of the mech operators. Much to Tovi's surprise, the platform landed directly in front of him and the operators took up the seats in front of him, separated by a short barrier.

Tovi caught Ryan's eye as he stepped off the platform, and Ryan gifted him with a practiced smile. If Ryan was surprised to see a Praxian, he hid it well. Not one to be intimidated by power and prestige, Tovi rose to the challenge and smiled back, expecting his pointed teeth to cause a reaction. Instead of scaring him away, Ryan chose the seat nearest Tovi.

"Hello," Ryan said, turning in his seat to address him. "I'm Ryan Randolf." Again with that charming smile.

"I know. They announced your name earlier." Tovi refrained from pointing out that he was celebrated almost daily in the feeds as an eligible bachelor and scion of House Randolf. It wouldn't do to stroke his ego. "I'm Tovi."

"Pleasure to meet you," Ryan said, and he seemed genuine. "This is Del Ashworth," he said, gesturing to a short woman who also graced the gossip corners of the net, which Tovi would never admit to reading. She was the daughter of another Omnia family, often seen in Ryan's company, stirring up gossip about a marriage between the two families. It all sounded incestuous to Tovi. She moved with grace and self-assurance. Her hair was wrapped in an aqua blue head scarf that complemented her rich brown skin. Compared to Ryan, she appeared plain in a white, high-necked ribbed shirt and matching slacks under a long black overcoat, but Tovi knew quality when he saw it, and her clothes were understated elegance.

"Pleasure, I'm sure," she said in a bored tone and turned her back to him.

"Don't mind her; she's just rude. They haven't found a cure for the condition yet," Ryan said with a conspiratorial smile, and she slapped his knee. "Are you in the market for a new mech?"

Tovi laughed. "I don't have the kind of credits required for such a beautiful machine. Plus, it's too pretty for a mech battle."

Del snorted a derisive laugh, and he imagined she was rolling her eyes. Ryan shot her a look Tovi couldn't read.

"I agree, it's a pleasure model, meant for status more than utility. Are you an operator, then?" he asked, his gaze not leaving Tovi's.

"I was in the Asset Protection Division. I haven't operated a mech since then, but I hope to do so in the future. My partners are keen to put a battle mech together."

Ryan's bright smile dimmed at the mention of partners, and Tovi felt the need to elaborate. "My business partners, that is. Not like romantic partners or anything, I don't have one of those. We crew a salvage vessel." Tovi wanted to fling himself off the stands, where he would no doubt suffer severe injury and not the death that would spare him his own embarrassment. He was usually better at this. Had Sierra worn off on him? He internally winced at the admission of salvage work. Salvage crews were regarded as the lowest of the low amongst the space-faring set, but Ryan's smile brightened. Maybe Ryan wasn't the stuck-up asshole Tovi assumed him to be.

They smiled at each other for longer than was socially comfortable and Ryan leaned forward, the smell of peppermint wafting in Tovi's direction. "I'm going to an after-party when this dog and pony show is over. Do you want to join me?"

Tovi blinked in surprise. Did he want to hang out with the physical embodiment of Omnia's ruling class? On the surface, the answer was no. Had someone presented him with this particular scenario as a hypothetical exercise in the absurd, it would have been a definite no. Faced with this charming specimen who wasn't repulsed or enthralled by Tovi's 'exotic' appearance and who had a shared interest in mechs made him question his own assumptions. Maybe they weren't *all* bad. Plus, it would be a lark and a fun story to tell the crew when he got back to the ship.

"*We're* going to an after-party," Del interjected. "And I don't remember you asking me if it was okay to invite a complete stranger."

"We aren't strangers. His name is Tovi, and he works in salvage," Ryan said with a smug, unbothered smile. Del turned to glare at him, and Tovi could see her scowl.

"I don't want to cause a problem," he said, loath to get in the middle of an awkward situation. Del glanced his way, and Tovi was surprised her expression wasn't one of scorn, but pity, and he didn't know what to do with that. People often assumed he couldn't keep up with the party scene because of his naive demeanor, but they soon learned he could go toe to toe.

"Not a problem at all. Right, Del?" Ryan turned to her, and she sighed, then nodded. "So what do you say?"

Having decided it would be a fun adventure and having taken far too long to answer, Tovi nodded his assent. "Yeah, that could be fun."

"Could be? I'll have to prove just how much fun I can be," Ryan said, his voice dropping an octave, and Tovi's stomach did a flip-floppy thing that had him wishing he wasn't surrounded by hundreds of people oohing and awing at the mechs on display.

"Do you mind if we stop by my place so I can change? I feel like a Christmas tree."

Tovi smiled at him, finding him surprisingly self-deprecating, and knew the rest of this cycle—and probably the next—was spoken for.

Chapter 6

A Royal with Cheese, Please

Sierra didn't buy Tovi's flippant attitude, but if he was willing to trade one devil for another, she'd let him do it. She had her own skeletons she didn't want waltzing back into her life anytime soon. Ryan was a weaselly pissant, and she'd clock him at every opportunity.

Tovi led the way into Hazel's office. Hazel didn't put out any chairs, as she didn't like people hanging around. It was standing room only in front of her massive desk, a faux-wood island in a tiny sea covered in crusty knickknacks, like a creepy plush bunny that was missing an eye and appeared to be willing its own demise as it leaned treacherously close to the edge of the desk. Someone should really put it out of its misery.

Same went for the person sitting behind said desk. Sierra had been channeling some of the rage she carried for Hazel and her bullshit business tactics when she'd floored Ryan. Hazel was somewhere between fifty-five and mummified; it was hard to tell. She moved like someone younger, spry with small dog energy, while her skin was scorched from too much time in what Sierra could only assume was her own personal tanning bed. She changed her hair out on the regular; today, it was bleach blond and cut in a bob. It gave her a disconcerting innocence that didn't comport with her true, ghoulish demeanor.

Hazel studied her computer screen, then sucked her teeth and shook her head. She tsked and tapped at the keyboard.

"Christ on a catamaran, Hazel, save us the theatrics and spit it out," Sierra said.

Hazel gave her an unamused stare. "Well, when I add up the total salvage, then subtract the rental fee, refueling fee, admin fee, storage fee, courtesy fee, and damage to the equipment, your debt falls from 2,732 credits to 2,530."

"What the fuck are you talking about? We brought in more salvage than the estimated worth of the ship."

"That was the estimated worth two months ago. Since then, the recycling cost of batteries and motherboard components has gone up. The cost to refurbish those units outstrips their resale worth."

Sierra slammed her hand on the table, making the trinkets tremble, but Cecil intervened before Sierra made a valiant attempt to flip her desk. "We signed the contract based on the salvage worth at the time, not the salvage worth now."

"Yes, but there's a clause that calls for renegotiation in the case of market volatility," Hazel said, unfazed as she daintily righted a dusty plastic frog.

Cecil grinned, baring his teeth. "You mean there was a clause that I removed during negotiations and you signed."

"I don't believe I would do such a thing," she said, sounding slightly less certain, her short nails drumming on the desk.

"But you did. Check your copies."

This was not a coincidence. Cecil had caught the clause before their signing and drafted an edited version. It just so happened that someone had let loose a screaming beetle in the office a few minutes prior to the contract signing, and Hazel might have been distracted in the face of high-pitched screeching that could strip paint.

She tapped at her computer, a frown pulling down the edges of her lips. Her expression twitched and jerked as she realized her mistake. "Well, you are right on this occasion, but there is extensive damage to the units, faceplates falling off, a lack of proper maintenance to keep the mechs oiled, and the food stains in the mech are atrocious, and we explicitly state no eating or drinking in the suits."

"You're the one who refuses to keep the mechs maintained. The oil leaks are from busted seals, and that's on you. We are not required to maintain the seals. We'd need an oil IV drip to make up for the loss," Sierra said.

"Your ill-treatment of the mechs is eroding the seals."

Sierra balled her fists to keep from using her hands to strangle Hazel's very wringable neck. "Don't even with this bullshit, Hazel. How do you ill-treat a fucking seal except not maintaining the machine?"

"Be that as it may, your credit comes to 350 units, and we'll subtract that from your debt of 2,732 you have in arrears for the previously undelivered salvage. Maybe if you handed over some of the undeclared items you keep, we could get you in the black. If we don't receive the funds in the next thirty cycles, I'll be forced to impound your precious ship. And you know I only do that as a last resort." Hazel twisted her face into a mask of condescending pity.

Sierra wanted to smack Hazel's mocking concern off her face. "You mother—"

Cecil placed a paw over her mouth to stop the flow of insults she was prepared to rain down on Hazel. A mouthful of course hair kept her gagged.

"We'll be in touch," Cecil said, giving her a forced smile, then ushering them out the door.

"Cursing her out isn't going to help, Sierra," Cecil said once they were outside, and he'd released his hold.

She wiped the back of her hand against her mouth then picked a loose hair off her tongue. "It'll make me feel better. Isn't that worth something?"

"No, and what did I tell you about eating in the damn mechs? If you give her an excuse to charge us, she'll take it."

"Are you really going to lecture us about having a sandwich while we work?" Tovi asked. Sierra appreciated the support, but they all knew his comment was directed at her.

"No, I'm lecturing Sierra about keeping it in her mouth."

She snorted a laugh and kicked at the ground.

"How hard is it to chew and swallow your food?" Cecil asked.

"I don't know, super hard?" she said.

"Come on, let's not take this out on each other," Tovi said. He seemed tired, a bit defeated, and it took all the self-righteous indignation out of her sails.

Cecil seemed to lose some of his steam too. "Okay, let's get the rest of this stuff on the market and see what we can salvage. I still say we should sell the cat."

Tovi shot him a glare, and Sierra was glad he had some pep in his step, but she couldn't help thinking that maybe Cecil was right. They were drowning in debt, and what was the point if Omnia repo'd everything of value they had? It had taken them ten years to afford the ship and get it into shape, and now Hazel, of all the scum to slither on the station, was threatening to take even that away from them. They could cut their losses and move on to another station, but they'd built something like a life here. Iz wouldn't go with them, not with Lana and her job on the station. Sierra knew she couldn't stop the inevitable; at some point, everybody moved on with their lives. She shouldn't get attached, but she wasn't ready to lose them; she loved her crew. Tovi's expression was crestfallen, like he'd already resigned himself to losing Lulu. Like he was so used to losing, he never had the chance to imagine winning.

"Not yet, Cecil. Let's see what we can do. We have thirty cycles to come up with the money," she said.

"Fine, but we'll need to disguise her," he said, pacified by her partial capitulation. "I broke up our skimming inventory and sent a list to the brokers we trust. I'll do the rounds."

"Thanks, Cecil," Sierra said and patted his furry arm. "We'll meet you at the club later."

He nodded and moved through the crisscross of people milling about the loading dock, scattering people as he barreled through.

"You okay, Tovi?" Sierra asked. He'd been quieter than she liked—never a good sign.

"Yeah, can we just go get a drink? I want to get out of this place and sit down somewhere familiar," he said.

Sierra knew just the place. The Star Hopper was a diner, the kind only frequented by locals and the occasional clueless tourist. It was tucked away in a working neighborhood where the apartments were too small to really live in, only sleep and fuck in the space that held a bed and a hot plate. Bathrooms and showers were communal, and everyone knew everyone's business. The diner was where people spent their off time shooting the shit and seeking solace in a heaping pile of chili cheese fries.

Sierra pushed open the door and walked back in time. Vintage booths upholstered in red, sparkly vinyl lined the walls, hugging chipped and well-loved teal tables between them. Tables and chairs inhabited the open space between the overflowing booths and the high counter with pedestal seats cradling weary laborers hunched over their burgers. The black-and-white checkered floors were peeling but clean, and her shoes squeaked as she walked to the counter. Marge, the owner, had a love of vintage movies from before the Expulsion, rivaling Tovi's obsession with Earth Before. There was no one alive who could attest to the diner's authenticity, only the media humans had squirreled away when they were shipped off planet.

Vintage rock music filled in the gaps between conversations, some loud and bawdy, others subdued and punctuated with long sighs. The third shift at the docks must have finished, releasing workers wearing their reflective vests back into the station to eat and drink until they fell into bed. They gathered around each other like screws to a magnet, small groups coalescing as more sentients arrived.

Sierra and Tovi chose a bar seat to get some space.

"Hey, lovelies, it's been a while. How was the salvage?" Marge asked. She was olive skinned, somewhere in her forties, with dark hair piled on her head and a pristine white apron hugging her candy-cane pinstriped dress.

They both made noncommittal noises.

"That bad, aye? Let me get you some milkshakes on the house," she said and wandered off to help another table.

"You didn't need to get involved with Ryan. I was taking care of it," Tovi said.

Sierra held up her hands. "Sorry, Tovi. I saw his pretty-boy face, and him laughing at you, and I couldn't help myself. What did he want anyway?"

"Offered us a job for a thirty percent cut," he said, absently tearing at the napkin wrapped around his utensils.

"The audacity is astounding." She chewed on a hangnail she'd managed to worry into existence. Stillness and tranquility were for losers, or people with less debts to pay.

"Yeah, well, now I'm not so sure. How are we going to pay off our debt?"

"We could steal his ship," Sierra said with a grin.

Tovi laughed, and she was glad to see him lightening up a bit. Any mention of Ryan and their stolen salvage sent Tovi into an emotional spiral. The betrayal had rocked his confidence. It didn't matter how many times they insisted he wasn't to blame—he took all the blame. But she didn't have an answer to his question. Their ship was rated for cargo and tows, and all legit salvage jobs came through the yards. While Hazel was a pain in the ass, she was the best of the worst. They kept their ears to the ground for any off-the-books work, but those came with greater risks.

"Let's see what Cecil can get for our skimmings. We almost got the mech operational, and we can take some dock jobs. Maybe a delivery job will crop up," Sierra said as Marge came back with chocolate shakes and set them on the counter.

"Thanks, Marge," Tovi said, the wattage of his smile turning up at the shake's arrival, and Sierra flashed Marge a grateful smile. He took a sip. "Goddamn, that's a pretty fucking good milkshake."

Marge's laugh was like the tinkling of bells. "Can I get you anything else, loves?"

"A couple of royals with cheese and fries, the usual," Sierra said. "Hey, if you know of any work kicking about, let us know."

Marge yelled their order back to the cook. "I'll let you know if I hear anything, honey."

"I'll pick up some shifts on the dock while we're station side," Sierra said.

"Hey, y'all," Iz said, coming up behind them. Their hair was down in microbraids that ombred from their natural dark brown to sparkling electric purple.

"Your hair looks amazing!" Sierra said.

"So sparkly," Tovi said, eyes wide as saucers.

"Thanks!" Iz said as Lana came up by their side. They grabbed a seat next to Tovi. "Talked to Cecil. Figured you'd end up here."

Lana was a broad-shouldered, heavily modified human with robotic eyes and a cat tail anxiously twitching behind her. She grabbed a seat next to Iz, wrapping the tail possessively around Iz's waist. "Sorry to hear about your haul," Lana said, glancing at Iz. "I have an uncle who needs some warehouse help. I guess people have been breaking in and stealing stuff. He's been short-staffed on second and third shift. I told him you know how to operate a mech and he was interested."

"Does he have his own mech?" Tovi asked.

"Yeah, you don't have to bring your own. He said you could drop by tomorrow, but he only needs one mech operator per shift."

"One of us should keep working on Archy anyway," Sierra said.

"You could pick up Lulu on your way to the job," Lana said. "I should be done reskinning her by then, and Iz fixed her mindsync. The antenna was broken." Sierra nodded and Tovi elbowed her. Apparently, her face didn't disguise her general dislike of Lana. There was something about her possessiveness that rankled.

"What's with all these long faces?" Iz asked.

"Ryan was snooping around," Sierra said. "Offered us some kind of job."

Iz's eyes narrowed, and Lana laid a hand on their wrist.

"What did you say?"

"No, of course," Tovi said.

Iz lifted an eyebrow. "Maybe we should hear him out." Sierra stared at Iz like they'd grown a second head just as Marge laid out two baskets with burgers and fries.

"Don't give me that. We might be able to turn it to our advantage. Keep your enemies close and all that," they said, stealing a fry from Tovi, who didn't complain.

"Sierra kneed him in the stomach, so I doubt he'll be back," Tovi said, dipping his fries in honey.

"That's good, means you'll be sticking around for a while," Lana said, and Sierra—for the first time—regretted assaulting Ryan.

Iz gave Sierra an appreciative nod. "If he does, then we'll know he's desperate. Finish your food. We're going dancing. I don't care if we didn't get paid."

Tovi smiled at Iz, took a big bite of his burger, and sipped his milkshake. Sierra took Iz's advice and tried to enjoy her meal. Thoughts of losing her livelihood and her home sat heavy in her mind, like a decommissioned mech. Worse than that was losing her crew. They'd be scattered to the winds if the ship was impounded, and she'd have to start all over again.

The day they'd bought the ship—and she'd moved out of her closet space of an apartment—had been one of the happiest of her life. After years of paying off her criminal damages and living paycheck to paycheck, the ship was a light in the darkness. It only took one bad job to put everything they'd worked for in jeopardy. All the old insecurities had piled on her since the day Ryan hijacked their salvage, and she couldn't talk about it to Tovi without him feeling responsible. They'd been best friends for over a decade, and nothing was going to get in the way of that, certainly not a bag of dicks like Ryan. She could admit to herself that kneeing Ryan had been the catharsis she'd needed.

They finished their meals and headed down to Scorcher's Alley, their favorite district on station to get a drink and dance until their worries faded into background noise. Sierra messaged Cecil, letting him know their destination. They ended up at Jolene's, a dark, disco-vibe bar playing throwbacks and serving watered-down drinks. They were a few in by the time Cecil showed up.

"How'd it go?" Sierra asked.

Cecil shrugged. "About what I expected, but I'm concerned about the AIcat. We should get her reskinned before she's spotted."

"Already on it," Iz said.

Cecil grunted and nodded, waving at the bartender for a drink. There were clear benefits to having a giant bear demand the attention of the bar staff. Nobody pretended they didn't see him.

"We have a job Lana set up for us. I'm not staying out as late, so I can take second shift if you want third," Sierra said to Tovi, who nodded in agreement. He had far more stamina and extrovert energy than Sierra. She didn't know how he did it. She was already overstimulated and wanted to crawl into bed with a book and some tea.

The dock work would be mind-numbing and a good distraction from her own thoughts. She liked working with her hands; it was grounding and something she understood. Moments like this, when the crew was in harmony and they let loose, it felt like home. Now, they were flirting with losing everything, and thoughts of the crew breaking up was an asteroid barrage she tried and failed to dodge. Sierra racked her brain with one harebrained scheme after another to pay off the ship's debt and keep their little family together. She sipped her drink while Cecil talked to the others, holding a giant drink with a swizzle straw and little pink umbrella that was comically small in his paw.

She turned around and leaned her elbows against the bar. Pixie sat on Iz's head like a purple, iridescent skullcap as Iz danced with Lana. Wrapped up in each other, they swayed to the deep, jazzy beat. Tovi came bouncing over holding an electric blue drink, the purple one long gone.

"Why y'all standing on the wall?" Tovi asked. He was in his element, and Sierra always envied his ability to put aside his worries when he went out dancing. She couldn't make the narrator in her head shut up.

"Just thinking."

"You're always thinking," Tovi said, yelling over the thumping music. "It can wait until tomorrow."

Sierra tossed back her second drink, which would be her last. She didn't want a hangover tomorrow, and it wouldn't help her relax anyway. Instead, she pulled a tablet out of her pocket and stuck it under her tongue. The pill was a mild relaxant that would do what the alcohol couldn't.

The song changed, and they made their way to the dance floor to forget about all the troubles that would be waiting for them in the morning.

Chapter 7

Blackmail Gone Stale

Del

Heard you were dropped by that salvage rat today.

Ryan

Don't believe everything you hear.

Del

I have video evidence.

Ryan

That bitch caught me by surprise.

Del

While you were trying to get in that Praxian's pants again?

Ryan

What a waste. I had a good thing going there. It's too bad he found my bug.

Del

Was it worth it?

Ryan

Getting their tech to find unclaimed salvage was worth it, pushed me up in the standings.

Del

Where are you now?

Ryan

Dieter is leading by ten points and I'm neck and neck with Aster.

Del

Your father's point system is seriously fucked up.

Ryan

I'm in a bind. You know those pirates I paid to make a problem disappear? They're blackmailing me. If Father finds out, all my hard work will be for nothing.

Del

I told you to be careful. They aren't as stupid as you think.

Ryan

Don't need an 'I told you so' at the moment.

Del

Reap what you sow, buddy.

I need to make the problem disappear.

I might have one or two ideas.

Do tell.

Chapter 8

Fight for your Right to Parley

Thirteen Years Ago

F or the millionth time, Sierra finished changing out the bearings on a commercial mech head, running through a diagnostic test to make sure it swiveled smoothly, absent the grinding sound it made when Targon brought it into the mechanic shop. She'd kill for a busted hydraulic arm or bent hatch to pound on; anything for a change of pace. Bonus if she could pretend it was Targon's ruddy face she was hitting with a hammer.

The head swiveled 360 degrees and righted itself, the glassy eyes of the camera reflecting her grease-stained face and the red handkerchief holding her hair back, a long brown braid resting on her shoulder. The machine shop had been a wet dream when she'd first arrived, housing four bays that were three stories tall and harboring busted mechs she could sink her hands into. She'd thought paying off her debt wouldn't be so bad if she had access to the massive hydraulic lift she was straddling, as well as every tool she'd ever lusted after and some she'd never heard of. The shine had decidedly worn off after she'd seen her debt diminish by mere increments in the last five years.

She climbed down from the mech and caught sight of Targon, a short, broad-chested man with red splotches on his face from never turning down a pint, something she was familiar with, coming from a family who drowned their sorrows in hard liquor. He was talking to one of his many henchmen lurking around the shop, then he retreated to his office. Sierra steeled herself, wiping her hands on a dirty rag, and followed him into the office, where he sat behind his sturdy desk, staring at his display.

"Come on, Targon, you got to give me a shot in the ring. You promised me last turn you'd let me compete," Sierra said, getting straight to the point.

Targon didn't spare her a glance. "I said I'd consider it if you met your quotas."

"And I met the ridiculous quota you set for me."

"And I'm considering it."

She threw the greasy rag down on his desk to get his attention. "If you don't let me compete, I'll audition for House Kibaya."

He glanced at her then let out a loud laugh, head thrown back and his hands covering his face as it grew redder. Sierra's jaw clenched, and she glowered at him.

"You really think you have what it takes to operate a mech? You don't have the talent or experience to compete in the ring. I didn't want to crush your pathetic little dreams, but you don't stand a chance. Save yourself the humiliation."

Sierra's heart plummeted into her stomach, where it thrashed in the acid pooling there. Her father's words came rushing back to her like a gravity wave. *You'll never amount to anything, so shut up and do what I tell you.*

All the voices in her head, whispering in the dead of night when she was alone in her bed, saying she wasn't good enough, now wore Targon's skin and echoed back to her in his grating, mocking voice. Was she really so pathetic, harboring delusions of grandeur? She was suddenly hyper-aware of herself, seeing her small, sad frame from above, how she imagined everyone else saw her—useless, embarrassing, annoying. Her father was probably laughing along with Targon, hand clutching a whiskey bottle.

"Even if you were any good at mech operation, you're impossible to work with. Don't you ever wonder why no one wants to hang around you, why you don't have any friends?" Targon was grinning, his joy at taunting her twisting her stomach.

Sierra was collapsing under the weight of his words, her shoulders rounding in a vain attempt to protect herself from the assault on her heart. At the mention of being a friendless wretch, she thought of Tovi, galaxies away and her only friend in the universe. What would he say if he was here? Targon had beat her into the ground for five years, isolating her and making promises he continually broke, then blaming her at every turn because he knew she didn't have better options.

Thinking of Tovi and how appalled he'd be if he was here made her realize how fucked up the situation was, and it had little to do with her. She straightened, drawing her shoulders back, turned on her heel, and walked away from Targon and his barrage of insults. She was going to try out for House Kibaya, consequences be damned. Targon's laughter chased her as she rushed out of the mechanic's shop and back to her cramped bunk.

She activated her sleeve, submitted the tryout application she'd filled out months ago, and took a steadying breath. She risked losing her work order with Targon; the moment he saw her in the audition tournament, he'd probably cancel her contract and she'd be royally fucked. This was her only chance to change her circumstances, and she'd have to give it everything she had.

Moments later, she received a ping on her sleeve informing her she'd be competing next shift. Sierra had heard House Kibaya didn't waste any time and suspected she'd be fighting soon, but not next shift; she only had about six hours to get ready. She took some deep breaths to try and slow her rapidly beating heart and tamp down the fight-or-flight response her body was belly-flopping into.

What if Targon was right, and she was about to make a fool of herself on interstellarvision? She could take what little savings she had, go down to the docks and see if anyone needed a mechanic, then ship-hop until she found a decent situation. Once she skipped out on the contract, she'd be blacklisted from most legitimate work and her debt would go to collections. Someone would come calling to collect one day, and she'd always be jumping at shadows.

No, she had to see this through.

You're not good enough. You're going to be the laughingstock of the mechverse. They'll be making fun of you for cycles, said a voice in her head that was a strange amalgamation of her father and Targon.

She paced the three steps her bunk would allow and grasped her head in her hands. "No, no, no, no, no! Shut up!"

She stopped pacing and turned to the cracked, narrow mirror taking up the entirety of her closet door, kitty-corner to her narrow bed. "You can do this." Her breath fogged the glass, obscuring her tense features.

Stuck to the mirror by a piece of gum was a photo of her and Tovi, posing with peace signs and arms slung around each other's shoulders. His smile was bright as ever, the one genuine thing she clung to. It was his voice in her head telling her that she could do this, and that one day she would pay off her debt and track him down, then they'd be a team again. *Assuming that's what he wants,* another little voice of uncertainty chimed in.

She shook that thought away and opened her small wardrobe, then pulled out the outfit she'd been working on, a black and green striped jumpsuit resplendent with buckles and straps she'd painstakingly sewed on by hand. Sierra took her time getting dressed, applying a thick line of messy black eyeliner and green mascara. Standing out was key to making an impression; they wanted personalities just as much as they wanted skill, and she knew she could never pull off a hero persona to save her life. Mech operators were entire personalities with back stories—mortal enemies, lost loves, and buckets of made-up drama to entertain the masses. The fights were real and the outcomes unplanned, but the personalities were extra.

The person who stared back at her in the splintered, flint-covered mirror appeared deranged, and she cracked a lopsided grin. There was only one thing left to do.

She packed her meager belongings, not trusting them in Targon's territory, where he could exact his revenge on the few precious objects she owned, namely the picture of her and Tovi and her tools—any self-respecting mechanic had a personal set. Everything tossed into a duffel, she left her bunk and the impersonal rooms that had been her shelter for years, hoping never to return.

Even after packing, she had a few hours to kill. She wasn't far from the battle ring, close enough to hear the fights on a quiet day, but she took a detour on her way to House Kibaya and stopped at an E-Z-Grow hair station near the crowded tourist area, using credits she couldn't afford to spend to let the machine dye her hair green and cut it to chin length. Her hair, now a green puff, completed her bad guy image.

She shouldered her pack with purpose and walked to the battle ring, pushing through oblivious tourists stopping in the middle of the street to stare at trapeze performers and pirate re-enactors vying for tips. When the tent came into sight, the crowd thinned, and she stopped short, staring up at the red-and-yellow striped tent, hearing the clash of metal as it seeped into the street. In all the years she'd been here, she'd not been inside, always watching the matches from her sleeve. Targon made sure she was working during the matches, and she only watched the replays after the battles were done. He sucked all the joy out of life like a demented vacuum.

Her feet were rooted to the metal street, the entrance to the ring towering over her.

"Are you coming or going?" a voice said from behind, making her jump and spin around and nearly crash into a tall, thin Black man wearing a powder blue suit. She immediately recognized him as Vandover, Captain and CEO of House Kibaya.

"Oh, shit. Sorry," she said, stumbling backward. "I'm going—into the tent, or I guess that's coming?" She was stammering, and she clamped her mouth shut.

His gaze took her in, like an ant under a magnifying glass. His expression gave nothing away. She felt the anxiety sweats coming on under his scrutiny, and she had an overwhelming desire to air out her pits for fear of smelling like rank BO. "You're here for the audition matches?" he asked.

"Yes, um, this upcoming shift."

"You're here early. Did you come to scope out the competition?"

More like scrape up the courage, she thought. "Yeah, didn't have anywhere else to be."

"Where were you before this?"

She wanted to make something up about fighting somewhere obscure, bolster her pathetic resume, but her mind was a blank. "I work over at House Targon, as a mech mechanic. Have done for five years."

An eyebrow twitched and it was the first involuntary move the man had made. "A debtor?"

"How'd you know?" She shrank back. Debtors got a bad rap; it was something she desperately tried to hide.

But he didn't answer her question. "I'll see you in the ring." With that, he walked around her, and she realized she'd been blocking the gateway to the battle ring, and her face reddened with embarrassment. She wanted to hit her head against something hard and unforgiving, repeatedly, until she forgot she'd made a fool of herself to the one person who could help her. *Grreeeeat.*

Sierra trudged into the battle tent, passed the rows of bookie boxes with smiling people taking bets from tourists and consummate gamblers alike, and showed her invitation to the terrifying white wolf with piercings lining her ears and cold blue eyes, standing guard at the ring entrance. She gave Sierra a bored expression and let her pass. Sierra thought she might be a compdroid at first, but she was too big, so she must be a Nhethian.

It took two seconds for Sierra to identify the other hopefuls, clustered together near the front of the ring, similarly dressed in outlandish outfits and staring pensively at the battle on display behind the safety glass circling the ring around the sunken amphitheater.

Sierra spotted someone she'd run into a few times at mech swaps, where she found used tools in good shape and got them in exchange for leftover parts she'd fixed up. Credits were nice, but they were a luxury, and sometimes parts went a lot further.

Sierra walked around the top ring, then down the aisle until she was in the same row as the other hopefuls. "Hey, it's Andy, right?" Sierra asked, trying to sound nonchalant. The person, broad-shouldered and taller than Sierra by a head with fawn pink skin and short, fire red hair that faded to orange, turned to her at the sound of their name then stood.

"Yeah, that's right, going by he/him today," he said, shaking her hand, and she saw the he/him pin on his dark blue collared shirt.

"Cool, I'm Sierra, she/her. Are you auditioning today?"

Andy gestured for her to sit down next to him, and she obliged. "I am. It's my second time. You?"

Sierra nodded. "I've never tried. I'm a bit nervous."

Andy shot her a smile. "Me too. Cool outfit."

Sierra blushed and relief flooded her. Maybe she wasn't ridiculous. "How does this work, then?" She knew how it worked—she'd seen it enough times—but she was floundering conversationally.

"Once this match is done, they'll bring out all the mechs and we'll get to pick which one we want. We'll then have to get it operating within three hours, and whoever's successful will have a two-minute match against whoever else gets done in time."

"No pressure, then," Sierra said, biting her lip.

"A stress-free environment, for sure."

Sierra watched the timer tick down and the buzzer go off on the rather boring match between two amateur fighters who were tangled up in each other's legs—embarrassing. The ring was cleared and the few spectators wandered out of the tent. Watching mechanics work was about as fascinating as watching paint dry.

Sierra studied the mechs as Vandover's crew rolled them into the ring, all of them sitting limply on hand trucks and dumped on the ground. She wanted one that only needed mechanical work. Her experience with electronics was nominal, and she'd likely end up strangling herself instead of fixing the problem. Some were shiny with badass weapons strapped to their back, but she didn't let that distract her. It didn't matter how pretty it was if she couldn't get it running. Then she saw it, a bucket of bolts, but the head swiveled as it was dropped, so no frozen bearings in the neck and its arms and legs were bent at rest, not straight and seized up, all good signs. It had a nasty gash in the front plate and one arm dangled a little too much. She hoped no one else picked it first, and avoided giving it too much attention, in case someone tried to steal it from underneath her.

Vandover came into the ring—the ring walls had been drawn up into the ceiling, leaving the area open—and waved the recruits forward. They lined up in front of him, a ragtag mix of people hoping to prove themselves, some more well off than others, with their expensive mech gloves sticking out of their pockets.

"Choose your mech," Vandover said without preamble, and Sierra sprinted for her mech, leaving others gaping and scrambling. She planted her hand on the mech's foot, staking her claim and ignoring the questioning glances from her competitors. A timer popped up on the marquee overheard. Sierra took that as a green flag and scrambled up the mech and into the frozen-open hatch with the gash in the center to run a diagnostic. As she plugged her sleeve in and set the diagnostic running, a crate of tools was rolled out to the center. Sierra saw a welder, a plasma cutter, extra wiring, ball bearings in every size, hydraulic pistons, and metal sheeting.

As suspected, she'd need to fix the hatch. It wouldn't operate unless it could shut and latch, a safety feature of all mechs, and the arm would need to be repaired, but that could come later. According to the rules, the mechs had to be operational and able to stand; it said nothing about functioning arms. Sierra figured she could always kick her opponents to death.

Time ticked down as she set to work on the hatch, occasionally glancing at her opponents and clocking annoyed grimaces and frustrated banging. At least she wasn't the only one. With half the time gone, she'd fixed the warping in the hatch by patching the gaping hole, allowing it to close fully, and she started on the broken latch mechanism. When that was done, she only had twenty minutes to work on the busted arm. It wasn't enough time, so she made a quick decision. The arm was nonfunctioning, making it a burden, so she grabbed the plasma cutter, pulled down her face shield, and cut the arm off at the joint.

She threw off the face shield and climbed into the mech, securing the door and firing it up, crossing all her fingers. It shuddered to life, lighting up the displays and righting itself to a full, straight-back sit. Sierra strapped herself in as the emergency lights nagged her to assume the secured position before it could stand. She straightened her gloves, and with a few practiced flicks of her fingers, the mech climbed to its feet, just in time for the buzzer to go off, signaling the end of their time. It was just her and Andy's mechs standing.

She opened the hatch and swelled with pride as it moved smoothly without a hitch, likely because she'd greased the shit out of the hydraulics. Alarms beeped as she removed the harness, and she turned them off before stepping out then staring down at the immobile mechs with triumph. Andy did the same, shooting her a thumbs-up.

"Congratulations," Vandover said from the ring floor. "Once the ring is cleared, the battle will begin." And didn't that sound ominous?

The other mechs were cleared out, leaving just her facing Andy as the ring barrier materialized from the ceiling, enclosing the two mechs. Andy grinned before climbing back into the mech and Sierra did the same. He seemed like a real cool person, but she couldn't let that affect the match. Targon was going to kick her out when he found out she'd gone against his orders, and then she'd be on the streets with her debt hanging over her. Winning was the only way she could ensure she had a place to sleep after this.

"You have two minutes to show us what you got," Vandover said over the intercom. With the hatch now closed, his voice was piped through the mech's internal speakers. People were streaming into the tent now that the competition had gotten interesting.

"Fight!" he yelled as the marquee displayed the two-minute timer. Sierra hadn't planned on getting this far, not wanting to jinx herself. She hadn't fought since her junkyard days and never in a mech; she'd just have to wing it. In the operator's seat, an entire mech at her mercy, she was more than ready.

She kept her distance, assessing the mech in front of her. It was short and stocky, with fists like hammers, but it had a bum leg that dragged. Andy took a wobbly step forward, then moved quickly, lunging at her, trying to overcompensate for the leg, and grabbed Sierra's mech around the waist.

Sierra didn't want to lose her advantage by taking the fight to the floor, so she wrapped her mech's one arm around Andy's waist and twisted to the side, slamming Andy's mech into one of the ring posts and loosening its grip. It fell to the side, but Andy didn't waste any time grabbing for Sierra's foot. Sierra stepped her mech back to avoid the grab and landed a kick to the mech's head, sending it swiveling in the opposite direction.

Sierra grabbed the other mech's arm, pulled, then counterbalanced with her body to swing the mech and throw it against the opposite wall. She misjudged the swing and slipped, crashing to the ground, but she'd managed to get some air on the mech, a hard thing to do with one arm and a one-ton mech.

Andy's mech was slow to recover, and Sierra took the opportunity to have her mech wave to the cheering crowd and make a muscle man pose with her one arm. The crowd ate it up; cheers rose and popcorn was thrown in all directions. When Andy's mech was up, the bum leg now frozen straight, he used the leg as a crutch, throwing the mech forward and landing a punch on Sierra's armless side, leaving her unable to block. She returned the punch with her mech's good hand, and they were locked in a clench when the buzzer went off, ending their ordeal.

"Fuck yeah!" Sierra whooped alone in her mech. That felt so fucking good. Even if she lost now and had no job to return to, it was worth it. She hadn't felt so alive in years.

The mechs were put in neutral, standing straight as soldiers. They opened their hatches, the industry-wide end to any fight where both mechs could still stand. She walked out on the hatch and saw Andy, a shit-eating grin on his face as he stared back. She put her hand on her heart and bowed in respect and he did the same. They turned and waved at the cheering crowd behind the protective barrier. It was a small crowd, but that didn't matter. Tryouts weren't scored or open to bets, only attracting die-hard fans.

After the cheering died down, they returned to their bedraggled mechs and Vandover's crew directed them to the warehouse for storage. Mech parked and powered down, Sierra opened the hatch then descended down the side, adrenaline coursing through her veins. She saw Vandover standing in the warehouse about thirty feet away, talking to Targon. Her blood ran cold. Targon was clearly pissed. She couldn't hear what he was saying, but the violent red of his face and the accusatory finger he brandished first at Vandover, then at Sierra gave him away.

Vandover peered down his nose at Targon. As far as Sierra could tell, he said nothing, or maybe he didn't move his lips much. Sierra hung back, embarrassed and ashamed. She knew Targon was listing all her faults and demanding she return to her work. She didn't know if Vandover was even considering her for the apprenticeship, but if he had been, he probably wasn't now.

Andy had climbed down and was watching the fight with curiosity. He shot Sierra a questioning glance; Sierra shrugged and pretended to poke at something on the mech's calf. Eventually, Targon must have worn himself out, leaving with his goons and shooting her an acidic glare.

Vandover walked over and appraised her, eerily silent. Andy stood pensively behind him, worrying the edge of his blue shirt.

"Oh my God, just say something already. It's like torture," she said, thunking her head on the calf housing.

"You should see me in an interrogation room," he said.

Sierra snapped her head up in surprise. Was he serious?

"I'd like to offer you an apprenticeship, you and Andy." Andy silently jumped up and down behind Vandover's back, punching the sky, then the air in front of him like a boxer, smiling like a loon.

"You serious?" Sierra asked, eyes trailing after the ghost of Targon, too nervous Vandover was pulling her leg to be excited. Plus, Andy was excited enough for the both of them.

"I've been regaled with your laziness, unprofessionalism, and incompetence. I believe only one of those is true. You asked earlier how I knew you were a debtor. Targon likes to pick up debtors because it feeds his ego to mistreat them. You aren't the first of his debtors I've taken on."

"So this is a pity hire?" she asked. "Not that I'm saying no. I have no shame, just curious." She was sure she saw his lip twitch this time, and she had a feeling she'd found a new personal project.

"You showed talent, and I can't fault your mechanical work or quick thinking in the ring. You have promise. If you stick with me, we'll turn that into something more."

"You got yourself a deal, sir," she said, holding out her hand. He took it and they shook on it.

Sierra couldn't hold back the smile that lifted her cheeks as Andy brandished two thumbs-up and a wicked grin behind Vandover's back.

Chapter 9

Beware of Boybands Bearing Gifts

Tovi didn't have any plans until third shift. He'd resurfaced from a dead sleep in the middle of first shift. Tovi had successfully suppressed the dread of Ryan's resurfacing with loud music, energetic dancing, and alcohol induced relaxation; he'd thoroughly enjoyed their outing. Sierra and Cecil had begged off hours before, then Iz and Lana went back to Lana's apartment, and Tovi stayed a little longer, dancing and chatting up the bartender before heading back to the ship.

He debated what to do after he'd poured himself a cup of coffee. The loading ramp needed repair and there was always work to do on the mech. He should check the readouts on their experimental salvage radar, but that thought came with unwanted memories and the ghost of Ryan's past made a run at the fences.

Space was vast, and it was difficult to find unclaimed ships. Iz and Tovi had created a system to concentrate their search in statistically likely places to find ships that had run into trouble based on stats from previous incidents combined with shipping lanes and distance to stations. The antennas they'd mounted on the ship scanned areas that were statistically significant, searching for anything that was warmer than the surrounding space or reflected a signal back to them.

It was a narrow signal, and they'd mostly found asteroids and space debris, but after months of scanning and manually reviewing data, they'd had a hit. They'd loaded up, rented the mechs from Hazel, and taken off in search of their quarry. By the time they'd arrived, an unidentified ship was leaving the vicinity and the chargers they'd planted on the unclaimed ship had turned what was left to rubble. They'd come back with nothing to show except the debt they'd owed on the rentals.

Tovi had been depressed at their exceptionally bad luck. It wasn't until weeks later, after he'd found the bug in his cabin, magnetized to the wall under his bed, that he'd realized it hadn't been a stroke of bad luck. He traced the signal back to the source, following it to Blue Dock and the fanciest personal pleasure cruiser he ever laid eyes on. He lurked in a dark corner, waiting to see who would show their face. When Ryan sauntered off the ship, Tovi's heart had plummeted. They hadn't been serious by any stretch of the imagination, but he'd *liked* Ryan, and they'd hung out a few times before rolling into Tovi's bed. He understood then why Ryan had insisted they go to Tovi's ship and his narrow bed when Ryan had an entire penthouse where they could stretch out. At the time, he'd thought Ryan was interested in his life, his work, and his crew, but that bubble burst abruptly.

Tovi had wallowed for a minute, feeling small and stupid, until Ryan came near his corner of deepest lurking, and Tovi punched Ryan square in the nose. The satisfying snap and Ryan's crumpled form had been an insufficient balm to his wounded pride and empty credit account.

He shook himself from the painful memory and changed into his coveralls. He pinged Sierra and found her in the cargo bay. He joined her on the loading ramp to inspect the damaged piston that had been acting up. Her tired eyes and sluggish movements told him she was suffering from a caffeine deficit.

"How was the rest of the shift?" Sierra asked, suppressing a yawn.

"It was fun. Got some free drinks."

"This is my shocked face," she said, her face unchanging. "I always have to pay for my drinks."

"It helps if you smile at people," he said.

"Ew, I'll pay for my drinks, thank you."

"Suit yourself. Are you going to glare at the piston or fix it?"

"If I glare long enough, it might fix itself, especially if I threaten to beat it with a hammer," she said, giving the piston the stink eye like it might take her threat seriously.

"Or I'll fix it for you."

"That also works." She handed him the spanner wrench she was holding like a club.

Tovi rolled his eyes and removed the housing covering the piston. "It might just need oiling."

Sierra's gaze shifted over his shoulder, out into the dock at his back. "Surely you can't be serious," she said.

"I am, and stop calling me Shirley," he said with a little laugh to himself, then he turned and his laughter died like a battery-drained mech when he saw who was headed their way.

"What the hell does he want now?" she asked.

Ryan was walking toward them, wearing a long camel-colored coat, a white turtleneck, and brown slacks, that knowing smirk on his face.

"He's dressed like he's auditioning for a boy band," she said, and Tovi snorted.

"You're not wrong."

"I come in peace," Ryan said, holding his hands up in surrender. "I want to make amends."

"You could pay us for the salvage you stole," Sierra said.

"I don't know anything about that," Ryan said, and Sierra laughed mirthlessly.

"You're a piece of work. Can I throw a wrench at his face?" Sierra asked, hefting a wrench in her hand that had materialized from somewhere in her coveralls.

Tovi waved her off. "There's no other way someone would have found a dead ship. Even if you didn't take the salvage, you bugged my room."

"That was unfortunate, and like I said, I want to make it up to you. I have a job that's perfectly suited to your expertise."

"Why do you need us? Can't your goons do it for you? Aren't you the Regional Controller?" Tovi asked.

"It's a delicate situation, and I'd rather not go through official channels. I'm willing to pay a premium for your discretion."

"We're not going to take the fall for your illegal activities."

"Nothing like that. It's totally aboveboard."

Cecil came lumbering out of the ship on all fours then stood to his full height. "If you're doing a paper-trail trick, there's a thirty percent uplift, and you'll have to supply all the necessary permits."

Tovi had no idea what Cecil was talking about. It must be something specific to Omnia, and he was grateful Cecil was there to negotiate.

Ryan narrowed his eyes at Cecil. "You're the Nhethian who used to work in our contracts department."

Cecil didn't respond, staring Ryan down instead.

Every fiber of Tovi's being wanted to turn Ryan away, but the impending impounding of their ship and Iz's earlier suggestion made him pause. "What's the job?" He felt more than saw Sierra's incredulous eyes boring into the side of his head. Ryan tilted his head appraisingly.

"A simple delivery run. I have a shipment that needs to get to Terrana quickly. I don't have time to go through official channels; too much paperwork. It's an exchange. You'll swap my goods for theirs and return them to me, then you'll be paid ten thousand credits."

Sierra let out a low whistle. "Ten thousand credits? You must be desperate."

"What are we delivering?" Tovi asked. He didn't trust Ryan as far as he could throw him, which was probably relatively far but not far enough. The mention of Terrana got his attention, though. It was an opportunity to see if the chatter on the net about Praxians on Terrana was true, maybe get a lead on his conclave.

"That's between me and my associates, and why your payment is so high for a fairly banal run."

"And here I thought it was our particular expertise you valued," Tovi shot back. "When would we take delivery?"

"The shipment will arrive next cycle and you will leave immediately upon its arrival. If the shipment is tampered with, the deal is off. If you don't return with the shipment, the deal is off. I will put you in touch with your contact when you accept my offer. I'm skeptical this thing you call a ship can make it all the way to Terrana and back," Ryan said, sweeping a cynical eye across the ship like he wanted to kick the cargo ramp to see if it was real or a cardboard cutout.

"You let us worry about that, darling," Sierra said, and Ryan frowned at her like he'd stepped in something sticky. Sierra was taking ample delight in pressing Ryan's buttons. Tovi was less amused and would rather Ryan made himself scarce before they came to blows.

"You can send us the offer in writing, and we'll get back to you." Tovi turned his back to Ryan to work on the piston. His back itched, and while every instinct born from his time in the service screamed at him not to turn his back to an enemy, he could see Sierra's eyes tracking Ryan's self-important gait and clicking shoes out of their docking bay.

"You should have seen his face when you dismissed him. I thought he was going to lunge at you. It would have given me the opportunity to try out my new hunting knife," she said, pulling a grisly-looking knife the length of her forearm out of an ankle holster and twisting it in the light.

"When did you get that?" Cecil asked, coming back to all fours. "I don't trust you with sharp objects."

"I got it yesterday, from a nice octogenarian selling tea leaves. And I'm glad too. If we're going to Terrana, I might need it."

"I immediately regret my decisions," Tovi said, leaning away from the knife. Sierra handled the knife with more confidence than skill—a dangerous combination.

"It's not the worst offer, sounds pretty straightforward," she said.

Iz came down the loading ramp and put a hand on Cecil's flank. Those two ran hot and cold, but they appeared to be on speaking terms today. Pixie was resting on Iz's shoulder, their purple legs undulating over Iz's chest and neck.

"That guy is a real prick," Iz said. "I wonder what his game is." They must have been watching the feed from the external cameras while inside the ship.

"I don't trust him," Cecil said, sitting on his back legs at the end of the ramp.

"You don't trust anyone," Iz said, patting his back.

Cecil grunted and scratched his ear with his back leg. "True, he's as slippery as everyone else. I'll review the contract and make sure it's airtight."

"He got one over on us last time," Tovi said. His skin crawled with the idea of having to work for Ryan.

"The money is very enticing," Sierra said, working on the housing for the piston with a wrench. "We could pay off our debt and get the mech running."

"Not if he screws us over again," Tovi said.

Cecil righted his porkpie hat, dark blue today with a feather sticking up on one side. "We'll just have to be extra careful, then."

"Is everyone on board with this?" Tovi asked, surprised no one was making a hard argument against Ryan and whatever his motivation was for offering them this job. He didn't buy his flimsy excuse about making things right; not that it was untrue, merely that nothing with Ryan was straightforward. Tovi had his own reasons for going; he'd take any opportunity to investigate the Praxian sightings if there was a chance they were from his conclave. He hadn't seen or been in contact with his family since he'd been shipped off Tapata seventeen years ago.

"Hell yeah," Sierra said, punching a fist in the air. "See it this way: we can get our pound of flesh from Ryan and make him squirm a bit. We could find some work on Terrana, maybe even get a delivery contract for the return to Octto station. If we have time, we could try and get into one of the mech tournaments."

"I hadn't really thought about it like that," Tovi said, Sierra's obvious excitement bleeding into him. If this was the best option available to them, he could work with that and turn it into something positive. He'd heard Terrana had an extensive trade network, and he had some hard-to-find items on his list, even if he couldn't track down any of his kind.

Iz clapped their hands, a delighted smile gracing their face. "I love this idea," they said. "Do you think you could get into a tournament without a mech?" they asked Sierra.

"A few of the houses have amateur tournaments anyone can sign up for, and they provide the mechs. Tourists love it. They can show off to their family or see what it feels like to operate a battle mech. They always lose, but it's entertaining for everyone, and people bet on random things, like how many body shots the amateur can get in or how many rounds they last. I even heard of people betting on whether the operators cry or vomit before it's all over. We can make money on the bets," Sierra said, bouncing on her toes in excitement. She turned her smile to Tovi, and he was filled with the same emotion—he'd do anything to get them back in a mech again.

"Something to think about," Cecil said, his dark brown eyes widening in interest. Cecil didn't have many vices, but he never passed up a good wager when the odds were on his side. "I need to see the contract. We're not signing anything unless he pays for expenses up front, and he needs to provide a manifest that's legit to customs and export control. That's not coming out of our pocket."

They moved through the ship and congregated in the galley. Sierra collapsed on a couch, and Tovi nudged her over to squeeze in. Cecil took up the entirety of the other couch, while Iz sat at the table, their current crocheting project lounging across the table in variegated pink and purple, like a psychedelic sloth. "You know, I've never been to Terrana before," Iz said, picking up their project where they left off, crochet hook in hand. "What's it like, Sierra?"

"Do you remember that pirate movie Tovi made us watch?"

"*Pirates of the Caribbean,*" Tovi said.

"It's like that, but with real pirates, of the space variety, running the show. The main tourist area has old pirate ships turned into tourist attractions, with rides and street performers. Behind the amusement park facade is a thriving community run by the houses. It used to be based on who owned which gambling house, but now they're diversified. Once upon a time, they had family names. Now, they quarrel incessantly, but they band together against outside influences for the good of the station. I haven't been there for years, but I can't imagine it's changed much," Sierra said, stretching out like a squirming puppy who couldn't get comfortable, draping her legs over Tovi's. She was half his size but could take up more space than physics should allow.

"Is there anyone you're excited to see again?" Iz asked.

Sierra was quiet for a moment, and Tovi was equally curious. She had been cagey about her time on Terrana, and he'd never found out why that was.

"There was Vandover. He was my debt holder for a while. I worked for him on the battle mech circuit before I left. He was kind to me. I can't say I always returned the favor. Then there's Andy—you know her as the Battleaxe—and she's still running the circuit."

"I follow her on the net!" Iz said in excitement. "Do you think I could get her autograph?"

"If she's not holding a grudge, then I'm sure she'd be happy to."

Cecil huffed then said, "Did you do something stupid?" Tovi shot him a glare.

"I didn't tell anyone I was leaving. I just left." She shrugged liked it wasn't a big deal, but her jaw was tight.

"That's a dick move," Cecil said, slouching in the couch, clearly unmoved by Tovi's glare.

Sierra snorted a laugh. "Correct. It wasn't my best moment, by far."

"Leave any jilted lovers behind?" Iz asked. Tovi recalibrated his glare toward Iz and let out a huff of air. "What? We should know if someone's liable to take revenge for a broken heart."

"No broken hearts," she said, then nibbled on her lip. "There was someone I had a thing for, but she had more fun goading me than anything else."

"Do tell," Tovi said, unable to help his curiosity. If she was opening up, he wasn't going to stop her.

She rolled her eyes as everyone leaned in like they were watching a scintillating episode of *Mechanizing a Starless Sky*. "She was the presumed heir of one of the pirate houses. We had a mutual interest in mechanics and mechs, but she was at odds with Vandover and enjoyed teasing me. I thought we had something special, but then I saw how often she used her charm to get what she wanted. I realized I was no different than anyone else, except she was somehow worse with me. We'd be getting along and really vibing, then she'd go cold and silent. I never knew where I stood with her."

"Does she have a name?" Tovi asked, fascinated by these juicy morsels.

"Her name was Mei, but she's since taken over the house and goes by Ching Shih. Some pirates choose a pseudonym, either made up or historical. In this case, it's been in her family as far back as anyone knows and was the name of an Old Earth pirate."

"You were keeping tabs on her?" Cecil asked.

Sierra picked at a hangnail, dropping her head to hide a blush. "I just saw it on the news. I wasn't net-stalking her or anything. She was older than me by a bit. I thought maybe she found me childish, and I doubt she remembers me anyway. If it's entertainment you're after, you should see what shows are playing on the asteroid."

Tovi didn't believe her for a minute—she was an accomplished net sleuth. Not even he was above checking up on his past flames, and Sierra was no different.

"Can we ride the rides while we're there?" Iz asked. "I always wanted to go as a kid, but my parents said it was dangerous." They rolled their eyes. Statistically speaking, it was one of the safer asteroid habitats—for tourists at least. The pirate community knew better than to chase off a significant chunk of their revenue stream, as well as their proverbial shield against retaliation from governmental and corporate entities.

"I don't see why not," Tovi said.

"Y'all are spending money we haven't made yet. You can spend your own money how you like, but we aren't spending our payout in advance of having it in hand. So, get out your paint and glitter," Cecil said. Iz was even more excited, if that was possible. They skipped out of the galley toward the storage lockers, intent on working on their art to sell at the markets.

"But your duties come first!" Cecil yelled after them, then grumbled his way to the flight deck.

Chapter 10

Dog My Cat Burglars

Sierra was many things—impulsive, easily distracted, often depressed and anxious—but one thing she wasn't was a morning person. It didn't matter that there was no such thing as mornings on a free-floating station.

The concept of a day or night was useless off-planet, and humans had conformed to the inter-galactic standard of time keeping. One cycle was the closest thing to a day, except a cycle was about twenty-eight hours long and was split into four, seven-hour shifts.

No matter the logic behind it, Sierra was slow to get moving after a sleep cycle. Getting up even earlier to stop by Lana's was a pleasure she could do without and an errand she'd prefer to sleep through, but Iz had asked her and she could never say no to them.

She'd napped for a few hours after Ryan showed up because she wouldn't have time later. Once she and Tovi did their dock shifts, they'd be headed out with their mystery cargo to Terrana. She drank two bracing cups of coffee, then threw her tools and snacks in a bag big enough to fit Lulu. Normally, she'd be fine with letting the AIcat follow her, but with Lulu's unsteady gait and no mindsync, Sierra preferred to play it safe.

Lana's apartment was a twenty-minute walk from the ship and Sierra was already running late, so she grabbed her magnaboard on her way out of the loading ramp and tossed it on the ground. It righted itself and hovered a few inches off the ground. The magnaboard used magnets to hover and minute body motions to speed up, slow down, and change directions. Sierra stepped on the board and pushed her front foot down to get it moving. She whizzed through the station, weaving around people and enjoying the artificial wind in her hair. Before she knew it, she was at Lana's apartment and she let out a sigh, flipping the board up and sticking it between her back and the backpack. It was a three-story apartment, about the max they could construct in the habitat, and painted a garish yellow.

"Fix your face, Sierra," she said to herself and tried on a smile. In the reflection of the apartment's glass door, her smile made her seem constipated, so she dropped it and shrugged. Some things were beyond her control. She pushed the door open and walked up the two flights of stairs to Lana's place and knocked on the door. After a moment, Lana answered, peeking out the narrow opening.

"Iz said you'd be stopping by for the cat. She's all done. Let me grab her," Lana said, not opening the door all the way and certainly not inviting her inside. She came back to the door and held out the cat, who blinked up at Sierra with owlish eyes. Sierra took off her backpack and set the magnaboard down, then unzipped the bag and took Lulu from Lana. She'd replaced the black fur with a black skin that shone like cobalt in the harsh light of the hallway and little white paws that Sierra wanted to gush over.

"Hi, Loos, I'm going to put you in here just until we can get you home." Sierra placed her gingerly in the bag and zipped it up, leaving a hole for Lulu to peer through.

"I was able to fix some of the damage, but she's unsteady. It's not a mechanical issue, so she'll likely always walk like that. Here's the original skin," Lana said, handing her the black pelt that was creepy collapsed on itself. Confusion must have been clear on her face because Lana added in a stage whisper, "I'd rather not have incriminating evidence in my possession."

Sierra took the pelt and put it in the front pocket of her backpack. She'd rather not have it either but chose to keep her mouth shut on the topic. Maybe Iz would want it for something.

"Thanks," Sierra said and felt increasingly awkward. They weren't on hugging terms, both harboring a mutual dislike for the other, so Sierra gave her an aborted wave. "See you around." She slung the pack onto her back, picked up her board, and retreated down the hallway, feeling Lana's eyes on her the whole way.

Lana's uncle Jimmy was an ineffectual, boring sort of individual. He'd droned on about safety and protocol, then spent even more time whining about missing stock. Sierra had zoned out after five minutes, imagining instead what she'd have for dinner. Maybe she'd go to the Ramen Palace and get the best miso soup on station, or she could pick up dumplings at that little corner stand on the way home. Her stomach rumbled at the idea.

"Here's the schedule for your shift. We need all this moved, and keep an eye out for anyone who doesn't belong in here."

"What exactly does that look like?" she asked, a little curious but mostly just annoyed.

"Out of place, like they're scrounging around for stuff that isn't theirs."

"So, like customs officials and station admin?"

He glared at her, and she knew she should reel it in or risk losing this job, and possibly pissing off Lana in the process.

"No problem, boss," she said and took the clipboard.

"You're mech three. I expect that whole roster to be done by the end of the shift or you forfeit wages."

Sierra gripped the clipboard and indulged in the idea of using it as a bludgeoning device and wondering whether it would fit up his ass along with the stick that had firmly lodged itself there. Instead, she saluted his back and wandered into the massive warehouse; rows and rows of shelves lined the soccer field-sized room. Some of the contents were in long-term storage on the far side of the warehouse, while the nearside was for high-turnover shipments. Anything headed out of red dock would pass through here first, waiting for whatever transport was scheduled to take it to its next destination. Same for goods coming into the station.

A short row of lockers stood along the wall, next to hangers holding coveralls and coats. She opened a locker and found someone's rank lunch fermenting inside. She wrinkled her nose then picked one farther down and set the backpack inside, along with the magnaboard. Lulu meowed once, and Sierra saw her eye peeking through the hole in the zipper. Sierra unzipped it more so she could stick her head out.

"I'll be working for a few hours. You might want to sleep and restore your batteries while I'm working." Sierra hoped Lulu understood. The mindsync still hadn't formed, and when it did, she'd probably make it with Tovi, since Sierra and Iz had their own companions and she seemed to prefer Tovi. If she could connect widely, then they'd all be able to talk to her. Based on what Cecil and Iz said, she was advanced enough to do that and more. Lulu seemed to get the gist and curled up in the bottom of the bag. Sierra shut the locker and used her sleeve to lock it to her sleeve's signature.

She walked along the back wall lined with mechs until she found bay three. The mech was in decent shape, if simple, used for loading and unloading storage crates and awkwardly shaped objects. It was tall enough to reach the top shelf of the warehouse, probably twenty feet in height when it was fully extended.

She climbed up the leg and used the code she'd been given on her sleeve to open the machine's chest cavity and climbed in. Sierra wrinkled her nose at the acrid smell of body odor and wished she'd brought an air freshener. What it really needed was fumigation—or a nuclear explosion. Inside, she familiarized herself with the controls. The machine had arm attachments that molded and conformed to odd-sized objects using gel-filled bags to disperse the pressure across the object. She'd used something similar before.

Sierra pulled on her gloves and connected them to the system. Using her gloves, she moved the mech forward into the warehouse stacks. She grabbed the schematics for the warehouse and reviewed the move assignments she'd been given. She took a few minutes to map out her assignments so she could ditch the clipboard and get to work.

Her first job was to prep cargo for a ship that would arrive for loading in an hour. It didn't take her long to move the half dozen crates to the loading zone, then load up the ship after it arrived and the customs officials inspected everything. Next, she was supposed to intake a shipment. She double-checked the roster, but the same name glared back at her. Omnia's Impound was bringing a shipment for export off station. She had no doubt the crates were filled with the salvage her team had recovered. They would ship it to recycling centers, like the one on her home planetoid where she worked her first mech job. She walked her mech to the station intake zone and saw Hazel's lackeys unloading four large crates. She waved when they made eye contact, then flipped them the bird.

"Have a nice day," she said through the intercom system of the mech. They stared at her, unamused, and finished their work in silence.

"Bunch of charmers," she said to herself.

Have you finally losst your mind? We can burn thiss place down if you're amenable, Rupert whispered in her mind, sounding far too enthusiastic about committing arson, as he slithered through her hair, and she questioned her own sanity.

"No, Rupert, I haven't lost my mind yet. When I do, I'll happily carry out arson with you. It's a good thing you don't have hands or tentacles, or we'd be in real trouble."

Sierra began the tedious process of moving and storing the transport cases according to the manifest in cargo hold thirty-two, before her next job of unloading a freighter that had just arrived. After that, she'd switch off with Tovi during the shift change.

As she turned down the row for hold thirty-two, she realized another mech was standing in the aisle, turned away from her. Sierra didn't remember seeing anyone else on duty for this shift, then she remembered the thieves. She grinned, glad to avail herself of any opportunity to take her frustrations out for a walk.

In hopes of taking them by surprise, she moved the mech quickly down the aisle. "Quietly" wasn't an option with a one-ton metal machine. When she was within ten feet, she saw the mech's head turn in the direction of her lumbering form, and a moment later, turn its body and lift its arms in defense. Sierra had the advantage of momentum and angled her pincer hands at the mech's neck, delighting in the metallic crunch as she squeezed, and the mech tried to jerk out of her grip.

"Now, now, if you move too much, I'll sever your head from your body, and what would you do without a brain?" she asked over the intercom.

It helped that the person's head was just under the point she'd gripped the mech's neck. Neck might be a simplification; it was the joint between the mech and the 360 camera, and crushing it wouldn't hurt the operator, but it was blood draining to watch metal crunching overhead and losing visuals. This close, she could see the pissed-off operator, and he looked like someone who could do damage, with beefy arms and something that was once a neck, but now there was nothing but muscle between shoulder and jaw. She spied a gun holster peeking out from beneath a heavy, forest green jacket.

He glared back at her, then the mech's elbow slammed into her chest plate, crunching in the protective cover in front of her. She took her free arm, closed the pincers, and jabbed it into the socket where her opponent's arm met its body, then opened the pincers, stretching and ripping the metal and electrical until the arm went limp.

It felt so damn good, and she reveled in the adrenaline. If she was back in the ring, it would have earned her two points to disable a limb. She missed the thrill of the fight, the lightning-fast assessment of the situation followed by even quicker decisions that could win or lose a battle. It was years of practice that built instinct, something she'd learned by doing and failing a hundred times.

Sierra heard and felt a thunking against her mech. She scanned her surroundings then saw a woman with short brown hair in a long black trench coat, like she'd come from *The Matrix*, with a bolt gun in hand. She shot again, and the bolt cut a hole into the mech and narrowly missed Sierra's hip. Sierra ripped her free arm from the lifeless limb and backhanded the woman, who went sprawling.

Her opponent's operational arm swung and jabbed its pincers at her breast plate, denting it farther inward, and dangerously close to her face. Now she was pissed. She opened the pincers on her free arm as the mech managed a second blow to her chest, tearing open the breast plate and grazing her side. She grunted at the pain, then punched into the other mech's arm, just below the pincers at the wrist joint.

The move trapped the arm across the mech's chest, and she pinched down to keep her grip. She pushed forward, crushing her pincer around the other mech's neck and forcing it to move back at a side angle until it tripped over its own legs and crashed to the ground. The person inside was trapped by his own mech arm and couldn't open the chest plate to escape.

"What the fuck are you doing?" Sierra asked over her intercom system.

The man glared at her and tried to use the mech's feet to buck her off, but he wasn't having much luck. It was obvious he wasn't overly familiar with mechs. You had to forget about hand-to-hand combat and all the physics that worked on the human body because mechs didn't move the same way. They weren't as flexible, and their center of gravity was different. Maybe this guy could take her in a fight—based entirely on biceps the size of a mech piston, she revised her estimate to *definitely* could beat her in a fight—but he didn't stand a chance in a mech.

"That's not gonna work, dumbass. Just tell me what you're doing and I might let you go before the port authorities show up. I don't own this shit heap, so I'm not that invested. You just pissed me off at the wrong time."

She was mostly curious and assumed he was one of the afore-mentioned thieves who'd been stealing cargo. He struggled for a few minutes more and Sierra waited him out, and eventually, he appeared to give up.

"We're here for the cat," he said through his intercom.

"Wait, what?" How the hell did anyone know about Lulu?

He didn't answer. Instead, he stared past her, and Sierra turned her camera to see what had caught his attention. Tovi was in the middle of the aisle, leaning over the woman who was laid out on the floor. Knowing Tovi, he'd be helping the sneaky fucker who'd tried to kill her.

"Tovi, that asshole tried to kill me," she said over the intercom. Tovi glanced up at Sierra and the woman moved, reaching for her bolt gun.

Sierra tried to open the hatch to her mech, but the damage to the chest plate made that impossible; she'd need to be cut out of the mech at this point. She returned her attention to Tovi, who must have kicked the gun away and was now fighting the woman hand to hand. Sierra wasn't overly skilled in freestyle fighting, but what she did know, she'd learned from Tovi, who, while they'd been separated, had earned money on the side through kickboxing tournaments. His skinny frame was lithe and feline, moving with understated confidence.

While she was watching him parry jabs and knee the woman in the ribs, she felt a shift in the mechs and turned her attention back to her own problem in the form of a pretzeled mech and the idiot inside. He'd released the arm she was using to keep him trapped in the mech. It had detached at the shoulder joint and rolled down the mech's body, leaving the chest plate free. He opened the hatch and jumped out. Sierra released the mech and spun backward to intercept the man. Tovi could handle himself against one opponent, but two was a tall order.

Then the lights in the warehouse went from pale white to red, and she heard a harsh siren blaring over the intercom system. Within moments, their two assailants disappeared. The man veered into the stacks, going where Sierra couldn't follow in the mech, and the woman turned tail and ran. She guessed correctly that Tovi was more worried about Sierra than the stranger attacking him.

"You okay?" Tovi asked, running toward her and yelling over the siren, hands covering his ears.

"Yeah, can you cut me out of here?" she asked. Before he could respond, they were rushed by port authority officers and what she assumed was private security in all-black tactical suits. Tovi raised his arms in surrender, and Sierra just stared at them.

"Nice of you to finally join us, but the people you want ran off," she said.

Overlapping voices shouted at her to disable the mech, which she did, but when they demanded she get out, she pointed to the caved-in mess that was the chest plate.

"Someone's going to have to cut me out," she said.

Chapter 11

Back Stabbin' Gum Flappin'

It took another hour for Jimmy to show up and vouch that she was employed by the company and review the tapes. Port authority officials cut her out and kept Sierra and Tovi in custody for hours. When they finally let them go, Jimmy laid into her.

"You cost me thousands in damages," he said, his face red as a tomato, and she was worried he might pop.

"You asked me to do security detail. That's what I did. Did you want me to let them walk off with your inventory?"

"I didn't mean get into a mech battle. You should have activated the alarm and called me." He was flailing his arms now, and she took a step back, out of chaotic slapping range.

"Well, that's not what you said earlier, and I'm not a mind reader."

"This is coming out of your wages, and you will never work for me again."

"Okay, whatever," she said, throwing up her hands, and walked past him while he continued to yell at her back. She didn't have the energy to argue with him, and it wouldn't make any difference. "I'm going to grab my crap and get out of your hair." She was incredibly grateful she'd left Lulu in the lockers or she would have been discovered in the mech, and there would have been probing questions. Sierra held her sleeve to the locker and it popped open. Lulu blinked up at her, waking from sleep mode. Sierra zipped up the bag around Lulu, then shouldered the bag and tucked her magnaboard under one arm. She kept her head down as Tovi led the way out of the facility, hoping no one would stop and question her about the bag, but most everyone had cleared out. Only a few tasers-for-hire were milling around, milking the clock.

"You're injured," Tovi said, pointing to her side after they were a few feet away from the storage facility. She'd been holding it, applying pressure and trying to ignore the throbbing pain whenever she let up. Every step jostled her side, and the pressure of the backpack wasn't doing her any favors.

"It was the mech pincers. It just grazed me."

"We should let Iz fix you up," Tovi said.

"You think Iz is going to be okay with that after I jacked up Lana's job?"

"They might not be happy about it, but Iz would never refuse you," Tovi said.

Sierra wanted to tell him what the man had said about Lulu, but she didn't trust they weren't being watched. She'd wait until they were back at the ship. She kept an eye out for anyone suspicious, which was a challenge—everyone appeared suspicious when she applied a critical eye. Instead, she decided to keep to well-trafficked areas over the shortcuts she'd normally use. Tovi threw her an inquisitive eyebrow lift, and she shook her head. Some people's gazes lingered longer than she liked, but they hurried passed them and made it to the ship without incident.

As the loading ramp slammed shut, she removed then unzipped the backpack and Lulu jumped out, swishing her tail in agitation. Her gaze focused on Tovi, and she wobbled over to him, rubbing against his legs. Tovi picked her up, and his whole body relaxed as she rubbed her face against his chin and he nuzzled her back.

"Can you check the chatter on the net and see if there's anything going around about Lulu? The guy I was fighting said he was after her."

"How's that possible? Unless there's another surveillance bug on the ship." Tovi's eyes narrowed in paranoid suspicion.

"We've been scanning for those daily. I don't think it's us."

Tovi nodded and tucked Lulu into the crook of his elbow. "I'll check it out," he said.

"I heard you got into some trouble," Iz said as they walked into the cargo bay, Pixie floating next to them, tentacles swirling anxiously.

Trouble! Pixie said, their voice all accusation.

"Sorry about that. I didn't mean to make a mess of things," Sierra said, hoping to head off a chewing out.

"And yet messes always find you," Iz said as they pushed Sierra's hand away from her side to assess the damage. "Follow me."

Iz led Sierra to the medical bay, and Tovi retreated to his room. She mouthed *thanks a lot* as he retreated, and he gave her a helpless shrug.

They entered the medical bay that masqueraded as a greenhouse. Long vines tumbled down tall shelves; the walls were alive with undulating greenery. Sierra was convinced she could feel her hair frizzing in the increased humidity, but she didn't mind when the smell of jasmine wafted under her nose, masking the antiseptic undertone that curled on the back of her tongue. Some plants were edible, like the lettuce and tanga root, while others were saved from trash cans or relinquished by derelict acquaintances. Squeezed in the middle of their miniature rainforest was a narrow medical bed, an even narrower counter to one side dominated by a sink, and vertical storage.

Iz had Sierra remove her shirt and pants, then sit on the cold medical bed. Iz worked in silence, cleaning the wound, applying glue to the cut, then bandaging it.

The silence unnerved Sierra. She thought Iz might be a bit miffed, but at the time, Sierra was running on adrenaline and rage and didn't bother with consequences. "I'm sorry if I made things bad with Lana. I didn't think it would be a problem," Sierra said.

"That's because you never think, Sierra!" Iz said, straightening up and pointing the medical scissors she was holding at Sierra. Okay, so they were mad. "How could it not cross your mind that getting into a mech fight with a mech that's not yours might end badly?"

"He wanted me to do security." It was weak and she knew it.

"And you took that as a blank check to do whatever you wanted. And yeah, Lana is pissed, but I'm the one who has to deal with that, not you." They slammed the scissors on the narrow counter.

"Let me talk to her. I'll apologize," Sierra said.

"That's not the point. You do this over and over, landing us in it. Lana's mad because I keep putting up with it, because it affects our relationship. She wants me to get a safer job, on station, where she doesn't have to worry if one of your stunts will get me killed."

Sierra blanched at that idea, her worst fear staring her down. She had attempted self-restraint, not wanting to push Iz away with a blatant accusation, but she'd had hours to sit in that room and stew on the sequence of events. If Iz was going to leave anyway, Sierra might as well throw the baby out with the bath water.

"I wasn't going to fucking say anything until I had proof, but how do you think a whole-ass mech got inside the warehouse? You think it just slipped under the door? Popped open a window? The man I fought said he was there for the cat. Who else knew about her?"

Iz was silent for a moment, their normally cheery smile turned down in a pensive frown, their braids creating a curtain around their turned-down face. "You think Lana set you up?"

"I don't know. Like I said, I have no proof, but someone told them where I was. I assume it wasn't one of the crew, so that only leaves Lana. Unless there's someone else who knows about Lulu."

"That's unfair. She was trying to help us out."

"Honestly, Iz, I don't care what Lana thinks about me. What I care about is being used and stitched up."

"Throwing yourself at the intruder didn't help the situation," Iz said. Behind the anger, Sierra could see the hurt, but Sierra wasn't sure it was all caused by her.

"Probably not. I've already apologized for overreacting, but I can't make this job safe, and it sounds like Lana wants to wrap you up in a little box and keep you under her pillow."

"That's between me and Lana. What I want from you is to make better choices."

Better choices, Pixie echoed, their round eyes squeezed into accusatory slits as they wrapped their tentacles around Iz's shoulder and neck, pulling themself against Iz's neck.

Sierra decided to keep her mouth shut after that. Maybe Iz was right this time, but she didn't go around making dipshit decisions all the time, not anymore. There was a time when she'd been much worse, when it didn't matter who she'd fucked over because no one stuck around and no one had her back. Her life had felt like a brief burst of light that would quickly extinguish, so she'd lived hard and fast. Then Tovi had come back in her life, steadfast as ever. Ten years later, after they'd pieced the ship together, Iz had come along, followed by

Cecil, each wanting something to call their own, a place to call home. Sierra desperately wanted things to stay exactly as they were, and Lana was doing her best to drive a wedge between them. If Sierra were more bloody-minded, she'd do something about it, but the only thing worse than everyone leaving was them staying under duress.

She resented the implication she would risk everything they'd built together to bust some skulls, but a small voice in the back of her mind wondered if that was exactly what she was doing, and wouldn't that just be fucked up? Iz finished their work and turned away from Sierra to clean up—a clear dismissal. Sierra murmured a thanks.

"What's all the yelling about?" Cecil's voice cut through the uncomfortable silence, and his head came into view through the doorway. He was too big to fit in the room with the two of them.

"Whoever I fought in the warehouse, they were after Lulu," Sierra said, avoiding the topic of Lana.

"Shit," Tovi said, appearing in the doorway opposite Cecil and reading from his sleeve. "I checked the message boards, and we need to get out of here ASAP. Word's getting around about an AIcat on the loose, and there's a finder's fee to bring it in."

"That didn't take long. Who's searching for her?" Sierra asked.

"It's a throwaway user ID. I can't trace it."

"We can load the cargo and leave immediately," Cecil said. "I say we should off-load the cat. She's more trouble than she's worth."

"She's disguised now and on the ship. And you never know, she could come in handy," Iz said, their tone subdued as they put away their medical supplies.

Cecil huffed but didn't press. "Everyone get ready for departure."

A ping sounded on Sierra's sleeve, and the screen displayed an unknown number. She hated unknown callers, but they were waiting for their contact on Terrana so they could arrange the exchange. She accepted the call, and the past came rushing at her in the form of a face she hadn't seen in ten years.

"Mei..." Sierra breathed out. She had fine lines at the delicate edge of her eyes and around her mouth, but her face was the same one she'd stared at too many times to count. Deep brown eyes lightening to a warm sepia at the pupils made richer by her golden-brown skin. Her black hair fell like a waterfall across her shoulders and forehead in long bangs. It was the same hair she'd longed to run her fingers through and looked soft as a cloud.

"It's Ching Shih now. As I'm sure you're aware. It's been a long time, Ser-Bear."

Sierra glanced around to make sure none of the crew heard the endearment, or she'd never live it down.

"You're our contact?" Sierra asked, unable to keep the astonishment and incredulity out of her voice.

"Isn't it a happy coincidence?" That knowing smile Sierra had come to love and loathe in equal measure graced her heart-shaped lips. "You left without a going-away kiss, or even a note. Don't you want to catch up, or were you going to avoid me on station?"

"I hadn't really thought about it." Sierra didn't like having this sprung on her; she hadn't had time to form a plan, mostly because she'd planned on avoiding it as long as possible.

"You look good. I like what you've done with your hair, and those tattoos are new. How low do they go?" Sierra blushed. The dotted stars tattooed on her chest did in fact go much lower than the cut of her tank top. Ching Shih's smile turned predatory.

Sierra cleared her throat. "Let's keep it to business. We have a job to do."

"As you wish. Once you arrive on Terrana, I'll send you the address for the exchange." Ching Shih's expression hardened as she talked about work, and Sierra missed the intimacy she'd purposely scattered like a flock of pigeons.

"We'll let you know when we touch down."

Ching Shih raised an eyebrow. "Don't worry, I'm keeping tabs on you."

Her tone sent shivers rolling down Sierra's arms. She kept forgetting who Ching Shih was now, and she likely knew all the comings and goings on the station.

"Right, I look forward to hearing from you," Sierra said.

"Ditto," Ching Shih said, that toothy smile shining through just long enough to see the predatory gleam in her eyes. Sierra was well and truly fucked.

Chapter 12

Doing the Time Warp Again

Sierra was growing more agitated about the prospect of returning to Terrana after the call with Ching Shih. Her past was rushing toward her like a gravity well. For nearly seven years, she'd lived on Terrana, an unincorporated freehold built into the interior of a large asteroid orbiting in an asteroid belt in the Bosqka System. By nature, it was inhabited by people that, for one reason or another, couldn't or wouldn't get citizenship or work on a station or planet.

There were parts of Sierra's chaotic past on Terrana that left her feeling humiliated and embarrassed—relationships soured by her insecurities and people who'd taken advantage of her loneliness. Her twenties had been a frantic attempt to keep her head above water, both financially and emotionally.

Do we getss to fight? Rupert asked, slithering over her sleeve as she tried to read a book in her bunk. He didn't like being ignored.

"Rupert, I'm trying to read here."

It'ss a bad book anyway. I can tell becausse you are making sstrange noissess from your food receptacle.

"It's called a mouth, Rupert. It's not the book, though. I'm nervous about going back to Terrana. When I left, I'd been working for Vandover, and I didn't give him any notice. It's possible he's carrying a grudge, and I feel shitty about that."

That wassn't very ssmart. Will you leave me without notice?

"Of course not! This was different, but yes, very stupid. I shouldn't have done that. I know snakes don't make mistakes, but humans do, and I've made a lot of them."

If you bring him a warm rock to cuddle with, he will forgive you.

"I'll bear that in mind."

I wish to fight. I would maim them, then sswallow them whole.

"I know you would, buddy." She ran her hand down his scales and gave up trying to read.

There had been good times too—the mech battles, the championships, the cheering crowd. She'd made friends, but she'd left it all behind when she'd bought passage off the rock to Octto Station. She'd thought about writing to Vandover a million times, explain why she'd left with no notice and no goodbye, but her explanation felt stupid and hollow. How do you repair something you crushed beyond recognition?

Sierra had hoped they'd end up back there eventually. There was no better place to re-enter the battle royale scene, but she'd have to be careful. She'd burned bridges on her way out, and pirates were known to hold grudges. And now one of them was a captain, with more power and sway than Sierra could imagine.

Mei had been the closest thing to a fling she'd ever had, and it wasn't even that. In hindsight, it was a one-sided crush on Sierra's part, mooning over someone who was playing an intricate and deadly game. Mei had always been out of her league, and Sierra cringed at the fool she'd made of herself. She'd have to start thinking of her as Ching Shih or risk a breach of etiquette.

Cecil had managed to negotiate the terms of the contract to include fuel costs and all the paperwork they needed to smuggle whatever it was they were holding. Tovi seemed more squeamish about the situation than anyone else. She didn't care what they were hauling as long as it didn't explode on the ship, and that thought had given her pause. They weren't allowed to open the shipment, but she made sure they ran all the usual tests to avoid an explosive incident.

They'd picked up the shipment at the same dock she'd been arrested in, ignoring the sour glare from Jimmy. She'd smiled and waved, having learned from her mother how very irritating it was on the receiving end. Loaded up and Cecil's checklist checked and double-checked, they left Octto Station and headed for the hyperstation. Their ship wasn't equipped for hyperspeed, being far too expensive for a cargo class 3 ship, which meant they had to use the public transit system.

It took two days to get to the station and another full day to wade through the tedious process of customs, paperwork, and inspections. Cecil knew whose palms to grease and had everything in order for their trip to Terrana.

They were all strapped in on the command deck, Cecil at the main controls and Sierra on navigation. Iz and Tovi were seated in the auxiliary flight seats. Iz was crocheting a blanket in pastels, and Tovi was watching a video on his sleeve.

"Is there anything else in the Bosqka System?" Iz asked, staring down at their project.

"It has three inhabited planets, two terraformed and one is the home planet of the Dorcaii," Sierra said.

"Busy system, makes sense there's a pirate outpost out there. Trade must be good. How long to get there once we jump?"

Sierra checked Terrana's orbit and distance from the node. "Should take about two days, assuming we don't run into trouble."

"Ever the optimist," Iz said.

Tovi glanced up from his sleeve. "Don't jinx it!"

"Just being realistic based on past experience," Sierra said.

"It won't be a problem with the paperwork, that I can guarantee," Cecil said.

The hyperstations used node points to bend space-time and send ships from one location to another, making it impossible to change course mid-transit. As they passed through the node, the only noticeable difference was the displacement of stars. It was like blinking and having them rearrange themselves while her eyes were closed, but instead, she was seeing stars hundreds of light-years away from those she was gazing at moments before.

Exiting a node was less chaotic than entering one. A voice came over the comm from the node station. "Identify yourself."

Cecil sighed. "*Who Wants to Know,*" he said with a vitriolic glance at Sierra. She smiled sweetly back.

"*I* want to know, and if I don't get your ship name, we will fire on you," came the irritated voice.

"That's our name, the *Who Wants to Know.*"

There was a pause. "Very droll. Transmit your authorization code."

It had been her turn to pick the ship name, and she'd been torn between *Why? Do You Want to Date?* and the *Who Wants to Know.* The latter won by popular opinion—not Cecil's, of course. Their authorization was transmitted to the node station, and moments later, they got the green light to proceed to their destination. She took another calming breath before unbuckling her belt.

She retreated to the mess, not in the mood to work on the mech. After months of effort, the mech was finally operational, and Sierra needed a break. She unfolded the couch from the wall and sank into it, propping her legs up and sprawling out.

They'd usually play video games in here or watch her favorite mech soap opera: *Mechanizing a Starless Sky*. It was hokey, the characters overacted, and many of them were sentient mechs, which didn't make any sense because then they'd be androids, not mechs, but whatever; she loved it anyway. Iz favored the table so they could spread out their crafts and Pixie could roam around the surface. Cecil usually took up the other couch, his snout in a history book or watching videos on how to code, his latest hobby, and pretending like he wasn't watching *Mechanizing a Starless Sky* even when she caught him staring.

Leaning back into the cushions, Sierra thought she should feel some kind of way with the mech done, like the universe had opened up a part of itself once locked away and unknowable to her, but everything felt the same. Even worse, she had an impending sense of doom. As much as they wanted to fight mechs, Tovi's words about spotting other Praxians on Terrana made her break out in a rash. If he found his conclave, he might leave, and their little family would break apart. She should be happy for him, and that made her feel worse because she selfishly wanted him to stay. A pathetic part of her was afraid he would choose them over her if it came down to it, and he'd leave like her family had. For once, she wanted someone to choose her.

"What are you moping around for?" Tovi asked, pushing at her legs so he could sit down. She swiveled to sitting but still resembled gelatinous goo, like Jell-O that had sunken in on itself. "Are you nervous about going back?" he asked.

Sierra shrugged. She didn't think she was nervous; she told herself it was fine. Terrana hadn't been her home. Only this ship had ever felt like home. "I don't know. I think I have too many feelings to parse them out. I kind of shoved them in a box to deal with later."

"And now you might have to open that box," Tovi said.

"Or I could ignore it and hope everyone else does too."

He nodded, lifting his brow. "Uh-huh, I wish you luck in your endeavors. And what about Ching Shih? You can't avoid her."

Sierra grumbled, "I plan to keep our interaction brief, business only. I wouldn't mind seeing Targon again and mooning him. I was so naive, I'd barely made a dent in my debt in the five years I worked for him."

"I'll never understand how the Consortium can have the authority to quarantine an entire planet and displace all its human occupants but refuses to interfere in unfair labor practices," Tovi said, annoyance lacing his words.

"Not in their purview, they claim. Feels like they only interfere when they feel like it. To be fair, I think they did the right thing with Earth. We were destroying the planet and all the other animals and flora. I think we ceded our rights to such a place. And I can't be entirely mad at the humans who ruined our second chance at a new world by making genetically modified animals, or we wouldn't have Cecil."

"I wish my conclave saw it that way. They truly believe humans have a right to Earth to do with as they please. Why they chose that hill to die on as Praxians, I'll never know."

"Same, though I think my family had nothing better to do and no prospects, so why not join forces with a deranged Praxian and go prancing aruound the universe spouting humanist nonsense? No offense to Patini; I'm sure she had a good reason to stay," Sierra said.

Tovi appeared pensive, not unusual when discussing his conclave. He held a flame for them in a way Sierra had snuffed out the day her family had abandoned her to follow the Earther movement. Her brother and her parents weren't worth her time, but Tovi had had Patini, someone who'd loved and cared for him, and the younger children of the conclave. He had loved and cared for them in turn. But in the end, his conclave left him to his fate without so much as a word in his defense, and since then, they hadn't reached out. What kind of family was that?

"She never said it, but I knew she stayed for the younglings. Patini was always watching out for them, and for me."

Sierra laid a hand on his shoulder. "She seemed like a nice person, even if she only ever gave me the evil eye. Turns out she was right, I did get you into a lot of trouble." Guilt always came knocking on that particular door, and she tuned it out.

"You can't take all the credit," he said and paused for a moment, chewing on his lip. "I've been hearing more chatter about Praxians on Terrana."

That got Sierra's attention. "Why didn't you say something?"

"I don't want to get my hopes up. Even if they were there, they could have moved on, and it could be anyone. What are the chances it's my conclave?"

"True, but you don't have to keep all this to yourself. Let us help you. You don't have to do it alone."

"It feels like I've been chasing a ghost for years. They're never there when I arrive, and I'm beginning to wonder if they existed at all, or if they were a figment of my imagination."

She wanted to say something, but it had all been said before. She couldn't make him forget the person who raised him, and she didn't want to. He wouldn't move on until he'd said his piece to her, and even then, she would always be his ghost, the problem he couldn't fix despite forever believing he should.

"Do you remember back on Zhital when you wanted a nose ring, but we didn't have the money to get it done right?" Tovi asked, and Sierra was taken aback by the abrupt change of subject, a deflection and distraction from a groundhog day conversation.

She did remember, and she chuckled at the memory. "Of course I remember. My mom had left her shitty jewelry behind when they'd left. I thought she'd be pissed when she came back to see her earring up my nose, but she never came back," she said.

"You were holding a nasty needle and I found you staring at a mirror about to shove it through your nose."

"Thank Hades you did. I would have ended up with tetanus."

"I was always the smarter one," he said, jostling her shoulder with his.

"Every time I see that spark of hesitation in your eyes, it makes me want to run and jump off a cliff headfirst, into whatever lies below, like a challenge."

"That's fucked up, you know that?"

"I know," she said, resting her head on his shoulder.

"Luckily, I made you sanitize the needle first, then you insisted that I had to do it because I had better aim and you would just mess it up."

"I did do that. I was too chicken shit in the end."

"You kept closing your eyes. You were going to poke an eye out," he said, shaking his head. Sierra laughed; she'd forgotten about that. She'd been too determined to piss off her mom and be bad-ass with a nose ring to think it all the way through.

"But you did it and it turned out amazing. Just a few missed pokes," she said, touching the side of her nose and the metal stud.

"It's one of the memories that made me laugh on my hardest days in the service."

His voice dropped an octave, and Sierra could tell he'd gone back there for a moment, to one of the bad days. "There was this time when the company disabled the oxygen on a mining vessel in the belt. We went in to clean up the mess and take their claim. There were bodies everywhere, just floating. It was my job to push them out into space, like they woke up one day and decided to go for a walk space side. No marks on their bodies, just frozen horror on their still faces." Tovi talked about his service as infrequently as she talked about her time on Terrana. They were both running away from their memories and toward each other.

"I thought about taking my helmet off and drifting off with them. It seemed like the easiest thing to do, but then a message popped up, and it was a photo from you. You'd taken a bunch of parts and made a massive spider-bot, just for fun, and sent me a pic because you knew how afraid I was of spiders."

She resisted making a snarky remark about her terrible timing and gave him the space to say whatever he needed to say.

"You'd spent weeks putting together that monstrosity just to poke fun at me. Knowing you were out there and thinking about me made me feel like I existed and someone might care if I didn't make it through."

Sierra's eyes stung, and once again, she said nothing. This time, she had no snarky comment waiting in the wings. She wanted to brush it off, make it out to be no big deal, but she couldn't. Anything she said now would feel forced or placating. She knew what it was to feel helpless, like she was slowly vanishing, one pixel at a time. Bad moments inevitably followed the good, like a rotating wheel station, and she'd learned to ride out the bad moments with varying levels of success.

"I was shocked you remembered that I hated spiders. I don't know why, but I assumed you'd forget."

"You're not as forgettable as you think," she said.

Sierra had held on to the memory of him like a lifeline for the years they'd been separated. It had taken time, but she'd eventually tracked him down on the net, four years after they'd been shipped off Zhital. She'd stared at the message for hours, ready to hit send, but fear gripped her tight. What if he hadn't wanted to see her again? What if he blamed her for what happened? Her heart would shatter into a million pieces. Finding him again had been a mission that kept her moving one foot in front of the other every day. She'd shut her eyes tight and hit the button, not knowing how far the message would have to travel and if he'd receive it. He had, weeks later, and her world had expanded, righting itself for the first time in a long time.

"Whatever's waiting for you on Terrana, I'll be with you. We all will," he said.

She had to swallow around the tightening of her throat, the sound loud in her ears. "Thank you," she said.

Chapter 13

The Imminent Approach of the Shit Hitting the Fan

Del:

> I'm hearing whispers about an MIA Alcat. That wouldn't be from your cleanup operation, would it?

Ryan

> My darling sister was kind enough to call me about that particular rumor. I put her off. Even a whiff of scandal and Aster comes for the throat. She threatened to take it to Father.

Del

> Is it, though?!

Ryan

> How do I know? All Alcats look the same. Could have come from any Omnia ship.

Del

If someone gets their hands on it, then we'll know immediately who's responsible when they check the ship ID. And if it's from *The Hope of Trappist*, then you won't have to worry about the spreadsheet anymore, he'll delete you, literally and figuratively.

Ryan

I'm on top of it, but I'm certain it was a rumor she started to get me in hot water. Can you have your flunkies track down the net address of the original posting?

Del

Already done, I'll send it to your sleeve.

Ryan

If it is her, then I can use it as leverage.

Del

And if it isn't?

Del

You still there?

Ryan

Then I'll have my hands full.

Chapter 14

This Bot is On Fire

Seventeen Years Ago

Tovi smelled the warm, buttery scent of sourdough bread, fresh out of the oven, its tendrils curling through the living room like the disembodied arm from the old Earther cartoons he and the kids watched every morning. It had a similar effect, catching his attention and drawing him inexplicably to their shoebox-sized kitchen with Leela in his arms like a forward-facing backpack, their pudgy little arms wrapped around his neck.

"Bread!" Leela exclaimed, wiggling to be let down at the sight of the steaming loaf. He set them down and Leela ran over to Patini and grasped on to her skirts, big eyes and wheedling pheromones begging for a fresh slice.

Patini's smile was quiet and full of warmth as she stared down at Leela. She was all angles and protruding bones with the fragility of an injured bird. The burn mark on her face was a smooth and rippled island in a sea of roughened skin. Her brownish red hair was braided away from her face as she worked. Patini rested her hand on the child's wheat-colored hair before cutting the bread much sooner than she should—steam from the open wound releasing like exhaust from a refinery stack—then slathered it with butter, making sure it wasn't too hot before handing it to Leela.

"Yummy!" they exclaimed even before taking a bite and toddling off down the hall.

"You spoil them," Tovi said, smiling at her and leaning against the tippy dining room table.

"I spoil you too." Patini set a plate in front of him with a warm slice of bread, equally slathered in butter.

He sat down and tucked in, licking his lips as the bread quickly disappeared. He should have taken his time. Now that his mouth wasn't full of soft, toasty bread, he couldn't put off the fight he knew was coming. If he waited much longer, he'd be late, and he hated being late, but he hated disappointing Patini more.

"I'm going out. I'll be back before dinner." He didn't make eye contact with her, instead pressing the pads of his fingers against the crumbs on the plate, then transferring them to his mouth.

"Where are you going?"

"Does it matter? Can't I just exist in the universe without a chaperone? It's suffocating, always being watched and monitored, every move I make."

"That's just the way things are. It's not our fault that we're hunted, but it is our reality," Patini said with the consternation of someone who was tired of having the same argument, and Tovi couldn't agree more, but neither of them budged. Water splashed on the floor as she plunged the cutting board into the sink. The faucet dripped at regular intervals, oblivious to the ratcheting tension in the room.

"Who is hunting us?" Tovi said, exasperation lacing his voice and flattening his ears. He stood abruptly, pressing his hands into the table.

"The Vengeance at the behest of the Praxian government for one, and outsiders."

The adults of the conclave were always talking in riddles, not saying what they meant, and Tovi had had enough. "You mean humans, the very people that idiot Tian has us chasing around the universe in search of a fairy tale. Those people?"

"Don't you dare say that. He provides for us while you're out with that girl who's going to ruin your life," she said, turning from the sink, hands clouded in suds, to confront him directly.

"Sierra's going to ruin my life? She's not the one who took me from my home planet, ostracizing me from my own people, and you think she's the problem? We're running for our lives from a boogeyman. He's keeping us scared and complacent with this made-up Vengeance nonsense. Can't you see that's what he wants?"

Something he'd said struck her, her lips pressing together, her eyes hard, and her ears up and alert, but her voice was soft. "You don't understand everything. I know you think you do, but you don't."

"Whose fault is that?" He turned and walked out of the kitchen, grabbing his duffel bag housing the meager assortment of tools he'd collected from the dump and resale shops, then hefted it over his shoulder before walking out. The front door creaked as it opened and slid shut with a resolute bang.

A few of the kids turned to him as he walked through the quad, an open area where the kids played between the circle of houses they communally shared in the compound. Tovi was no longer a child, having gained the ability to control his hormones and choose male sex characteristics after reaching adulthood, but he still played in their games, carrying them piggyback through the conclave or pretending to be a horse and trotting around with a bundle of laughing kids on his back.

Tovi could appreciate Patini's concern, but he wouldn't live his life in fear because shady people wanted to cash in on the big credits black market developers would pay for a Praxian test subject. The kids needed their protection; he, however, was an adult, and he'd live or die by his decisions.

Zhital, the planet they currently called home, was at the ass end of space, too small to catch the attention of the Consortium of Planets. It was a moon of Chepital and comparatively the size of a compdroid. It had been terraformed, mined to death, abandoned by the company who'd paid for its development, and converted into a dump and recycling center for the host world and passing ships. Factions and separatist groups favored places like this. Largely ignored, they were able to amass weapons and followers, easy in a place so economically depressed that it only took a flick of the wrist to stir up tension. There'd been whispers about the Consortium showing unprecedented interest in Zhital as the factions became more ostentatious with their rebellion. It was the reason Sierra's family had packed up and left, leaving her behind in their haste.

The native soil was a sickly yellow color; patches poked through the long-neglected road system. Compounds lined the street, their gates tightly locked or left open and rusted where they had been abandoned. The sky was gray, clouds forever circling the moon, obscuring Chepital and any glimpse at a better life.

Tovi walked down the road, kicking yellow pebbles until they broke apart like chalk. The strong smell of foul trash was an ever-present byproduct, but it grew heavier and more cloying as he neared an old part of the dump that had been left to decompose years before. It was where he'd met Sierra, along with the other neighborhood kids who used the old dump as a playground. Nothing was more exciting than going on treasure hunts, unearthing buried treasure in the form of toys thrown away by the children of Chepital.

He climbed through the hole cut into the fence and over the first mound of rusted trash, flattened by the feet of hundreds of kids who'd passed through. Tovi spied a cluster of teenagers and adults in the packed down area they'd cleared for their impromptu ring. Word had gotten around, and they had a good showing for their matches and were making a decent scratch selling tickets.

Sierra crouched over their robot, a squat, four-wheeled thing with an articulating saw arm measuring two feet wide and just as long. Scratches marred the pale skin of her hands, probably from another fight, and her brown hair was a frizzy mess that she kept pushing away from her face. He sat down next to her and pulled a hair tie out of his duffel, handing it to her.

"You're a lifesaver," she said, taking the tie and pulling her hair up into a sloppy bun.

"When was the last time you washed it?"

"The power was cut, so maybe a week," she said absently.

"Your parents haven't been in contact?" He knew he shouldn't ask. She would have said if they had.

"Not since they fucked off to God knows where. Wouldn't tell me in case I blabbed to the government or whoever they think is after them. Not that I care," she said, waving her screwdriver in the air like she could parry away her irritation.

He worried about her living on her own in that apartment. She'd eventually be evicted and on the streets, and Tian had flat-out refused to have her in the compound. They both worked in the waste plant, operating cheap mechs to move the trash and sort the recycling, but it wasn't enough to live on. "You could have gone with them. This place is a dead end."

Her eyes hardened and he winced, expecting her to go off on a rant, but then she suddenly seemed immeasurably sad. "I honestly didn't think they'd leave without me. I said I wouldn't go, that I didn't want to leave, and I thought for sure they'd make me go. Instead, they just left. I keep thinking they'll come back for me, like this was all some kind of fucked-up lesson, but I don't think they're coming back." The fear in her eyes stopped him cold. Sierra had always been strong-willed and feisty with her words and her fists, but under all that was this vulnerable, terrified adolescent.

He wrapped his arms around her and held her tight. She folded into him, pressing her forehead into his chest.

"We'll figure something out. I'm not going to leave you," he said.

She nodded against his chest, then abruptly stepped back, glancing around to see if anyone noticed her moment of weakness. "We both go down together," she said, and he nodded. It was a pact they'd made as a passing joke whenever one of them had done something seriously stupid.

"Who did you wrestle this time?" He pointed at her cracked and cut hands.

"Does it matter?" she asked, her face a storm cloud. When she focused on his face, her expression morphed into suspicion. "Did you fight with Patini again?"

Tovi sighed. "Yes, same shit, different day."

"She means well, though."

"I just want to live my own life, on my own terms."

"You and me both. Did you bring the camera? We might have a shot at entering the system's robobattle competition with this fight."

"I did," he said, pulling out the camera he took from the conclave. It was Tian's, but according to Praxian social norms, everything was part of the collective, and Tian was a dick, so he didn't care. It was far better than anything they had at hand.

"Okay, great! I collected viewing fees from this lot, made some pocket change. You'll be happy to know I finished our secret weapon."

"The flame thrower?"

"The flame thrower!" She jumped up and down, throwing her hands in the air.

"Awesome. I'll record if you fight."

"Deal." She removed the controller from her backpack and turned it on, driving their bot in a circle and testing the saw. "Someday we'll be mech operators fighting onstage to a cheering crowd. We'll have all the food we want—and champagne."

"And we'll have our own mechs with cool weapons. We could buy a ship and tour the universe, see all the planets," Tovi said, imagining flying through space to any destination he wanted to explore.

"Ready?" the operator of the other mech yelled from his side of the flattened training area. He had a three-wheeled mech with a hammer slung out the back that would crush anything as long as his aim and timing was right.

"You bet!" Sierra said, jumping up and punching the air.

Tovi turned on the video recorder and set it up on the tripod. He wanted his hands free in case she needed help. The two bots squared up a few feet apart, and once both operators nodded, the fight began with the two bots facing off, neither making the first move.

"His three wheels make him less stable and easier to topple if you hit him just right," Tovi said, keeping his voice low.

Sierra's gaze was focused, but she nodded at his words. "I want the fucker to make the first move."

"I don't think he's going to." The two dozen people, mostly teenagers and some adults, were whooping and hollering for someone to do *something*.

"Ah, fuck it," she said and rushed the mech forward. It sped over the uneven ground as she swerved sharply to the left to avoid the falling hammer from the three-wheeler. She rammed into the side of the bot and extended the little saw, cutting into the body of the bot. It backed up, out of reach, and angled itself for another hammer drop. Fluid dripped from the body of the mech. She might have nicked the fuel line or a brake cable. The hammer fell on their front left wheel, smashing it nearly flat.

"Dammit," Sierra cursed. "Fine, take this." She pulled the trigger for the flame thrower, and fire burst forward, covering the bot in a thick flame. Tovi expected it to die out when the flame thrower petered out, but the fluid it was dripping caught fire and the bot exploded.

"Oh, shit, that's nuts," Sierra said, a maniacal grin on her face.

Tovi rushed over with the fire extinguisher to put it out but grew panicked when the fire appeared to spread.

"What the hell?" Sierra said.

"It's the plastic in the ground. It's on fire." Tovi desperately sprayed the ground around the smoldering bot, but it was spreading faster than he could contain and the heat pushed him back. The extinguisher sputtered and died, and he threw it away. "We need to run." He grabbed Sierra's hand and ran back to their supplies. He picked up the camera and threw it in the bag.

"What about our bot?" she asked, shoving her supplies in her bag and staring longingly at their bot, flames licking around its base.

"Leave it. It's too dangerous."

She didn't argue, but her eyes were desperate and sad. They gathered their things, and Tovi hauled Sierra to her feet.

"Halt! Stay where you are or we will fire on you."

Tovi searched for the source of the sound and saw five drones flying overhead, encircling them, their guns pointed directly at them. Everyone else had disappeared.

"How did they get here so quickly?" Sierra asked, her voice trembling.

Tovi dropped the bag and raised his hands in the air. "I don't know. Don't you dare run. They'll mow you down."

Sierra, face defiant in a scowl, dropped her bags and followed his lead. "Someone stitched us up."

Tovi could only agree. Anyone who knew what they were getting up to could have turned them in for a reward or an exchange of favors.

"My conclave will come for us, don't worry. We'll figure this out," Tovi said.

She slowly lowered her hands. "No one's coming to save me, Tovi."

"Don't you fucking run, or I'll kill you myself." The curse word got her attention. She cursed as a fluent second language, but he only did it when he needed someone's attention. "I'll follow you."

"You wouldn't dare," she said, eyes narrowing in his direction.

"We both go down together. You promised." He'd thrown her own mantra back at her. She always said it in jest, but he was dead serious, and he did his best to convey his intention with a hard stare.

"Raise your hands, or we'll shoot," the drone said. The voice was human, meaning it was being remotely operated.

Sierra slowly raised her hands back up. It wasn't long before armed guards roughly pushed them to the ground and restrained them. They were shoved into separate vehicles. Through the smoke and the unnatural shadows flickering from the growing fire, Tovi saw the scared expression that Sierra was trying to mask with anger.

He never imagined it would be years before he would see her again.

Chapter 15

There's no Place like an Asteroid Base

Tovi had seen and infiltrated his fair share of asteroid habitats, but he'd never seen one this large. The asteroid called Terrana was gray, covered in a layer of pumice-like dust. Underneath had been a metal-rich core, systematically mined and hollowed out from the inside and converted into a habitat as the lucrative materials were excised. It was shaped like a giant peanut that spun in orbit to simulate gravity. Asteroids couldn't handle gravity replicators, and as unsanctioned satellites, the inhabitants couldn't get their hands on one if they tried.

As their ship approached, Tovi saw the hivelike structure of the habitat where it broke free from the asteroid's center. Underneath the gray surface of the asteroid, the habitat expanded like an anthill. Cecil maneuvered the ship to match the spin of the asteroid and flew through the plasma barrier that kept air inside the habitat. The space traffic controller sent them an authorization confirmation and parking directions.

Tovi could see the large transport ships parked nearest the exit, three in total, and they were about ten times the size of their ship and likely used to regularly supply the asteroid with food and supplies.

Cecil flew past about a dozen medium class 2 ships before arriving at their designated spot with the rest of the smaller class 3 ships, and Cecil set them down with the smallest of bumps as their landing gear was snatched by the safety docking arm.

"We headed out?" Tovi asked.

"We have some time before we meet Ching Shih. I'm taking Iz to the market so they can sell their artwork while we're here. If you want help getting to your destination, you're welcome to join us. You have any plans?" Sierra asked.

"I want to ask after any Praxians in the area. The market is as good a place as any to start."

"What are you going to do?" Iz asked Sierra.

"I'm going to stop by the ring, see if they have any amateur events going on."

Can I come? Lulu twined between his legs. *I want to see the pirates.*

"Not this time, Lu." He was being precious with her, but they'd only just established a mental connection, and he was worried he'd lose her in an unfamiliar environment. She was also easily distracted, and he could see her running off, her curiosity getting the best of her.

But Rupert and Pixie are going, she whined into his mindsync.

"Next time. We'll work on getting you comfortable on my shoulders." He patted her head, and she took a swat at him. "Don't be like that." She sauntered in the opposite direction, tail and nose up in the air. He promised himself he'd make it up to her when he came back with a new toy.

"We have to go through the Port Authority to get our disembark clearance. If you have contraband, put a little effort into hiding it," Sierra said.

They left the ship in Cecil's capable paws, exiting down the cargo ramp and closing it behind them. They crossed the wide hangar to the exit that took them to a hallway with signs directing them to the Port Authority and was the only way into the interior of the asteroid.

The hallway dumped into a room lined with stations, each with an attendant on duty to collect the necessary forms and fees. In the center of the room were rows and rows of uncomfortable hard-back chairs and things that resembled chairs for sentients lacking legs, or bones for that matter. The lighting was dim and a bulb flickered overhead, reminding him of an unsavory bar he'd frequented on Octto in his early years. Tovi was grateful for the low light. Based on the acrid smell, he didn't want to know why his shoes were making sticky noises against the floor. He suspected more than a few species had overindulged and their stomachs had retaliated as they'd waited for clearance.

Lucky for them, Cecil had submitted all their documents electronically, and Tovi hoped it would save them time. They took a number and sat together with a dozen bored or hungover sentients.

Tovi decided the best use of his time was to do a little sentient-watching while they waited. It usually took a good twenty to thirty minutes to get all the paperwork in order and receive their clearance to go back and forth between the ship and the interior. Sierra was on his left and Iz on his right, both tapping away on their sleeves, not paying much attention.

Tovi watched a hardened badger, the sentient kind, not a comp-droid, arguing with an unsympathetic authority agent. The badger's snout was scarred and he was missing half an ear. He was on his back feet and baring his teeth, a growling rumble coming from deep in his chest as he argued over the fees with the authority agent. The agent wasn't intimidated, which Tovi assumed had something to do with the very obvious security ports installed in the wall behind the agent, thinly veiling the pellet guns that would subdue the badger if things got too heated, but that was unlikely. The badger knew how far he could press before he went too far; a being who had survived that much damage knew how to survive tedious logistics and an avalanche of paperwork.

At another station, a pair of Taconites stared blankly at a distressed agent tapping furiously at her console. Taconites didn't have vocal cords, nor did they communicate through speech; instead, they used telekinesis to override computer systems. They'd commandeered the agent's computer and were communicating via text. Governments had to put up with a certain level of data leakage when it came to Taconites. There was little they could do to stop them, and everyone in the known universe relied on Taconite mining technology for precious metals and rare elements.

Taconites operated as a pair. No one knew why exactly, but Tovi had never seen one alone. Their pale skin was amoeba-like in its translucency and their bodies were unable to maintain any one particular shape, more of an amorphous blob. They were impossible to read through body language, except their changing colors that might or might not allude to their emotions—no one really knew for sure. He'd only ever spoken to a pair once when they'd taken over his sleeve to ask him directions. He tried to respond with words, and when there was no reaction, he typed his response and the Taconites left without so much as a thank you. His smile had held no charm for them.

Sierra leaned over in her chair so she could whisper to him without being heard. "What do you think they're saying?" she asked, her eyes trained on the Taconites.

Tovi considered for a second. "We have a shipment of purple sparkly slippers for delivery," he said in a robotic voice.

The agent was typing, her face pinched, and Sierra picked up the hypothetical conversation. "Purple slippers are on the list of approved goods for resale, however, sparkles and/or glitter are restricted when shipped from Taconite airspace due to the glitter embargo," Sierra said in a low voice, holding up a hand to cover her smile.

"The glitter is sourced off planet through legal trade agreements with the glitterati," Tovi said.

"Is that real?" Iz asked, their purple, shimmering backpack reflecting in the light. "If it is, how do I join?"

"If it was real, you'd already be president," Tovi said.

"Chief Glitter Officer," Sierra said.

"Sparkle in Chief," Tovi said.

"That's my new title, until otherwise notified."

"Noted," Tovi said.

The rest of the occupants were mostly human, some so gene modified, they barely resembled humans, with grafted horns, glowing skin, slitted eyes, and tails of every variety. This sector of the known universe was culturally enamored of gene splicing and body modification, and the Consortium didn't regulate human populations on free-holds. Tovi hadn't taken an interest in body modification, mostly because they'd never been tested on Praxians and he didn't fancy being a test subject, but he enjoyed the species-watching and seeing the interesting ways people found to decorate themselves. Clothes were Tovi's favorite pastime; he was a sucker for anything shiny.

An attendant called their number, approved their paperwork, then sent access files to their sleeves so they could come and go without incident. Tovi was more relieved than he expected to be. Places like this were particularly shrewd, but they wanted their pound of flesh like anyone else. He felt the assignment from Ryan like a weight he was more than ready to remove from his shoulders. Even if they made it through this job unscathed, Tovi would never trust him.

The three of them passed through the secured doors leading into the main building. The dim lights of the Port Authority office had ill-prepared his eyes for the artificial sunlight that shot down from the dome ceiling of the main atrium. From this side of the honeycomb windows, he couldn't see the stars from space, as the lights reflected off the glass. The lighting effect was fascinating and beautiful in its own way, like the sun was just over the horizon. It didn't feel like they were in space at all.

The atrium was large enough to fit three class 1 cargo ships under the tall and rounded ceiling. Tovi had to blink away the lights so his eyes could adjust, his second eyelid automatically closing out the harshest light. People were moving perpendicular to them along a large thoroughfare that ringed the atrium. On the other side of the crowd was a circus. He wasn't being hyperbolic; there were actual acrobats performing in front of an amusement park with a circus tent, everything pirate-themed. Acrobats wore eyepatches and peg legs with checkered shirts and handkerchiefs for hats. Tovi could see a pirate ship ride and a cardboard cutout of a group of pirates surrounding an overflowing chest of gold with the heads cut out. A group of teenagers were sticking their heads through and making funny faces for a photo.

It was jarring in light of the real, honest-to-God pirates lurking behind the cheery facade, and he wondered what they thought of this bastardization. He'd find it a bit degrading, but pirates weren't the most scrupulous of people. It was hard to believe cutthroat pirates of the modern, space-faring variety existed when presented with this candy-coated confection of a theme park, but maybe that was the point. Surrounded by happy families and reinforcing the belief it was an ode to a bygone era made it all the easier to operate under everyone's noses. Filling the place with innocent civilians wasn't a bad way to shield themselves from external threats.

Tovi shook his head. He was spending too much time around Sierra, and his thoughts were becoming just as cynical as hers.

They jostled through the crowds, bumping into people who stopped abruptly to take a picture of a CompParrot squawking in a fake palm tree that was listing to the side at a precarious angle. Sierra led them through the crowd until they came to a wide avenue headed into the asteroid and bisecting the main tourist thoroughfare.

"What a zoo," Iz said, brushing off their pink puff sleeve. "Isn't there another way inside?" they asked.

"Nah, they set it up like a casino. You have to go through the tourist trap if you come into the commercial docks. It's all about eyes on the merchandise," Sierra said, unfazed by the tumult.

They headed down the avenue, its wide street accommodating merchants lined on either side selling imported fruit that sounded deceptively otherworldly, like yumma fruit and dama root. Both were genetically engineered and grown in greenhouses; there was nothing remotely exotic about them. Other booths sold souvenir trinkets, costumes, and toys.

Iz scanned the crowd, doing some kind of incomprehensible math, taking in all the booths, the people running them, and the shoppers they attracted. They were in their own world, analyzing the situation. Tovi and Sierra could have disappeared in a puff of smoke, and they wouldn't have noticed. Tovi exchanged a knowing glance with Sierra, who quirked a smile in acknowledgment. After a few minutes combing up and down the market street, they came to a stop in front of a booth selling bracelets and jewelry. The table wasn't packed but had good walking traffic. Iz caught the attention of the attendant and exchanged words Tovi couldn't hear, but he guessed Iz was suggesting a cut of their sales in exchange for booth space. Moments later, Iz began unpacking their artwork with a self-satisfied smile.

"They're happy as a clam," Sierra said to Tovi. "What's your plan?"

"I'm going to ask around, put out some feelers. I have a few lukewarm leads. Based on the amount of attention I'm getting, they probably don't see many of my kind," Tovi said, and it was true. It was easy to differentiate between the locals and the tourists. Tourists were visibly shocked when they locked eyes with him, some skittering away in the opposite direction, others outright staring. Locals glanced in his direction, but their gaze didn't linger. Tovi suspected it was more out of self-preservation than anything. Staring too long at the wrong sentient could have unpleasant consequences.

"I'm headed to the ring. They should have some kind of amateur battle matches. With any luck, there's one coming up," she said. "Don't get in any trouble."

"I could say the same to you," he said.

"I never cause any trouble," she said, attempting an innocent smile that was devious when paired with her sharp gaze.

He waved her off, and she disappeared into the crowd. He had no such luck with that particular talent, being a head taller than everyone else. Tovi wandered through the market, examining what was on offer and striking up conversations with anyone who was receptive, and struck out at the first few booths. As he moved farther back, the wares became less superfluous and more applicable to discerning customers—cubbies for smuggling contraband and sharp weapons hidden in broom handles and hair accessories.

At a booth selling compdroid merch, he found a giant fly cat toy that flew up in the air and bounced around the floor. He parted with the credits and pocketed the toy for Lulu, hoping she'd forgive him.

He kept an eye out for a talker, someone with loose lips who traded in information. He passed by two stands where the owners were either busy or their posture suggested he should buy something or keep moving. At a shop selling zero-grav rated cooking supplies, pots and pans hanging from a makeshift rack with utensils stuck to them to show off the magnetic power of her products, was a woman chatting with a customer. She was human, or human adjacent, light-skinned with long blonde hair and wearing a floor-length black dress.

He remembered Cecil griping about their burned pans, thanks to one of Sierra's attempts to make mac and cheese that went awry. He perused the options, picking one that was similar in size. He balked at the price, remembering the sad state of their coffers, and chose one a little smaller.

"Find something you like?" she asked, her last customer having wandered off.

"Yeah, I'll take this one," he said, handing it to her. "I was also wondering if you had some information for sale. I'm happy to pay full price."

Her gaze sharpened. "What kind of information is that?"

"Nothing heavy. Have you seen some of my kind in these parts lately? I'm searching for a friend."

"For information like that, I recommend you purchase this pan instead," she said, pulling down a larger pan with a thicker bottom and sturdy handle. It was more like a weapon than a kitchen implement. He glanced at the price tag and tried to swallow his consternation.

"For fifteen percent off that price, I think it's a great deal," he said.

"I can swing that," she said with an experimental swing of the pan. "Get it? Like the pan?" It was an effort to smile instead of roll his eyes.

"Yes, quite witty," he said, sending the credits to her sleeve. "Now about that information."

"I've seen a few of you around, or maybe it was the same one multiple times. Hard to say really. You all look so much alike."

Tovi gritted his teeth to maintain the smile and hold his tongue.

"You should really talk to LaLooka. She helps refugees and such, runs a café over in Little Marseilles called the Cobbler's Daughter. They serve cobblers, you see, but they're shaped like little boots. Get it?"

"Adorable," he said. "Anything else you can tell me?"

"It's funny, we used to see more of you, but lately, it's like they all disappeared. I remember one, a few weeks back, he, she, or they bought some of my synthetic honey, seemed to really like the stuff. Not much of a talker, though."

Tovi's heart ran like a ring train. "Did they have a burn scar on their head?"

"Now you mention it, they did. Looked like an old injury, healed over but pretty visible. I wondered at the time how they got such a nasty scar. Must have been an interesting story, but I'd never pry. I'm not that sort of person, you see. And they didn't seem very friendly, thought I might spook them and lose a customer."

Tovi tuned her out. She'd been here, and recently—Patini. He ran hot, then cold, at the thought of seeing her again. If there was anyone he needed to apologize to, to make amends to, it was her. He both yearned for and dreaded confronting her again. She'd been the closest thing to what humans regarded as a parent.

Praxians were communal by nature, but those communities could change rapidly and without warning, people leaving and others joining. Relationships were not predicated along familial lines, but instead by mutual interest. Children belonged to the community and would stay in the care of whichever adult felt the most attached to the child, and that person frequently changed.

Tovi assumed that was why Praxian children were painfully cute, and he knew for certain they emitted pheromones that instilled a sense of attachment and affection. As soon as Praxians were old enough to alter their sex characteristics, they would stop emitting the pheromones and become an adult member of a conclave.

Patini had been his caregiver, along with half a dozen other children in their conclave before he reached adulthood.

He'd felt trapped in the conclave, taken from his home planet as a child and unable to return. Tian had convinced the conclave to leave Prax when Tovi was twelve and follow his idiotic beliefs, promising them eternal life and riches if they helped humans return to Earth and the fount of eternal life.

Tovi hadn't expected to feel remorse, not alongside his resentment. How those two diametrically opposed feelings flourished within him, he couldn't understand. It didn't matter to Praxian law that he'd been removed as a child; he'd have to jump through nearly impossible hoops to go back due to Praxian isolationist policy. It was a deep wound he couldn't shake, and yet, he missed Patini. She had raised him, loved him, and he'd let her down, left her to take care of the younger kids on her own. More than anything, he needed to know she was okay.

And now there was a chance he'd finally tracked them down. Whether Patini and the conclave would be receptive to his overtures kept him up at night. She could turn him away, shun him to his face this time. He told himself this was a reaction he was prepared to receive, but the coiling anxiety in his chest left him unsure. There was only one way to find out. Tovi left the clerk with a wave as she continued her one-sided conversation and pulled up the map to find Little Marseilles. He checked the time and cursed his luck. There wasn't enough time to follow the lead before their meeting with Ching Shih. He tamped down his sense of urgency; he'd waited this long, and a few hours wouldn't make any difference. At least that was what he told himself as he headed back to the ship.

Chapter 16

What Goes Up Must Come Down

Sierra wound her way through the crowds. She was relatively certain she could remember her way through the station to the fairgrounds. Little had changed since she'd been away. The rides were all the same and the storefronts had changed some, but they offered the same array of cuisine and sweet treats tourists loved, from burgers to soft serve. Lucky for her, the pathways were clearly marked in case her memory failed her, which it was wont to do. She followed the signs and the crowds pointing to the fairgrounds until tall, wide columns framing a massive yellow-and-red striped tent rose in front of her. Ten years and some changes had passed since the first time she'd stood in this spot, in awe and trepidation of what awaited her, and like déjà vu, she was back here again, just as excited and full of dread as before.

Just like back then, all her hopes for the future were in that tent, financially and professionally, but this time, she had her autonomy. She had to remind herself that she didn't need this to work out; she wanted it. In theory, protecting her heart and remembering it wasn't essential might keep her from crushing disappointment.

The hammering and crushing of metal on metal rose above the din of the crowd, prodding her forward with greater urgency, not wanting to miss a moment of the action. She paid for a ticket and pushed through the sluggish mob of people to the stairs leading down into the bowl of the theater. Everyone was standing and shouting as the two mechs in the large circular ring pummeled each other. Sierra slipped into a row and brushed past annoyed fans—ducking a tossed popcorn bag thrown at her head—and found an empty seat. She hadn't seen a live fight in years and had forgotten how loud the affair was with shouting people and scraping metal.

The smell of the crowd—with their hotdogs oozing mustard and ketchup and beer sloshing out of thin-necked bottles, spilling over with the force of shaking fists—mixed with oil and a whiff of ozone.

In the ring was a familiar mech, one she'd fought before, though it had changed with time and obvious success. Once upon a time, it had been fighting a losing battle with corrosion, but now it was hot-rod red with gold detailing. It was tall for a mech, which Sierra always thought gave it a high center of gravity, but the downswing of its telltale battle-axe gained immense momentum.

She remembered the almighty concussion she'd suffered at the hands of the mech dubbed the Battleaxe. They were in the throes of the third round, and Sierra cursed her luck for missing the bulk of the battle. Round one was her favorite, as she preferred hand-to-hand combat. She'd always scored the most points in the first round, when her body was fresh and adrenaline was pumping. The mechs could use inert weapons in round two; no tricks, just hammers, knives, spears, and the like. Round three was fun from a spectator's perspective, but inside the mech housing, it was another story.

Onlookers waited with bated breath to see what the mechs would spring on their opponents, placing outlandish bets. In the third round, they could use an ultimate weapon, a seemingly unfair advantage for anyone with the means to craft a superior weapon, but that rarely went to plan. A mech operator would only get the drop on their opponent during their first battle with the weapon. Every subsequent opponent would strategize and compensate, but they never knew what could be coming for them, unless they'd managed to bribe someone for the information or planted a bug to listen in.

The Battleaxe always had some variation on the axe, even if it didn't use the axe's obvious blade. She'd once seen it electrocute a mech, taking it down without a single swing. Today, the blade was illuminated so brightly as to blind its opponent at the right angle, and from Sierra's vantage point, it was doing an admirable job. She wasn't familiar with the opposing mech, which had a wide, squat body with powerful arms and sturdy legs, trading agility for strength. She found the matte-black body and the silver lines tracing down its sides uninspiring and pretentious, leading her to the obvious conclusion that the operator was a tool.

A glance at the scoreboard told her it was called the Roughneck and there were thirty seconds to go in the round. It jabbed at the Battleaxe with a long spear, its movements brash, feeling the ticking of the clock and physical fatigue after three five-minute rounds. It wasn't the same as boxing, but operating a mech in battle was laborious and the hits were hard.

The Roughneck sprang its secret maneuver in the last thirty seconds, and Sierra understood why it had waited. It thrust the spear toward the Battleaxe's knee joint, too far away to hope to land a blow, except the end of the spear jettisoned forward, its flat blade hurtling past the Battleaxe's defenses and spearing through the knee joint with a ripping sound as the wires were severed. The Battleaxe lurched, staying upright thanks to the blow being just to the inside of the knee, leaving it partially intact and robbing the Roughneck of the fall points that might have secured the match in their favor.

A horn signaled the end of the fight, followed by a chorus of screams from the crowd, a mixture of elation and indignation as the Battleaxe was declared the winner. Sierra was incomprehensibly pleased to see the Battleaxe win, even after being on the receiving end of its wrath a distant lifetime ago. She pushed through the crowd, an idea forming and bringing a grin to her lips.

She popped out of the tent and jogged down the street to the nearest liquor store. There were half a dozen on the street, catering to the winners and the losers. She bought a cheap bottle of something calling itself red wine, but at her price point, it was undoubtedly as synthetic as a liquid could come. She snagged a cheap black ball cap off a rack. The clerk, a bored twenty-something wearing a black mesh top and cargo pants, offered her a bag pinched between slime-green painted nails. She waved the bag away, walking out of the shop holding the bottle by the neck like a bludgeon and pulling the cap over her blue hair.

Sierra vividly remembered the back entrance to the ready rooms at the stadium and followed the tent around the side. She pulled her new ball cap down low but walked with long strides like she belonged there. As she approached the administrative block housing the private rooms, a crowd was waiting, excited fans hoping to glimpse their favorite mech operators and get an autograph.

She pushed her way through, holding up the wine bottle like a torch through the darkness. The bodyguards—two large, imposing sentient wolves—blocked the entrance with their aggressively relaxed bodies, slinky and imposing.

Sierra brandished the wine bottle. "Got a delivery for the Battleaxe from an admirer," she said, not stopping her approach. She didn't know these particular guards, a relief if there was one. She'd never gotten along with the security detail, and if she was absurdly lucky, she wouldn't run into the head of security.

A dark gray wolf sniffed and glanced at the door, and Sierra took it as an invitation to keep moving. The second wolf, nearly snow white, was licking its haunches and paid her no mind. The crowd protested her easy passage and the wolves continued to ignore them, their presence deterrent enough.

Sierra opened the door leading into the administrative wing, smiling to herself. She was greeted by an empty hallway stretching in either direction. Noises came from the right side of the hallway, where it spilled out into the arena. People were talking over one another, and she couldn't hear anything specific or pick out a familiar voice. She turned to her left, scanning the placards on the doors until she came to one emblazoned with *The Battleaxe she/her* on the digital readout. She didn't hesitate, pressing the door open and then slipping inside.

The room had changed since the last time she'd been here. A maroon curtain separated the room in two, presumably to offer the operator privacy while they got ready when they had visitors. The organizers and managers would sell used toothpicks if they could, and they had no qualms with invading the privacy of operators by charging top dollar to customers who wanted a pregame chat in the operator's private room. Sierra was relieved to see the bank of chairs lined against one wall was bereft of butts. The Battleaxe didn't much like visitors, but operators didn't often get a choice. The rest of the room was painted red with gold accents, just like the mech. The carpet was plusher than Sierra remembered, and an overstuffed red couch perched against the far wall, clothes thrown haphazardly over its scrolled armrests detailed in gold cord and stitching. The room smelled of flowers, and she guessed there were a few bouquets hidden behind the curtain.

"What do you want?" came an annoyed voice from behind the curtain.

Sierra cleared her throat. "Special delivery for the second baddest bitch to bust skulls this side of the black."

The curtain ripped aside, revealing a half-dressed human with murder in her eyes. Sierra had known her as Andy, using he/him pronouns, but she changed names and pronouns as much as she liked. Her dark brown hair was tied back in a bun, sweaty wisps clinging to her forehead and cheeks. She had a wide face and fat body, currently wearing a half-discarded bodysuit, unzipped and bunched at the waist with the empty sleeves hanging by her sides.

"You son of a bitch," she said, her voice half whisper, half accusation.

"I'm happy to see you too," Sierra said, holding her arms out for a hug and brandishing the wine bottle.

Andy rushed at her, and Sierra thought she was about to lose her life as Andy aimed for her waist. Expecting to be thrust into the wall, she squeezed her eyes shut and tensed her body. Andy wrapped her arms around her midsection and hauled her into the air.

Sierra wasn't sure if she was being hugged or having the life squeezed out of her. "Are you trying to kill me?" Sierra squeaked out, all the air crushed from her chest.

"I haven't made up my mind yet," Andy said.

"I brought you wine," she offered feebly, her feet dangling off the ground. "I'd rather not smash it over your head."

"I suppose we could drink it before I kick your ass," Andy said, finally setting her back on solid ground.

"That's going to bruise," Sierra said, arching her back in an attempt to pop her vertebra back into place.

"You deserve it," Andy said, taking the bottle from Sierra, untwisting the cap and then taking a swig. "God, this tastes like shit. Couldn't you get something nicer?"

"I thought it was a nice touch, you know, for old times' sake," Sierra said. Andy lifted a skeptical brow. "Also, I'm broke."

"What a surprise."

Sierra flopped down on the couch. "Are you still going by Andy?"

"For the moment," Andy said, taking another swig. "How did you get past the pack?"

"Creatures of habit. People were always sending you wine, and they assume no one would be stupid enough to risk getting caught out."

"Except you," Andy said.

"Exactly," Sierra said, flashing her most annoying smile.

"What brings you back to this dump?"

"Got a job going. We have a few cycles of shore leave, thought I'd look you up."

Andy didn't seem convinced. "Budge over," she said, and Sierra retracted her legs so Andy could sit on the couch. "What do you really want?"

"I'm hurt. Can't I visit an old friend?"

"An old friend you haven't kept in contact with for the last ten years."

"You didn't contact me either," Sierra shot back with more malice than she had anticipated.

"Touché," Andy said, passing Sierra the bottle, and she took a swig, then made a face.

"You're right, this is shit," she said and took another.

"Out with it," Andy said.

"I was wondering if there were any amateur matches coming up. Was hoping to make some credits while we're asteroid-side."

"You're a hot mess, you know that?"

Sierra shrugged. It was true; she couldn't deny it.

Andy sighed, holding out her hand for the bottle before leaning back against the couch. "We have them throughout the week. Next one with open slots is six cycles from now."

"Think you can put in a good word for me? I didn't exactly leave on the best of terms."

Before Andy could answer, the door banged open, making both of them jump. In walked the very man she'd been trying to avoid, Ian Vandover. Pushing in behind him was a very large, very white wolf with a row of hoop earrings lining the underside of her ears. In a single bound, she was on top of Sierra, teeth exposed in a predatory grin, and a rumbling growl vibrated from her chest and through Sierra's body.

Sierra's eyes dilated, and all the breath evacuated from her lungs. The last time she'd been in this position, she'd lost a large chunk of her shoulder that had to be regrown—she still had the scar. The memory of Kaylo's teeth ripping into her flesh brought her into a cold sweat, and she felt a panic attack coming on.

"I can smell your fear, taste it on my tongue. It's delicious," Kaylo said, drawing out the word "delicious" like a succulent indulgence. She licked the side of Sierra's face, her rough tongue swiping across her cheek like sandpaper and leaving a trail of saliva. "It was a mistake to come back here and deceive my pack."

"S-sorry?" Sierra managed to get out, hoping she wouldn't embarrass herself by vomiting on Kaylo's white pelt. Rupert slithered out like a shot and hissed at Kaylo, making her rear back.

Let me maim her, he said.

If she comes at me, feel free to do your worst, she said through their connection.

"Kaylo, let her up," Vandover said from somewhere behind the wall of hair and muscle.

With an indignant sniff and a last show of teeth, Kaylo backed off Sierra, circling ominously between her and Vandover. It was space enough for Sierra to take a deep breath and fight off her instinct to vomit and run like an idiot from the room. Rupert wrapped protectively around her neck, mouth open and fangs protruding.

"If it isn't Van the Man," Sierra said, trying to relax back into the couch and appear nonchalant instead of petrified. She was pleased to note she hadn't pissed herself, a humiliating win.

"What are you doing here?" he asked, his eyes narrowing in her direction.

"I was in the neighborhood. Just came by for a chat," she said.

Vandover always reminded her of mobsters in old movies, dressed to the nines and exuding a calculating menace. He was a tall, barrel-chested man with dark skin and shrewd eyes. He wore a suit like a second skin, his signature pocket watch chain draped over his chest and tucked into the breast pocket of his vest. Antiques like that, ones with real mechanical hardware, were rare, and by extension, expensive. Conflicting feelings of shame and affection warred one another as Vandover's eyes drilled into her. She desperately wanted to crawl behind those eyes and see what he saw, know what he thought of her.

"She's wanting to fight in the amateur league," Andy said, her approach less subtle than Sierra was hoping for.

"Are you now?" The light in Vandover's eyes brightened, and Sierra was feeling like a canary who was not only in a cage, but trapped in a coal mine. He checked something on his sleeve; the expression in his eyes was calculating, and Sierra was tense in anticipation. "You're in luck, we had someone drop out of our headliner match. Nerves got the better of him."

"The next match?" Andy asked, sitting up straighter. "That's in three cycles."

"Are you serious?" Sierra asked, knowing the answer. Vandover was always serious when it came to business.

"Better not waste any time," he said, walking out Andy's door like he hadn't handed her a golden opportunity to sink or swim—again.

Chapter 17

The Subtle Art of Herding Cats

Tovi hadn't made it halfway up the ramp before Sierra was on top of him.

"Any luck?" she asked, jumpy as a rabbit.

"I got a lead I'm going to follow up after the job."

"That's great," she said. He wanted to tell her what he'd learned, but Cecil came into the cargo hold, passing Iz where they were working on the mural, all their paint supplies laid out. Pixie was floating above them, working on the upper section, three tentacles wrapped around individual paint brushes. Cecil's black velvet cap with a red feather rode low over his brow in a no-nonsense manner. He was in management mode.

"What's the plan for the drop-off?" Cecil asked.

"Hey! I haven't told him the good news. We got a fight!"

"Heck yeah," Tovi said and high-fived her. He hadn't expected she'd be successful out of the block, since persistence, not charm, was her defining feature.

"What did I say? The job comes first. Stay focused," Cecil said.

"You're such a party pooper," Sierra said, pushing at his furry shoulder. He didn't budge. His huff blew her hair away from her face. "We're supposed to meet them at a warehouse in D block. I have the address somewhere," she said, poking at her sleeve to pull up the information.

"Got you this," Tovi said, handing Cecil the heavy pan. Cecil hefted the pan in his paw and assessed it with an appraising eye.

"Did you get me this so I'd make you that bread you keep talking about?"

"I wouldn't say no," Tovi said with a smile.

Lulu poked her head out of one of the lockers and sniffed the air.

"Hey, Lulu, I got you a present," Tovi said, pulling the toy out of his pocket. She snuck back into the locker, her tail sticking out and writhing. "Don't be like that. At least take a peek."

She turned around but didn't leave her hiding spot. He set the bug down and pressed the button. It flew a few feet in the air before coming down, skittering on the floor, and then flying up again. After a pause, Lulu shot out and made a valiant attempt to capture the bug. Tovi smiled, happy he'd done something right.

Lulu glanced over her shoulder at him. *I accept your apology, this time*, she said before scampering after the bug. One small disaster averted.

"We should leave someone outside the warehouse, in case things go sideways," Tovi said, taking a derisive satisfaction in learning something from his last encounters with Ryan.

"You got it. I'll dig around for some information on the building. We'll swing by the place and see where I can set up." Iz said, sounding distracted as they stood up from the floor. Iz was usually the one on lookout duty, thanks to their uncanny marksmanship and lateral thinking in a crisis. Tovi sensed there was something not quite right by the tension in Iz's shoulders and their flat tone.

Iz packed up their work, Pixie mimicking them and stuffing their work in Iz's bag. Their tentacles floated beneath them. Sierra caught his eye and looked pointedly at Iz with a raised eyebrow. Tovi glanced at Iz, shoulders slumped and eyes on the ground. He followed Iz out of the cargo bay. Knowing Sierra was also concerned about Iz gave him confidence to ask them what was on their mind.

"Everything okay, Iz?" he asked, jogging up beside them.

"Yeah, why wouldn't it be?" Iz said, snapping back at him.

Tovi held up his hands. "I don't know, you're not your normal, cheery self, thought maybe you'd like to talk about it."

"It's personal," they said after a moment. "And sometimes I don't have the energy to be 'on' all the time."

"Okay, I won't pry. If you want to talk, I'm here," Tovi said. It wasn't like Iz to hold anything back, but he'd respect their wishes. Turned out he didn't have to wait long. They took a few steps, then leaned against the wall and slumped to the floor like a discarded toy.

"It's Lana," they said, crestfallen. He followed her to the floor, back to the wall and shoulder to shoulder, and waited for them to continue. "Sierra said some stuff earlier, about Lana trying to control me, and it's been bothering me."

"Don't take everything Sierra says to heart. She can be impulsive," Tovi said, fully aware of the way Sierra's words cut too close to the bone.

"But she's right. I was mad about it because I don't want her to be right. I really like Lana, but she's been trying to convince me to give up the ship and get a job on station. I thought she was worried about me, my safety and all that. Now, I'm not so sure. I think, maybe, she just wants me all to herself. She keeps saying she can't watch me put myself in danger, it's too hard on her and she wants me to be safe."

"What do *you* want?" Tovi had his concerns about Lana. She was controlling and often tried to keep Iz from the rest of the crew when they were on station. There was always some excuse as to why they couldn't meet up, and he had a sneaking suspicion she'd been dropping poison into Iz's ears about the crew.

"I don't want to leave the ship and give up my share. Is it really any more or less dangerous than a station job? People are hurt all the time on station."

"Did you tell her that?"

"Yes, but she kept pushing it. Wouldn't let it go. On top of that, there's the incident with Jimmy. I've had time to think about it, and Sierra might be right. Lana was the only one outside of the crew who knew about Lulu's existence. If it's true, and she leaked the information about an AIcat on the station, that means she set Sierra up. I don't want to believe she's capable of that."

Tovi was reminded of Ryan and his betrayal—though they'd never officially dated—but he could appreciate how Iz felt because what did that say about their own character and judgment if it was true? He nodded, not having much to offer and what was done was done.

"I just... I don't want to be alone, and compared to the other sentients I've dated, she's been great. What's wrong with me?" Iz dropped their head into their hands.

Tovi wrapped an arm around their shoulders. He wanted to say something about how they weren't alone because they had the crew, but he stopped himself, knowing that wasn't what they were talking about.

"I get it, being alone is hard sometimes."

"I'm sorry, that was rude of me."

"Not at all. You know I've made my share of mistakes. Whatever you decide to do, we'll be here for you. I'll be honest, she does seem a touch controlling, and Sierra can be astute, if lacking tact on such matters."

Iz snorted a laugh. "An elephant has more grace than Sierra."

"Yes, but she's *our* elephant."

"Don't let her catch you saying that; she might take it as a challenge. We should get going before Cecil yells at us. Sorry to fall apart on you there," they said, wiping their face free of tears.

"I'm a mechanic. You can always come to me if you're breaking down," he said with a cheesy smile.

They stood and Iz swatted his shoulder. "That was terrible, but thank you anyway. I needed a good cry, I guess. It's been bouncing around my brain since we left the station."

"Seriously, though, you can always come to me if you want to chat about what's going on. And whatever you decide to do, we'll always have your back."

"Thanks, Tovi," Iz said, gracing him with a watery smile. "What about you? Did you find anything on your conclave?"

"Nothing concrete, but I'm working on it."

They continued down the hallway, Tovi keeping his arm around their shoulders until they'd dropped off their supplies and Iz left the ship. He felt a little relieved himself. Iz was too good a person to end up stuck with someone who kept them like a shiny trophy. Their need for love and affection was too easy to exploit, much like his own.

Chapter 18

My Heart Goes Boom Boom Boom

Sierra's background check on the drop-off point showed it as a warehouse in a quiet, industrial part of the asteroid mostly used for long-haul freight storage. In Sierra's experience, it was the kind of place for shady deals of this caliber. When Iz returned from their reconnaissance, the crew gathered in the galley.

"Iz, did you find a good vantage point?" Sierra asked.

Iz was bent over the table, checking out a map of the area. "There aren't any windows, but I saw in the building schematics there's a vent Pixie can sneak into. Better for her to sneak in so no one's the wiser about her snooping around. I can set up on the roof next door and use their surveillance video to keep an eye on y'all," they said, pointing to a nearby building. "If we're lucky, they'll leave the door open when we get there, and I'll have a better shot. There is a back entrance leading to two offices, then a hallway into the rear of the warehouse. It's the only other way out."

Sierra nodded. "If things go sideways, fall back. Plan is to show up with the goods, do the exchange, and return to the ship." She said it like she was reading the air quality report, but she could tell everyone was wound tight.

"Thoughts?" she ventured, feeling like she was supposed to be more inspiring but falling short. Having an egalitarian ship structure left them lacking when it came to inspiring speeches and anything requiring singular leadership skills. She'd never been the most charismatic of people. "Let's get this pile of crap out of here. I'll feel better when this part of the job is over." Her mind was too cluttered; she needed to scratch something off her to-do list so she could reorganize her mental furniture into some kind of order—at the moment, it was a garbage dump.

"I'm headed out to get in place before our contact shows up," Iz said. They were dressed like a Hello Kitty assassin. Their black overalls had a sparkly sheen in the right light and their long-sleeved undershirt was black with little cat-eared skulls and crossbones running down the sleeve like a macabre lace-up. Their hair was pulled back in a high ponytail, their purple braids falling over their shoulders. "I'll let you know when I'm ready." They shouldered a bag full of God-knows-what and left through the cargo bay.

Lulu had scrabbled up Tovi's clothes and was standing along his shoulders, pressing her face against his ear.

"Not this time, Lulu. It's too dangerous," he said. He paused. "You're doing a great job, it's not that. I don't want you to get hurt. We'll take you out when we're not doing a high-stakes deal." Hearing the one-sided conversation common with compdroids was disconcerting, but she was obviously making an argument to join them. "No, I don't think you're going to mess it up. If something goes wrong, you could get hurt."

He couldn't coddle her forever, but Sierra could appreciate the sentiment. It took her months to let Rupert accompany her. Not that they could truly stop them. Compdroids were sentient and therefore autonomous. It was a mutual attachment that kept comp-droids with their partner. Lulu hopped down and wobbled off, still not entirely coordinated. She didn't get what she wanted, and Tovi sighed. Sierra gave him a pat on the shoulder.

The three of them gathered their supplies. Sierra wore her usual casual attire—boxy gray shirt and cuffed black cargo pants. She attached a holster to her leg, which was her preferred highly visible sidearm placement. She checked her knife before stowing it in the harness at her belt. Tovi wore burgundy pants with more zippers than she could count and a fitted black shirt with a harness for a gun under each arm. He threw on a loose-fitting leather jacket over top.

Cecil put on a vest he'd picked up last year; it looked sharp, with shiny buttons on the front, but had armor plating. He didn't carry weapons normally because most weren't adapted for paws larger than a human head. They had a remote firing system Iz had modified to fit Cecil's body, but that felt like overkill, and there was no way to hide the contraption. Walking through a tourist area with a heavily armed Nhethian was hardly subtle.

Sierra got the anti-grav lift out of storage and loaded the crate. Hovering off the ground, the case came up to her chest, and she stood on the platform housing the lift controls, a simple podium design with a few basic controls. Sierra steered the lift from behind and Tovi hopped on top of the crate, dangling his long legs off the front. They lowered the cargo ramp and drove out of the ship, securing the doors behind them. Cecil walked on all fours next to the crate, sweeping his head back and forth as he walked, his eyes sharp.

They made an interesting threesome as they moved through the tourist areas. People followed them with their eyes, a Praxian and a giant Nhethian in a fantasy world full of pirates. It would give them something to talk about, no doubt. Sierra was the least interesting of the mix, and she didn't mind one bit. They drew less attention as they moved out of the tourist area and into the business side of town. She kept an eye out for anyone she recognized. Since she'd been back, she kept one eye open for someone she knew from back then. It was like tensing for a jump scare that might never come.

It wasn't long before they came to the warehouse. It was a squat building, only two stories tall, but wide. A large door was left open, big enough to fit a mech into. Through the door, she glimpsed a loading area in front of long rows of storage. Sierra checked the time; they were ten minutes behind schedule—early, in her book.

"Guess they're waiting for us," Tovi said. He hopped off the front of the crate and unzipped his jacket—game on.

Tovi moved to Sierra's right and forward, and Cecil stayed close to the case at her left. They entered the clean, neatly organized warehouse, stacked high with crates and larger products covered in canvas like industrial ghosts and lining the walls. The loading area to the front was clear, leading to four rows of tall shelves scraping the ceiling. She didn't see anyone at first, squinting to look farther back into the dimly lit room.

"To your right," Tovi said, having given up on getting her used to clock position long ago. A figure emerged from the stacks, flanked by three others carrying a black, metal crate, which meant there were more hiding in the wings. As they came into view, Sierra sucked in a breath.

"Good to see you again," Ching Shih said. Seeing her on the sleeve didn't do her justice, and Sierra couldn't contain her shock, despite knowing she'd be seeing her in person. The feeling was overwhelming, and she was suddenly aware of herself in ways that made her painfully self-conscious.

Ching Shih's short black hair reflected the cool blue light like a cobalt curtain. Sierra knew it would feel like silk between her fingers. The bob, angled long around her face, accentuated her jawline, which was even sharper now with age. She wore a pair of high-rise cropped jeans and a long camel-colored coat. Why was she so perfectly put together? By comparison, Sierra felt like a caricature of someone who had their shit together, and she fought the urge to smooth her hand over her plain gray top, like she could make her hand an iron and magically remove all the wrinkles. But it was her eyes, velvet brown, sharp and assessing, that brought back the old feelings of longing. When Ching Shih looked at her, Sierra knew she had her full attention. It was like a big cat had found a tasty morsel and Sierra was tempted to let Ching Shih consume her.

Sierra broke eye contact before she said something stupid. She didn't see any weapons on Ching Shih, but it would be a mistake to assume she was unarmed. Her three companions were armed to the teeth with rifles slung over shoulders and handguns visible in exposed harnesses. Sierra was brought back to reality as the warehouse doors rattled closed behind them, shutting out the filtering light from the asteroid, leaving only the overhead fluorescent lights. Sierra had considerable doubts as the heavy door slid closed with a resounding clang.

"And I'm very pleased to see you again," Ching Shih said, giving Sierra a rakish smile. "That's what you're supposed to say back."

Sierra's flush returned and Ching Shih's smile widened. "I do hope you plan to fight while you're here. It's always a *pleasure* to see you fight. You have such a unique style, a bit... chaotic but so fun to watch."

"Sometimes you need to cause a little chaos to get things done," Sierra said, rolling her shoulders back and trying to get a grip, fighting the blush heating her cheeks. The way the word *pleasure* rolled off Ching Shih's tongue was sinful. "You have a tidy place here." So tidy, she had an inclination to scuff the well-polished floor with the toe of her boot. Ching Shih considered her for a moment, like she was sizing up her worth in a single stare, and Sierra had no idea whether she measured up.

"We're here for the exchange," Sierra said. "I believe everything's in order with your payment." She rested a hand on the plastic crate in front of her. She was spit-balling, having no idea what was in their crate or the one sitting innocuously next to Ching Shih.

"Yes, Ryan. A real charmer, isn't he?" She placed a hand on the crate her crew had set down next to her. "This is our end of the deal. You won't mind if we verify the contents of our payment?" Ching Shih asked, running her fingers through her hair, and Sierra tried not to stare. Sierra knew how dangerous she could be, and she shouldn't let her guard down.

"Go for it. We're just the messengers here." Sierra's hand was on the anti-grav controls, and it took real effort to keep motionless. Something about having the crate between her and three people holding rifle-style impact guns provided a false, if reassuring, sense of security.

Cecil moved in closer to Sierra, silent and ominous. He'd been itching to know the crate's contents since it had come on board.

Ching Shih moved to the front of the case and tapped on a small screen. She held up her sleeve, transmitting the access code Ryan sent her upon their arrival. Sierra heard the click of the lock. Ching Shih grasped the case's lid and pulled it open. Sierra didn't have a great view from the opposite side of the wide case, but when Ching Shih pulled out a very new, very shiny gun with a muzzle the size of her fist, Sierra's intestines turned to liquid.

"They say it's the newest in concussive force technology. It'll scramble your brain but won't breach a hull by accident."

"Cool, that's neat. Now, if you'll just open this door, we'll take your crate and be on our way," Sierra said, her eyes not leaving the terrifying weapon, which came in handy when it was suddenly pointed directly at her.

"The thing is, you have something we need. Turns out our deliverables are missing a key ingredient, namely one AIcat that I have on good authority is in your care. My crew is generally very capable, but when they counted the carcasses of ten cats, they didn't recognize one was a compdroid and not the tenth AIcat. For this deal to be completed, we'll need that AIcat. The other nine were quite destroyed, but just imagine what a fully functioning AIcat would go for," Ching Shih said with a smile.

Sierra didn't wait for her to keep talking. With her hand on the controls of the anti-grav machine, she pressed a command and the crate-barreled forward, hitting Ching Shih and making her grab the crate or be crushed underneath. Sierra hopped off the anti-grav machine, nearly twisting her ankle as she hit the ground, and ran for the warehouse shelves, hoping to get cover. A tall woman in tactical gear was nicked by the case as it careened wildly without an operator, and she went down spewing bullets at random. Cecil was on top of the second person, a stocky guy Cecil stepped on and sent sprawling. Tovi was running in the same direction on the other side of the warehouse, his gun out and firing at the third pirate.

With no one at the controls of the anti-grav machine, it drove erratically through the warehouse. Ching Shih had pulled herself on top of the case, looking determined and maybe a little annoyed—admittedly more enraged than annoyed. Sierra watched as the unmanned machine careened toward a bank of shelves, and her breath caught. She didn't want to give Lulu to Ching Shih, but Sierra didn't want her dead. Sierra lost sight of Ching Shih then heard the deafening screech of metal.

Inside the stacks, Sierra's first instinct was to climb up. She scrabbled over a crate and up to the second story. She activated her sleeve and sent an open call to the group. "Iz, things went sideways. Do you have eyes?" She wanted to relay an array of insults, but they had more pressing issues.

"I have eyes on you. There's an exit out the back, but I'm sorry to say there's three more people coming from that direction. Backup, presumably."

"Hear that Tovi, Cecil?" Sierra said, her eyes scanning the ground.

"Copy," Tovi said.

Sierra heard a clang and swung around, bringing up her gun. Cecil was climbing deftly to the top of the shelves behind her.

"Copy," he said.

Sierra scanned the back of the warehouse and saw three people running into the room from a hallway. They all had guns; none as intimidating as the one Ching Shih had pulled from that damnable case, but they likely fired non-combustive bullets that could kill in close proximity and break bones otherwise. They fanned out, one heading down their aisle. She gestured at Cecil, trying to convey her meaning through a series of hand motions.

Cecil stared at her like she'd lost her mind. She then pretended she was pushing on a nearby crate after counting down from three on her fingers. He nodded, getting the gist of what she was saying, and positioned himself behind a crate that was nearly as tall as Sierra. She got on her hands and knees to peek over the side, giving her a better view of the approaching pirate. He was scanning the ground, sweeping his gun back and forth, the light above the sight illuminating behind boxes. He glanced up occasionally, but he seemed jumpy, whipping his head around to check his back, afraid he'd be hit from behind.

What he hadn't expected was a giant crate falling from above, thanks to a signal from Sierra and a violent push from Cecil. There was an explosive crashing noise, and Sierra peered over the edge to see the man's arm sticking out from beneath the crate, unmoving.

"*What was that?*" Tovi asked. "*Everyone okay?*"

"We're good. One of the three new arrivals is down."

"*I got one too,*" Tovi said. "*With a little help from Pixie.*"

"Sierra! I'm just trying to do a deal here. There's no need for all this." Sierra could hear Ching Shih but couldn't see her. Sierra gestured for Cecil to walk away from her. If they were caught, she didn't want them to go down together. A rain of bullets slammed into the shelves and dented the wall behind where they'd just been.

"Dammit, Phil. Don't use live rounds. What's wrong with you? Excessive damage comes out of your paycheck, and if you hurt a hair on her head, I will kill you myself," Ching Shih said in a voice Sierra could barely hear.

She was moving quietly across the shelf, trying not to give away her position, when she felt a muzzle on her back. She raised her arms slowly, dropping her weapon. An arm came around her waist and pulled her knife free, and she glared. That knife was brand new, and she hadn't even had a chance to break it in.

"Now, you're going to climb down and get your mates together," said a gruff voice. He must have been the third backup. Sierra looked over the edge and saw Ching Shih with two of her crew, guns pointed at Sierra. She couldn't see any way out of it and climbed down to the floor.

"Honestly, the cat ran off as soon as we got back to the station," Sierra said to the sour-faced Ching Shih. Her jacket was wrinkled and stained, her hair rumpled.

"That's not what I heard," she said. "I've done some digging and found out you're in the red and your ship is in danger of impound. I can make that go away."

It was a very tempting offer. Lulu had been the source of one headache after another and now Sierra was staring down a pissed-off Ching Shih.

Her opportunity to fuck up the situation further was cut short as a blast sent Sierra flying through the warehouse, tumbling with debris and fire. Pain flared through her body before everything went dark.

Chapter 19

This is Fine

Tovi was at the back of the warehouse, Pixie floating above his head scanning the room for combatants. Pixie had descended on a pirate who'd snuck up on him from behind and covered his face with their tentacles, blinding him long enough for Tovi to hit him with a stunner.

You'd be dead without me, they'd said airily in reply to his thank-you.

Tovi had pulled the unconscious man behind a crate when he saw a flash of light followed by a deafening explosion that tore through his ears. He covered his ears as shrapnel came flying from the other side of the crate. He felt something soft and oddly squishy covering his face. His double eyelid protected his vision until he realized it was Pixie. He pulled them off his face and wrapped them in his arms, shielding them with his body. Heat washed over him, and the air was thick with smoke and the acrid smell of melted plastic. He coughed, covering his mouth with his shirt. Metal tearing and bending assaulted his ears with the clatter of debris. He watched burned wreckage hit the back wall of the warehouse and tumble to the floor.

What idiot set off an explosive? He'd thought Ching Shih's House had better training than indiscriminate bombing. He only hoped his team had been as far away from the blast as he was. He tried using his comm but only received static. Pixie was a quivering mess latched on to the fabric of his shirt. He zipped up his jacket to keep them covered.

He ventured a look over the crate and was shocked by the massive hole ripped into the far side of the warehouse where the loading door once stood. Exposed metal beams were pushed outward, and torn pieces of metal sheeting hung precariously above the gap. Flames crawled over the debris littering the floor, mangled plastic chunks from the casing and canvas creating solitary bonfires.

The whole structure was deeply compromised. Tovi's brain went on autopilot. He had to get everyone out before the roof caved in. He grabbed the man on the shelf and hauled him into a fireman's carry and picked his way down the shelves, the structure rickety and swaying dangerously back and forth.

Ash fell around him, some of it falling like tiny flames scorching his cheeks, hands, and the back of his neck. The metal was hot under his hands as he moved down the shelves. He squinted through the smoke and saw two unmoving forms—people who'd been close to the center of the blast, their bodies flung away. In the back of his mind, he begged for them not to be Sierra. Cecil would have been obvious from any distance. Tovi set the unconscious man down at the back of the warehouse, away from the flames, and ran toward them, starting with the one closest to the epicenter.

The heat and smoke were oppressive, a persistent barrier pushing him away. He didn't stop to assess their status, fearing the instability of the structure and the fire spreading through the warehouse. He grabbed under the person's arm and pulled them away from the smoldering fires, a trail of blood smearing the ground. When he came to the second person, half rolled on their side, he grabbed them by their tactical vest and dragged them both to the back of the warehouse.

The first man was unresponsive, his face burned beyond recognition. Tovi checked for a pulse on his wrist and felt nothing. The second person, the tall woman from before, was breathing, but it was shallow. Her right side was severely burned and mangled.

He needed to get them out of the building, but his training told him to check for other survivors first. Help should arrive soon; no one could ignore a blast of this size, especially inside an asteroid base. It could compromise the hull of the station and the smoke would need to be mitigated. The air scrubbers could only do so much; the asteroid would smell of smoke and plastic for weeks.

Tovi moved through the warehouse, searching for other survivors and his own crew. He found one other person, alive and conscious but wounded. He was stumbling down the adjacent aisle, his gun held in his hands. When he saw Tovi, he tried to raise the weapon, but doubled over coughing, blood splashing the ground. Tovi came up next to him and wrapped his arm around his back, holding him up under his armpit.

"You're going to be okay," he said, yelling into his bleeding ear. "Let's get you out of here."

He helped the man into the hallway that led to the back entrance. Once outside, he set the man down against the side of the wall.

"Oh my God, are you okay?" Tovi turned to see Iz, untouched by the blast.

"I'm okay. I haven't found the others yet. Can you help him while I go back in? There's two more I need to get out," he said, then remembered Pixie. He unzipped his jacket and Pixie, seeing Iz, released their droopy tentacles from his shirt and floated, ash-covered, into Iz's comforting embrace.

He went back twice to retrieve the two unconscious pirates who had a pulse, depositing them next to the first man, who was now slumped against the wall. Iz had their bag open and was applying emergency stabilizers to the man's neck and head. Tovi didn't stop, returning to the building and the last aisle he hadn't checked. A large, dark form moved halfway down the aisle.

"Cecil?" Tovi yelled, hoping to God it was Cecil. He choked on the smoke. His second eyelid helped keep his eyes from watering terribly, but not entirely. As he grew closer, he saw Cecil's hat had long blown away, keeping him from communicating in a way Tovi could understand.

He put his hands on Cecil's side, checking for any injuries. Cecil turned to him, his eyes wide as he let out a low, distressed moan. Tovi held Cecil's head between his hands. "It's going to be okay, buddy. Are you injured?" Cecil shook his head, then swung it toward a hunk of metal. It was half of the crate holding the weapons, ripped apart and smoldering. He lifted it with his massive paws, flipping it back and over.

Underneath, Tovi saw Sierra, half covered by a man lying face down on top of her. Tovi rushed forward and flipped the man over, searching for signs of life and finding them lacking. He moved to Sierra next. She was face down, her hair a disheveled mess of soot and debris. Her head was turned to one side and a gash in her cheek spilled blood.

Her arm was twisted at a terrible angle, definitely broken, but in how many places he couldn't tell. His heartbeat was so loud in his own ears, it sounded like a dull roar. She couldn't be dead. He wouldn't allow even the possibility, but his heart wrenched painfully. He reached down to find the pulse in her neck. Where he expected to contact skin, he felt scales—Rupert wrapped around her neck.

She sstill breathess, Rupert broadcast to Tovi's implant for the first time ever.

He'd been wrapped around her neck, assuring himself she lived. That more than anything brought tears to Tovi's eyes. Cecil stared at him imploringly and gestured with his head to his back. Tovi nodded.

He turned her over, slow and careful, unsure of the extent of her injuries. She likely had a concussion and, judging by the blood trickling from her ears, perforated eardrums. Internal injuries were unknowable, but she wasn't bleeding from anywhere else. He picked her up and placed her on Cecil's back, who wasted no time in carrying her out the back door and into Iz's capable hands.

Tovi fought the urge to run after her, to make sure she was okay with his own two hands, but his medical knowledge was limited. He'd only get in the way. He needed to check if there was anyone left alive. The building was falling apart around him, and it could cave in at any moment. The clanging of metal falling from a great height punctuated his thoughts. He hadn't found Ching Shih yet and would not leave until he had.

He circled the wrecked case, the smoke thicker here and making it hard to see. He found another body, the head caved in and impossible to identify. He'd nearly given up hope, his lungs filled with steel wool, when he saw someone crawling out from under a pile of debris—Ching Shih. Her teeth were gritted as she used her forearms to pull herself forward. Tovi ran up to her and pushed the debris off her legs. They were badly burned and at least one was broken. There was a good chance her hip was damaged as well, a life-threatening injury.

"It's okay, I'll get you out of here," he said. He was considering the best way to move her when the structure around him shuddered violently. He hauled her up, wrapping her arm around his shoulder, and lifted her. She screamed, then clamped her teeth shut. She was incredibly light; Tovi was able to run out of the building as it crumbled around them.

Outside, he panicked when he saw the area deserted, then he realized Iz had the forethought to move everyone away from the compromised building. They were across the street, next to a nearby building. More people had gathered and were watching the building fall apart or caring for the injured occupants. He was surprised by the half dozen locals tending to the wounded. It felt like he'd been in the burning wreckage for hours, but in reality, it hadn't been long at all.

Tovi set Ching Shih down. She yelped and groaned as her leg and hip met the ground. Her face was colorless and her breathing ragged.

"My people," she ground out.

"Three survived. I'm sorry, I couldn't get the others out."

She didn't respond. Her eyes were tightly shut and her face smeared in sweat and ash. She turned her head to the side and opened her eyes. Tovi followed her gaze to an unconscious Sierra, tended to by Iz.

"How is she?" Tovi asked.

"I don't know. I don't have the right tools with me. They all need a hospital." Iz waved their arm to encircle the row of mangled bodies in various states of unconsciousness and distress. Iz's shirt cuffs were pushed up their forearms, their hands and sparkly overalls covered in other people's blood. As if summoned by their words, emergency crews arrived on the scene. Ambulances pulled up, unloading stretchers and heading straight for Ching Shih.

"They..." She pointed a finger at Sierra then the rest of his crew. "They come with me."

The emergency crew didn't bat an eye at Ching Shih's demand, and Tovi didn't care so long as Sierra survived. He watched her chest rise and fall with shallow breaths, her ragged clothes ash-covered and dangling from her limp body. As they loaded her on a stretcher and hauled her away, he tried not to remember the last time a fire had separated the two of them for a small eternity.

Chapter 20

Impatient Patients

At the hospital, they were checked for injuries. Tovi had inhaled a detrimental amount of smoke and ash and was given an oxygen mask with nanobots to clean his airways. He had burns on his hands he didn't remember getting and a few cuts the doctor covered in self-mending bandages. He was sitting up in a medical bed, the machine beeping next to him as his lungs reassembled themselves. Cecil was in a reinforced bed next to him with his own oxygen mask. He had some singed hair, and his paws were burned from swatting burning wreckage. He'd apparently been overturning everything in his path in search of Sierra.

Turned out Cecil had been as far away from the blast as Tovi, but on the other side of the room, while Sierra had been staring down a gun across from Ching Shih. Tovi's clothes were torn and gray from the soot. Cecil's vest was intact, and once it was removed, the fur under the vest was the only part of him not ash gray. It would have been funny in other circumstances, but Tovi had a deep hysterical desire to laugh in the somber clinic—anything to break the tension.

Iz was the only one not a dusty mess, but they were streaked with blood from applying first aid. They sat between their two beds in an uncomfortable chair, petting a traumatized and quivering Pixie.

Rupert had taken up residence around Tovi's arm like a bracelet. Tovi was not partial to snakes, but he'd do anything for Sierra, and when the medics had tried to remove Rupert from her, Tovi had to coax him off her neck and onto his arm.

I will kill them if they do not ssave her, he'd whispered into his ear, and Tovi did not doubt him.

They'd been deposited into a private room with four stations, two left unoccupied until Sierra joined them. *When* not *if* Tovi kept repeating to himself. The walls were painted a pale yellow, like stained teeth. Everything smelled smoky, but underneath that was a sourness he couldn't shake that made him queasy. They left the privacy screens open, keeping an eye on every nurse, doctor, technician, and hospital staff who came in at odd intervals. They were jumpy as a bunch of cats. Waiting on news about Sierra was driving him around the bend. He distracted himself by making sure Rupert was okay, doing a system diagnostic, anything to pass the time.

"Do we have any idea what happened?" Cecil asked, pulling off the oxygen mask and letting it dangle below his chin. He'd managed to scare someone into getting him a translator, a ribbon-wide necklace that expanded around his neck. His voice was gravelly from the smoke and the cheap translator.

Iz was staring intently at their sleeve. They hadn't torn themselves away since they'd arrived, and Tovi knew better than to interrupt Iz when they were in investigatory mode. "I'm reviewing the footage, but I think it came from the case."

"How's that possible? We tested it for explosives when we brought it on board," Cecil said.

"I don't know. We used all the tools we had available, but if the weapons were a new technology, it tracks that the explosive might be as well."

"This all comes back to Ryan—again," Tovi said. "I should have trusted my instincts." He balled his hand into a fist and pressed his fingernails into the flesh of his palm, wishing it was Ryan's neck he was crushing. Tovi wasn't naturally a vengeful or violent person, but that version of himself was hard to visualize beneath the river of rage that washed over him.

"We didn't have much of a choice," Iz said.

"We did, though. We could have found another way to pay Hazel, even if it meant taking a loan from someone else. Most people want to be paid back; he wants us dead."

"While I'm loath to say it, I don't think we were the intended target. He was very specific about being on time. Not only were we late, our departure was delayed by Ching Shih," Cecil said. "On the flip side, that was always a possibility, and he did it anyway."

"Do you think he knows about Lulu?" Iz asked.

"If Ching Shih knows, it won't be long before someone at Omnia catches wind of the situation, and they'll hunt her down. I told you we should have off loaded her."

"She's family," Iz said.

"She's a liability," Cecil countered, and Iz glared at him.

"It's too late now no matter how you slice it," Tovi said. "We need to regroup and come up with a plan." Tovi's brain wasn't firing on all cylinders. The adrenaline he'd been high on had worn off hours ago, and now he was tired and his body ached. Only the rage kept him going.

"Any chance we could wheel Sierra out of here and return to the ship without Ching Shih noticing? Maybe she's forgotten about us. We could pull the plug on the operation and go into hiding while we figure this out." It sounded dumb to his own ears, but right now, he wanted everyone back safe.

"Unlikely," Iz said. "There's been one of Ching Shih's crew sitting outside since we arrived. They haven't tried to stop us coming and going, but they're keeping an eye on us. We don't even know how Sierra's doing. They haven't updated the case file."

"It's the personal touch," Cecil said, devolving into sarcasm, a sign he was running thin on patience. "I'll be right back." He removed the oxygen mask and slid off the bed, moving to the door like a bear on a mission.

Iz shot Cecil a glance with a raised eyebrow. "I'm not going to stop him," they said to Tovi. "How are you holding up?"

"Tired. I can't think straight."

"I'd be worried if you could," they said with a wink. "But you should get some sleep. We'll probably be here for a while."

Tovi couldn't possibly sleep, not without news of Sierra. "What if Ching Shih has me killed in my sleep?" he said, half kidding with a weary smile.

"I'll protect you," they said with affection.

Cecil stormed back into the room, followed by an attendant. "You should really be in bed, sir." Tovi was impressed the attendant was only mildly terrified and was holding her ground. Not a particularly smart move, in Cecil's condition, but brave nonetheless. Cecil grunted and sat on the floor, staring at her, obstinate as always.

The attendant huffed and consulted her sleeve. "It seems the patient in question is in recovery. She has a fractured ulna and radius, concussion, and pulmonary contusion," she said without inflection enough to tell if this was a good or bad condition to be in.

"And?" Iz asked. "Her prognosis?"

"She'll survive. Her arm is in a regenerative cast, her concussion hasn't led to brain swelling, and the nanobots are working on the contusion now. It will take some time to fully recover."

"Thank God," Tovi said and let his head fall back on the pillow. "When can we see her?"

"They'll bring her here shortly."

"Is there paperwork we need to sign? And where can I see an itemized bill?" Cecil asked.

"You will need to fill out discharge forms, but this is all under Ching Shih's account. You won't be billed." They were all struck silent, and the attendant took the opportunity to return the way she came.

"That's not good," Cecil said. "What does she want in return?"

"Maybe she's doing it out of the kindness of her heart?" Tovi asked, suddenly unbearably tired. Sierra was going to be okay; that was all that mattered. He heard Cecil snort as his eyes grew heavy and sleep stole him away.

Chapter 21

A Truce Born of Treason

Everything hurt, from the top of her head radiating down to her toes; like a shockwave, every nerve was on fire. She didn't want to open her eyes, afraid she'd see the world burning around her and her body too leaden to escape the flames.

She couldn't parse what she was hearing at first, a jumble of noises that felt both too loud and not loud enough at the same time. After a minute, she could discern voices, speaking far away, too far to hear what they were saying, then they grew closer. At the sound of Iz's voice, her eyes snapped open. And she once again regretted all her life choices as the light stabbed at her sensitive eyes.

"Hey, don't push it. You nearly died back there," Iz said. "I'd ask how you're feeling, but I have a pretty good idea."

"What happened?" she tried to ask, only then realizing she had an oxygen mask on her face and her throat was scorched. Iz handed her a glass of water and helped pull down her mask so she could drink.

"Something exploded, something inside the case. Ryan set us up, again."

"That fucking prick," she said, then coughed, searing her throat.

"Cecil's trying to work out the logistics of pulling his fingernails out from a distance. I'm sure he'll come up with something."

Sierra's eyes focused a little better, and she saw Tovi unconscious in a hospital bed facing her own, an oxygen mask over his mouth. Her throat closed in sudden and smothering fear. "Is everyone okay?" she managed to croak out.

Iz placed their hand on Sierra's wrist. Sierra turned her hand palm up despite the pain so Iz could hold her hand, interlocking their fingers. Iz was putting on a brave face, but beneath their calm eyes, Sierra could see the water churning. "We're all okay, some burns and scrapes. You took the brunt of the blast."

"Are *you* okay?"

Iz hesitated. "When the warehouse exploded, I thought you were all dead. The blast was immense. I suddenly felt I was alone in the universe, and I wished I'd been in there with you. I honestly don't know how you survived, but I'm so grateful." Tears trickled down their cheeks, a dam breaking. Sierra wanted to hold Iz, wrap her arms around them, but she could barely move. Instead, she squeezed Iz's hand, a paltry substitute. The door opened and Cecil squeezed through, stopping when he saw Sierra.

"Hey, Cecil. Good to see you. Could you do a laid-up lady a favor and give Iz a hug for me?"

Cecil didn't hesitate; he wrapped the small human in his giant arms until Iz fairly disappeared into his fur. They clung to Cecil's neck until their sniffing died down. "Glad to see you're awake," he said over Iz's head.

"Glad to be awake. What about Ching Shih?"

Iz pulled away from Cecil with a whispered thanks and dried their cheeks. "Tovi managed to get her out, some leg injuries notwithstanding, and a busted pelvis."

"Of course he did." She wanted to roll her eyes but even the thought was painful. "I was seriously considering giving Lulu up. I didn't see another way out," Sierra said.

"The situation has changed drastically," Iz said. "And now we have the space to come up with a plan. We have Lulu's old skin; all I need is a cat-shaped robot to create a decoy. I'm not entirely sure what to do with that. If anyone opens it up, they'll know it's a robot."

"We can work with that. If Ching Shih wants the cat to blackmail Ryan for the explosion, we can give her the decoy and get out of Dodge before anyone's the wiser. I guess we'll have to wait and see. How long until I can get out of here? I don't like hospitals."

"Until you can move on your own."

There was a knock and someone she didn't recognize in tactical gear and a rather large gun walked through the door. Cecil reared up to his full height, a growl emanating from his throat.

"That didn't take long. If you're going to kill me, could you make it quick? I have a splitting headache." She was too damn sore and pissed off to play games.

The pirate's closed-off face was her only response; he came to the side of the bed, holding out a tablet. Iz snatched it up before Sierra could attempt to raise a hand. Sierra was tense, waiting for an attack she couldn't defend herself from. The pirate stepped back, and Sierra turned her attention to the tablet Iz held for her and saw Ching Shih's bruised and battered face staring back at her. Cecil crowded in on her other side to see what was on the tablet.

"You look like shit," Sierra said.

"You're not looking too hot yourself," Ching Shih said. Sierra hadn't even considered her own face. The pain was so universal, it took her a moment to clock the stinging of her cheek and the bandage covering the side of her face.

"Fair point," she said. "What's the damage?"

"You weren't kidding about sowing chaos. I lost four people in the explosion."

"I'd feel bad, but you were planning to toss us out an airlock or bury our bodies in the compost."

"Don't be dramatic. I was trying to strike a deal when you used an anti-grav machine as a bulldozer."

"By pointing a gun at my face?"

"I wasn't pointing it at your face. That would be incredibly dangerous. It was aimed above you, and it wasn't even activated."

"Who's being dramatic now?"

Sierra thought Ching Shih had tried to shrug, but all she accomplished was a grimace, and it plucked at Sierra's heart.

"With the recent turn of events, I now have different priorities, namely making Ryan Randolf pay with his life. How would you feel about teaming up to make that dream a reality?"

Sierra was furious she'd let Ryan get the drop on them again. She had to tamp down her desire to make Ching Shih pay for her part in this mess, because she'd been played too and suffered heavier losses. She swallowed her indignation and focused on the practical. "Is it safe to say you're not interested in the cat anymore?"

"If you can get Ryan here, then I can forget the cat existed."

"Is this you offering us a job?" Cecil cut in.

She seemed to mull this over. "I will pay you two thousand credits and forget about the cat if you can bring me Ryan."

"Let me talk to my team and see if we can come up with some ideas." There was too much to consider and not enough brain power available to her.

"I owe Tovi a debt. He got me and some of my crew out alive. In exchange for my crew, I've paid for your care." Her voice was solemn, like she was speaking a prayer or an incantation.

Ching Shih had always been fair—for a pirate. Sierra didn't appreciate being shot at, but she needed to direct her rage to Ryan. Any deal they made with her was a relatively safe bet in the face of mutual revenge.

"How are you bearing up?" Sierra asked. She told herself it was an act of reciprocity, not genuine concern for the woman who once made her feel like the center of the universe.

Ching Shih seemed surprised, but it was hard to tell around all the swelling. "I'll survive. If you get me Ryan, I'll make sure you can pay off your debt."

"That is an offer I don't want to refuse," Sierra said. "I may have half a plan, but it's hard to think when my body's rejecting itself."

"I can appreciate that," Ching Shih said with a wince. "I'll be keeping an eye out for any movement on the asteroid with a whiff of Ryan's involvement. At the moment, the news is reporting an explosion, but they've left out our names at my request. Keep me informed." Ching Shih nodded to someone Sierra couldn't see, and the screen went black.

Sierra looked up, eyes searching for the pirate, and found him next to Tovi's bedside, staring down at his sleeping form. Sierra's blood ran cold and Cecil snarled.

"Hey, you lay a finger on him, and I'll kill you," Sierra said, devoid of snappy analogies.

He turned to her with a lifted eyebrow, walked toward her and took the screen with surprising grace, then walked out the door.

"Not much of a talker," Iz said.

"A real conversationalist." Sierra scrutinized Tovi. "Just minor injuries, you said?" He hadn't moved since she'd woken up, and she itched to go over there and reassure herself he was safe and unharmed.

"He was very tired but wouldn't go to sleep until he knew you were out of danger," Iz said with a warm smile in his direction.

Sierra felt something moving by her feet. She jerked and yelped as pain shot through her body. Then she saw the slithering form under the sheets. Rupert slid up her fingers and around her forearm and squeezed, an action she'd come to recognize as a hug.

"Hey, buddy, how are you?"

I will find thiss Ryan and kill him.

"You and me both. Glad you're okay, though." She wanted to reach out and reassure him, but moving was too much for her.

"Get some rest," Iz said. "The nanobots work faster when you're not moving around. You should feel a lot better if you get a few hours in."

"Is that a promise?"

"You betcha," Iz said, their smile sincere despite the tightness around their eyes.

"You should rest too. Ching Shih can pay for one more bed."

Iz waved her off, going back to working on their sleeve, leaving her to sleep. Sierra wasn't going to fight. She wanted nothing more than to sleep off the pain.

Chapter 22

A Bird in the Hand...

Sierra woke to a dimly lit room, absent of Cecil and Iz, and was surprised to find Iz had been right. Instead of a searing pain throughout her body, it was now a dull ache. She couldn't have been more appreciative of Ching Shih's generosity in paying for their care. She would never have been able to afford the rapid healing technology; it would have taken weeks to feel like this, and even then, she might never have fully recovered.

She didn't know the extent of her injuries, and she was afraid to ask. She took stock of her body, like poking at a canker sore. There was a tightness to her chest, and when she tried to take in a deep breath, she could only manage short sips, like her lungs had shrunk. Her arm was in a cast, and she gave it an experimental lift. Whatever the fancy cast was made of, it truly deadened the limb, which felt like a mech arm with broken hydraulics. At least she couldn't feel the pain. There was a dull throb on her cheek and the sticky tightness of a bandage. Everything sounded like it was coming down an echoing hallway.

She didn't know how long she'd been out, but it didn't really matter. Now the plans they had before would never come to fruition. The world had turned itself upside down and shook her out. She didn't quite know where to go from here. Her bravado with Ching Shih was based almost entirely on drug-induced hysteria. The exhaustion and pain had set her on autopilot. She had no clue what to do.

Across the room, she saw Tovi was awake, staring at her, his face a question mark. "Oh, thank God. I don't think I could have stayed alone in my own head for one more second," she said.

Tovi laughed. "I feel that. It's good to see you awake," he said. "We were worried for a moment there."

"You know me, I'm like a bad penny," Sierra said. In her head, she added the addendum: *not worth much, but I keep turning up*. She knew he wouldn't appreciate the self-defeating humor and figured she would spare him.

"How are you doing?" she asked. "Iz said you had some injuries."

"Oh, I'm fine. I was a little burned. Turns out carrying multiple people is harder on my body than I had initially thought."

"We got a little thank-you note from Ching Shih to send your way. We can thank her for all of this, it seems," she said. She waved her hands around the majestic surroundings they found themselves in.

"She didn't need to do that."

"You did pull her ass out of a burning building, so I feel it's well deserved. Plus, we can use as much help as we can get, and I think she can use some as well."

"Ryan?" Tovi said.

Sierra could hear the question mark and the exclamation point in his voice, maybe also a drawn-out ellipsis. It held everything they were feeling simultaneously, which, for her, boiled down to wanting to murder Ryan. Though she wouldn't consider it murder—more like justice.

"Yeah, I was just thinking about how I have no idea what to do with that situation. Ching Shih has offered to pay off our debt if we can deliver Ryan to her."

Tovi winced. "I wouldn't want to be at the business end of whatever she has in store for him."

"Neither would I. The trick is getting him here. It'd have to be something very particular to get him to come to a pirate asteroid. I mean, the man can't even handle our ship, and it's significantly cleaner than most of these places. I think he also objects to the company in general, as well as in particular," she said.

"You're not wrong about that. He thinks his shit don't stink," he said. "Cecil thinks he hadn't intended to kill us, but also wasn't opposed to that outcome. Had we arrived on time and left immediately, we would have been out of range of the explosive," Tovi said.

"Lulu is the only real bait we have. Omnia would be furious if they found out some of their most coveted tech was wandering out in the universe. Iz kept Lulu's old skin and said they could put it on a robot as a decoy. So something-something build a plan around that?"

"That's a start. I'm sure Cecil and Iz can fill in the something-something."

"Smart idea," Sierra said. "I guess we can keep them."

"Cecil flipped over burning wreckage to get to you."

"Stop, my heart might explode," she said, feeling like a soup of warm squishy feelings threatening to boil over. "Where are Cecil and Iz anyway?"

"They went out to do something. They were very clandestine about what. Cecil's paws were a bit singed, but they managed to heal up fast enough with this rapid heal stuff they got going on here. Never got to use any of this when I was in the service. Too expensive, I suspect, for lowly soldiers like myself."

"I hope they come back soon. I'm ready to get out of here. What the fuck happened to my sleeve?" Sierra asked.

"I think the nurses had to cut it off you," Tovi said with a pained expression.

"Goddammit, I was really hoping I could keep that one for longer than six months."

"That's why you shouldn't buy expensive ones. Do you want me to send a message for you?" Tovi asked. "I have mine. It's a bit worse for wear, but I'll call the crew back and see if we can get out of here."

"I have to fight in, like, two cycles. We need to get everything ready."

"You gotta be kidding me," Tovi said. "How are you going to fight? Your arm's all... like that," he said, waving at her broken arm.

"I don't need to have my whole arm; that's what the gloves are for. I can move my fingers." She wiggled her swollen fingers experimentally, because she hadn't been entirely sure she could move them. "I'm not giving up now. I highly doubt Ryan's going to pay us since the goods were destroyed, even though he was the one to destroy them. We can't count on it, same with Ching Shih's job. If we win the match, we could skip out and pay off our ship," Sierra said.

Tovi shook his head. "Let's see what the crew has to say about it. I've sent them a message. I don't think they've wandered too far off; we're just a bit paranoid at the moment. By the way, when I woke up, there was a note in my hand. I assume you didn't put it there."

"A note?" Sierra asked. "No, I don't know nothing about it."

"It only said 'thank you' on it. I can't believe someone used a piece of paper for that. Could've just sent me a message."

Sierra remembered the pirate staring down at Tovi. She thought he was going to hurt him, but she guessed his stony expression was what passed for affection or concern, possibly gratitude. She didn't know; his face had been like unforgiving steel. Maybe one of the people Tovi had saved, or Ching Shih herself, meant something to the man. Something enough to send Tovi a silent thank-you. It was hard for her to think that someone with a face like a rock cared enough, and she told Tovi so.

"That's awfully nice," Tovi said, his eyes going soft and gooey like they did when he was reading a romance novel.

"You're a pretty stand-up dude apparently," Sierra said. "You and Cecil dragging my ass out of a collapsing warehouse."

"I have a sinking feeling your survival had a lot to do with one of Ching Shih's people taking it to the face and blocking you. Had he not been standing between you and the blast, I don't think you would've made it."

"That's a comforting thought."

The waiting was killing her. She was a hair's breadth away from throwing a tantrum when there was a knock at the door. Probably another nurse to check her vitals.

What walked—or, more accurately, ducked—through the door was a Sisthmeya, a ten-foot-tall birdlike entity with eyes the size of dinner plates, appearing like the most innocent creature in the universe with perpetual puppy dog eyes. It would be a mistake to fall for the illusion; the hooked beak between those watery eyes crushed the rocklike shells of their prey on their home planet of Daduda, making a human skull barely a snack. Based on the short head feathers surrounding a skinny S-shaped neck and muted blue feathers covering its body and folded wings, this was a female Sisthmeya. Their long, greenish-brown legs, the color of dirty moss, ended in four birdlike toes with vicious, tearing claws. Under all the plumage, Sierra glimpsed the shine of a weapon, probably a remotely operated weapon that could take her out without the Sisthmeya moving a muscle.

She introduced herself as Sistemsisa. That wasn't the noise that came out of her beak, but it was what the translator offered. "I'm with station security investigating the incident at the Ching Shih docks," she said, her long tail feathers sweeping the ground behind her, making Sierra nervous she'd take out the equipment. "I need to interview everyone involved. You were the only one in your crew seriously injured in the blast."

Station security was made up of sentients from across all the major houses, affecting a cloak of impartiality, when, in reality, it made them painfully partisan. Sierra's interaction with them had been minimal when she'd lived on the station, as interhouse issues were outside their purview and were handled internally. Station security managed broader issues, like explosions that could space thousands of entities and put a damper on trade and tourism, their two biggest economic sectors.

"Now might not be the best time. I'm recovering and my memory is fuzzy, on account of the concussion." Inside, Sierra was panicking. No doubt Sistemsisa had already spoken to Ching Shih, who had given her a heavily edited version of events, one she hadn't relayed to Sierra. By all accounts, the explosion had come from their delivery, making them the obvious suspects. If she could buy time and figure out what she was supposed to say, it would save them a lot of grief.

"I find it's best to gather data while it's fresh. If you think of anything later, you can amend your statement."

Shiiit. "I don't remember much from before the blast. We were on our way to do business with Ching Shih. I remember entering the warehouse, but it's all a blank after that. Next thing I know, I'm in the hospital and everything hurts."

"What is the last thing you remember?" Sistemsisa asked.

"Just the warehouse doors shutting," Sierra said, and thought that was the safest move.

"I see. Do you know the source of the explosion?"

"No, but I intend to find out. Whoever blew up the warehouse nearly killed me and my crew. It's my first priority." That came from an honest place, and it was better if she stayed there.

"What were you delivering?"

"I think it was labeled mech parts. I can't remember. Our business manager has all that information." *Let two giants stare each other down,* Sierra thought. Cecil was much better at this, and she wished fervently he was here to help her out. Instead, she had Tovi staring at her wide-eyed from across the room. At least he'd have time to come up with a better lie.

"You don't know what you were carrying?" she asked incredulously.

"We normally do salvage runs. This was a one-off. We needed the cash, but we aren't entirely stupid; we did check to make sure the case wasn't armed before we left."

"Where did you pick up the shipment?"

"Octto Station, that's our homebase." Why, for the love of God, was she prattling on like this? She didn't need to know that. "I'm sorry, but I'm feeling ill. Is there anything else you need?"

Sistemsisa considered her for a moment. "Your ship is being booted as we speak and will remain so until my investigation is complete. We take such incidents very seriously, and if you are found to be responsible for the blast, you will be tried for murder and attempted murder of everyone in the sector." Sistemsisa delivered this possible version of her future matter-of-factly. "If not, you'll be free to go."

"That's... very reassuring. I can tell you, we were not responsible for the explosion. What's the use of money if I'm dead? My family was in that building, and there's no one outside of it who would benefit from my death." Now they were stuck on the asteroid, eviscerating the possibility of escaping the asteroid to regroup, which had been a reasonable option.

Sistemsisa moved on to Tovi, and Sierra unapologetically eavesdropped. He claimed to have been talking to one of Ching Shih's crew members near the back of the warehouse when the bomb went off. A good lie, since there were enough dead crew to make corroboration impossible. Sistemsisa left, her tail feathers an organized chaos threatening to smash into everything but touching nothing.

Sierra let out a breath, and she and Tovi had a tired conversation with their facial expressions. It didn't take much longer for Cecil and Iz to return to the hospital room, fill out the paperwork, and get them out the door.

Sierra was happy to be out of the stale antiseptic smell of the hospital and into something that might have been misconstrued as fresh air, but she couldn't tell if it was the memory of the fire or if the whole asteroid smelled like burning metal and plastic.

They were quiet and contemplative on their way back to the ship. Once they were inside, they circled around the mess, everyone buried in their own thoughts.

"We appear to have numerous problems," Cecil said. "Not much we can do about station security at the moment. That leaves the Ryan situation. We don't have to take Ching Shih's job."

"About that," Iz said, looking up from their sleeve. Pixie was glaring at the screen from their shoulder. Sierra was surprised to see a hardness in Iz's face, and she found she didn't like it one bit. "There was a message waiting for us. Encrypted and sent to the ship. It's from Lana."

Sierra glanced around, afraid of saying the wrong thing and hoping someone else would jump in. Silence reigned as Iz synced their sleeve to the screen in the mess.

The video popped up and Lana was center screen. Her eyes were rimmed red and her cheeks were puffy like she'd been crying. "*I want to start by saying I never meant for all this to happen. When you brought home the AIcat and said Sierra would be picking it up, I made an impulsive decision to try and steal the cat. The people who'd been breaking into my uncle's warehouse are... associates of mine. I sent them a message about the cat, telling them when Sierra would be alone at the warehouse.* She stopped and took a shaky breath. *When they didn't get the cat, they posted about it on a forum. It has taken wings, and I was picked up by some people I suspect were from Omnia. They threatened me and my uncle with criminal charges. In exchange for their silence on my activities, I told them where they could find the AIcat. Warning you is the least I could do. Please know, I did this because I wanted to build a life for us, and selling the AIcat would have made that possible. I'm sorry, and I have no right to ask for your—*"

Iz cut the video. "It's just more of the same after that." Their voice was hard. Sierra knew that expression; she'd never seen Iz wearing it like an ill-fitting suit. Pixie had turned a deep purple and was ready to murder.

Cecil raised a hairy paw and placed it on Iz's shoulder, and the dam broke and Iz folded into Cecil. Pixie retreated and hovered a few feet away, then whirled out of the room. Sierra and Tovi exchanged a look as they gave Iz time to let it out. Iz stepped away from Cecil and wiped at their eyes. "Sorry, let me blow my nose, then I'll be okay."

"Take your time," Tovi said.

"No, we have to figure this out." Pixie returned with a square of pink cloth in their tentacles, and Iz took it gratefully before wrapping Pixie in a hug, like a teddy bear.

"Omnia knows about Lulu, then," Iz said. "They'll destroy her if they find her. A ship's AI has too much information and they aren't allowed outside the ship. By all rights, she should have immediately imploded when the central AI went down in the attack."

"Doesn't she fall under AI sentient laws? Since she can make decisions, she should be allowed to survive on her own recognizance," Tovi said.

Iz shook their head. "Not with ship AIs. The main AI is considered the host. Without it, the AIcats are like severed limbs, unable to function properly. According to AI law anyway."

"That's fucked," Sierra said.

"If we could find a way to destroy a decoy so they think it's taken care of, that would work," Cecil said, and everyone turned to stare at him with shocked expressions. "What? She's grown on me."

"You're such a big softie," Iz said with an affectionate smile, and he glowered at them.

"And she's worth more to us in one piece."

"There it is," Sierra said.

"So we lure Ryan here with the cat, then let Ching Shih take him into custody?" Tovi said. "Then what? Broadcast the cat's destruction? That seems too contrived."

Sierra thought it was cute Tovi believed Ryan would only be arrested. "We could stage a fight, and the robot cat gets destroyed in the fire fight," she said.

Cecil was nodding thoughtfully. "That could work. If Ching Shih's on board, then who would be the best candidate to start something?"

Sierra groaned. "Vandover. He's the obvious choice. Everyone knows I used to work for him. He would be the person I'd ask to have our backs during a deal like this."

"That's good, isn't it?" Iz asked. "Since you're friendly with him."

"We used to be..." She had no idea where she stood now, and she wouldn't blame him if he wanted nothing to do with her.

"It's believable that Ching Shih would crash the party to get revenge on Ryan, and that you asked Vandover to do security detail. Between the two houses, there'll be enough chaos to destroy Lulu's body double. And there will be enough witnesses to confirm its destruction," Cecil said, then surveyed the beleaguered crew. "We're all tired and upset. Let me send a message to Ching Shih for a meeting. In the meantime, everyone should get some rest."

"I'll see y'all tomorrow. I'm going to lie in my own bed for a while, turn my brain off, then on again, to see if it'll reboot," Sierra said.

Sleep sounded excellent to her abused body and exhausted mind. Sleep was better than replaying—over and over again—the explosion, the noise, and the fleeting moments of panic before she was battered unconscious. She only hoped that when she closed her eyes, she wouldn't relive that nightmare.

Chapter 23

Stuck Between a Rock and Hard Head

Tovi was tired and worn out from the events of the last cycle, but he couldn't keep his mind from gravitating back to Patini and the lead he hadn't followed up. When Sierra went for a nap, he retreated back into the station in search of the Cobbler's Daughter.

It was a bright, cheery shop with blue awnings, like happy blue eyebrows over two wide-eyed, retractable windows. On either side of a bright blue door stood circular blue metal tables big enough for two coffees and a scone, hugged by well-worn chairs. The area was less crowded, and the unselfconscious ease of the pedestrians told Tovi this was a neighborhood spot instead of a tourist attraction, one of those places a good netsurfer would gush about with hyperbolic enthusiasm. Tovi hadn't expected places like this on a pirate asteroid. He'd been watching too many stellar dramas with their predilection for grungy, atmospheric pirate dens on economically depressed hunks of rock.

A chime rang from somewhere in the back as he pushed open the front door, a faux-wood number with inlaid glass, painted blue to match the awning. The inside was a sea of white tile punctuated by pops of blue napkins, blue pillows on bench seats, and sea landscapes in thick white frames. The smell of warm buttery bread and flaky pastry filled the shop, reminding him of Patini's kitchen, where she'd bake fresh bread for the week. The kids would gobble it up in a few days, to the consternation of the other adults, but Patini would just smile in that quiet way of hers and make another loaf. She'd toast the bread and spread it with butter, and for a real treat, she'd sprinkle sugar on top. The shop smelled just like that, but sweeter, with notes of raspberries and blueberries baked into the cakes.

Three kids were at the counter, grasping at pastries from an older white human woman with gray hair piled into a bun on top of her head before running back to their parents. The woman he assumed was LaLooka smiled, revealing deep laugh lines. She brushed the crumbs off the counter with the dirty end of her blue apron.

She made eye contact when the door chimed, and the smile slowly melted off her face like gelato in a hot cargo bay. He watched her body language close off as she turned to the side, like she was bracing for a blow. Tovi was startled by her reaction. A mixture of self-consciousness and resentment jostled for dominance, old feelings he never shook off entirely. His initial reaction was to be indignant, but he knew he wouldn't get what he wanted if he was hostile—that was what she was expecting. Instead, he dug deep for his winning smile. Like stretching plastic wrap across his face, it was smothering.

"Hello, ma'am," he said, dipping his chin in greeting.

She swallowed and worked her mouth, as if weighing her words on her tongue, her eyes flitting to the families eating their snacks and sipping their coffee. "How can I help you?" she settled on.

"I'd like one of your most popular cobblers, if you don't mind."

She appeared briefly confused before moving to the case weighed down with sweets, many he'd never seen before. Her eyes never left his as she pulled out a lightly browned triangle pastry with orange goo seeping onto the paper. She placed the pastry in a bag, not asking if he wanted to eat it in the shop. He took a step forward, closing the gap between himself and the counter, and her shoulders tensed.

"Ma'am, are you okay?" he asked.

She hesitated as she was folding the top of the bag. "What are you doing here?" she whispered, keeping her eyes on her work.

"Buying a pastry? I think maybe you're mistaking me for someone else. People often confuse me for others of my species. They say we all look alike."

"I think you should leave. Take this and go," she said, thrusting the bag in his direction.

"Ma'am, I'm here to find my family. Someone said you were the person to talk to."

Her eyes hardened. "Get out," she said. Her hand slipped below the counter, and Tovi realized she wasn't as vulnerable as she first appeared. He imagined she had a bat or a pulse gun strapped under the counter, and he didn't want to wait around to find out if his suspicions were correct. He backed out of the shop, holding the pastry bag in front of him like a buttery shield, the eyes of the curious patrons tracking his strange exit. Outside, he took a steadying breath as the door swished shut behind him.

The expression in her eyes spoke volumes of fear laced with defiance. Tovi had encountered more than his fair share of xenophobia in the universe; it was inescapable no matter a sentient's origin. Even if a particular breed of alien didn't have the genetic imperative to fear the unknown and the other, they were feared by others. A universal society was made of the component parts of the least of it. He was met most often with suspicion and curiosity. The lack of Praxian representation throughout the universe meant most people had never seen one and only knew of them through media depictions, like the news and movies, but more often than not as a plot point in intergalactic space operas. Praxians played the role of devious ne'er-do-well, often plotting against the Consortium. The void Praxian secrecy created was filled by the imagination of salacious writers with baffling ideas surrounding Praxian sex practices and characteristics.

Tovi had once downloaded a well-reviewed romance novel with a Praxian lead, hoping it would be an honest and positive representation he could relate to, and what he found horrified him. He wasn't sure it was physically possible to accomplish some of the sexual positions posited in the text. The character was an amalgamation of the worst stereotypes. By the time the main character punched a guy for merely looking at his "soul mate"—a thing Praxians didn't entertain—he'd been ready to throw his sleeve against the wall.

This level of hostility was something altogether different, and something he'd only seen in xenophobes who made their xenophobia their entire personality, something he was hard-pressed to associate with the woman who had been described to him as something of a safe space for refugees.

Tovi had never met her before, so it couldn't have been personal, unless she confused him for someone else. Which wasn't a bad sign—that meant she was in contact with other Praxians, giving him some level of hope—but the fear was concerning. Who had scared her so badly? Praxians were generally pragmatic, a trait that didn't necessarily preclude violence—if anything, it could justify it—but who would want to intimidate a small band of heretics? They were harmless weirdos, by all accounts.

Or had his conclave warned LaLooka about Tovi? Maybe they hung up his photo like a mugshot behind the counter. Was it possible they had excommunicated him so thoroughly? There wasn't a precedent for him to follow in this case. Praxians had left the conclave and been snubbed, but he hadn't exactly left of his own accord. He hadn't been able to track them down, but that didn't inherently mean they were avoiding him specifically. It was just their way.

Now dread sat heavy and heaving in his mind, like a lung struggling for air. He'd known, intellectually, they could reject him, and he'd convinced himself he was ready for that rejection, but now he knew he was not ready, not prepared to have his conclave turn their backs on him. He loved his friends and the family they'd created, but it didn't make the rejection less poignant or personal. His conclave had watched him grow up, known him as a child, been privy to his juvenile mistakes and unfiltered joys. It felt as if those moments would dissolve into vapor without witnesses. Why it mattered, he didn't know. It just did.

He shook himself from a creeping downward spiral. He couldn't stand outside a quaint café, staring into the distance, without attracting unwanted attention. Plus, he couldn't be sure he was interpreting the situation correctly. She could have confused him for someone else, and if that was the case, there was trouble brewing. He briefly considered adhering a piece of tape to his shirt and writing "Hello, my name is Tovi, your friendly neighborhood Praxian," but he suspected it would have the opposite effect.

He decided instead to case the place, like a normal, well-meaning individual with no homicidal tendencies. He strolled down the lane, searching for anything approaching an alley. With space at a premium, alleys were a luxury for the movement of supplies and goods. All the shops he passed had retractable walls or glass doors to take in deliveries, leading Tovi to conclude there was only one way in and out of the bakery—through the front door.

He strolled for a little while longer to confirm his suspicions before circling back to the bakery, finding a smoke shop a few doors down where he casually bought a magazine and sat at a table in view of the bakery, but far enough away to be missed at a casual glance. He opened the magazine and quickly realized it was the swim edition of *Physical Dynamics Illustrated* when he was greeted by the toothy smile of the intergalactic swim champion, one Ursula De'genis of the Martalates, a water-faring species similar to the mermaid in human folk legend, but with much larger teeth and anterior feet.

He kept an eye on the storefront, and in surprisingly short order, LaLooka appeared through the doorway of her shop. Tovi hid his face with the magazine, avoiding jerky movements and hoping he was far enough away. He had good eyesight; most Praxians did, compared to the short-sighted nature of human eyes. He glanced over the top of the magazine and watched as the woman, a satchel thrown over one shoulder, departed in the opposite direction.

Tovi stood, leaving behind the magazine. He followed her down the street before she took a turn down a narrow street. As they moved farther away from the commercial district, the streets felt more like hallways, growing narrow and pressing in on him. He had to get closer to the woman than he liked, risking getting caught but not willing to lose this opportunity. He lost sight of her at an intersection and stood considering his options, then he heard a strangled yell come from his left.

Running on instinct, he headed that direction. Fighting the urge to run after the sound, he moved slowly, glancing around corners before moving forward, drawing on his years of experience in the resource wars. He followed the noise to a claustrophobic narrowing of the alley. He was nearly on top of them when his brain registered what he was seeing: a tall Praxian, similar in build to himself but broader in the shoulders and hips, had the woman pressed against the wall, his hands grinding into her shoulders and her feet dangling freely.

It was now abundantly clear who LaLooka had confused him for, but how she thought they resembled each other, he couldn't fathom—Tovi was far more handsome. She was terrified; the bag she'd been holding was dumped on the ground, and her head was turned away with her eyes tightly shut. The Praxian's head whipped in his direction, and he released his hold on the woman, who dropped to the ground and crumpled with a shocked release of breath.

The Praxian was on top of him before he could think, diving for his legs. Tovi twisted away from the lunge and ran into the opposing wall. He understood why the Praxian chose this spot for a confrontation; there was nowhere to run or move in the narrow alley. The Praxian regained his footing and lashed out with a kick aimed at Tovi's side. He was able to block with his forearm, but the blow hit and he staggered against the wall, dislodging a piece of crumbled rock. He grabbed the rock, hiding it from the Praxian's view with the side of his body. When he came in low for a tackle, Tovi brought the rock down on his head. The Praxian collapsed to the ground like a sack of potatoes.

Tovi waited for movement, for the Praxian to stir, but he stayed slumped on the ground. Tovi moved over to the woman, who was sitting and staring at him wide-eyed.

"What do you want?" she asked.

"I want to see if you're okay," he said, but he didn't venture any closer, holding his hands in front of himself so she could see them.

"You followed me."

"Yes, I told you at the shop, I want to find my friends, and someone told me you might be able to help."

Her stare was guarded. He shrugged and turned his attention to the Praxian. Tovi couldn't make her believe him, and after being attacked, he couldn't really blame her. The Praxian's skin was a dusty yellow-gray color; his family was probably from the midlatitudes of Prax, an affluent area housing the capital and where much of the continent's food was grown.

He patted down the Praxian's pockets, pulling out a retractable knife he repatriated to his person, before feeling around for anything useful. He saw the woman out of the corner of his eye stand on shaky legs.

"What are you doing?" she asked.

"Searching for anything useful. Is there someone you want to call? Not sure what justice looks like on this particular rock."

"I have some people coming to help out," she said, and Tovi thought that was a warning for him as much as the other Praxian.

Something caught his eye on the Praxian's neck, poking out from underneath his collar. Tovi hooked a finger on the collar and pulled it down to reveal a nesting diamond tattoo where his neck met his back.

"What is it?" the woman asked. His surprise must have shown on his face.

"I thought it was on old caregivers' tale—a kind of boogeyman. It's the tattoo of the royal Praxian guard trained to track down dissidents and bring them to justice," he said, hearing the voice of Patini in his head, telling the story of *Denetia and the Vengeance.*

She'd take on a low, sinister-sounding voice, the one that always had Tovi leaning forward, cross-legged on the floor and holding his stuffed Valax, eyes wide and hanging on her every word. A century ago, Denetia had been the partner of Emporia XXIV for a time, an outsider from the island of Devoria off the west coast of the central continent. Emporia XXIV had met and bonded with Denetia while on a tour of the island. When she was inaugurated as the elected figurehead of Prax by the governing body of the Praxamore, she brought Denetia home with her.

By all accounts, they were well matched and in a harmonious union, until Denetia had recorded the Emporia's secrets that she unwittingly revealed in her sleep and passed them on to a group of rebellious Praxians. When her deceit was uncovered, she fled off planet and sold her information to the highest bidder, exposing Praxian secrets to the universe.

The Vengeance, as the tale goes, were highly trained enforcers whose only task was to protect the home world from outside threats, even when those threats came from within Prax. When the Vengeance tracked her down and threw her into space, a true desecration and insult—no longer a citizen of her home world; her body would not be allowed to nourish the earth of her ancestors. When Patini described the Vengeance, they were dressed in yellow, the color of purity, with nesting diamonds across their chests, like an eye within an eye. The same symbol was tattooed on the back of the Praxian's neck.

Tovi had thought the story was told to scare Praxians from dissent, then adopted in their conclave to justify their constant transience through the universe, forever running from a ghost. Confronted with the symbol, he didn't know what to think, nor did he have time. He realized something else was off, and too late, he noticed the body was no longer breathing easily—instead, his muscles were tensed. Tovi tried to step away, searching for the rock. The Praxian quickly moved to his feet and threw a knee to Tovi's stomach, connecting hard and sending Tovi crumpling to the ground.

The Praxian went for the knife in his pocket, only to realize it was gone. His eyes connected with Tovi's, cold and calculated, a streak of red blood oozing from the wound on his forehead. Before either of them made a move, the sound of people approaching their snug, impromptu battle ring sent the Praxian running after a brief glance at Tovi.

Tovi felt him commit his face to memory, like a body scan, and he shivered with dread. Moments later, a mixed group rounded the corner, armed with pulse guns. Before a syllable left his mouth, Tovi was hit with a stunner, and his world blacked out to nothing.

Chapter 24

I Hope this Email Finds you Well

Tovi's head felt like it'd been hit by the butt of a gun, and his mouth was drier than Praxian sand. He blinked, and light stabbed at his corneas. His inner eyelid saved him from the worst of it, but not enough. It took a few moments for him to remember what had happened, then assess his situation.

His arms were cuffed behind his back, and he was lying on a surprisingly soft carpet. When his eyes adjusted to the light, he saw he was in a spacious office, with a nice, faux-cherry desk standing in front of him. From his vantage point on the floor, the desk blocked the occupant. A whistled tune filled the space between them, a song Tovi wasn't familiar with.

The carpet he'd been face down on was an ocean blue color with a thick pile. A bookcase covered the wall behind the desk with as many knickknacks as books—model ships inside glass jars and strange antique dolls. Tovi assumed the door must be behind him. He smelled the pungent odor of a cigar. He'd gotten used to the aroma in the corp, where his compatriots smoked like it was a hobby, trading tobacco and arguing over where to get the best leaf.

He tried to reach for his sleeve, but it was gone. He tested his restraints, but they were high-grade cuffs. Out of options, Tovi admitted defeat and struggled to right himself with his hands cuffed behind his back. He levered himself up to a seated position, causing his hair to fall in front of his face, and he shook his head to clear his vision.

"Welcome back, sunshine."

Of all the people he was expecting, it wasn't Ching Shih. She looked about a thousand times better than she had when he'd found her in the rubble, gritting her teeth and dragging herself. He'd had loads of respect for her in that moment, as she'd refused to give up despite the perilous situation. Her hair was cut even shorter now, removing the singed and burned parts. Her legs were contained in white healing wraps.

"Where am I?" he asked.

"In my office, of course. You created quite a stir."

"Sorry, ma'am," he said. "How did I end up here?"

"I did say I was keeping an eye on everyone's movements, and that included your misfit band of scavengers. Good job I did too. That other Praxian was prowling around after you were tased unconscious."

"Any reason I'm tied up, ma'am?" he asked.

"Standard procedure with my crew. I'll have you released. Can't do it myself, doctor's orders, and you can call me Captain. You know, I don't meet a Praxian all my life, despite sailing the black waters for three decades, and in the course of a year, I've had more than my fill."

"Where? I'm searching for my conclave." He hoped she had a lead he could track down. He considered leveraging Sierra in the conversation, but he wasn't sure whether that would elevate or diminish him in Ching Shih's estimation.

She gave him an assessing stare. "You're very polite for a prisoner, you know that? They are in hiding with a group who specializes in smuggling anything for money. They don't want to be found, not by you or anyone else."

Tovi traversed warring emotions. Patini was here, maybe in this very building. It was the closest he'd ever been to locating her, but she didn't want to be found. There were multifaceted reasons for her reticence, especially in light of the Vengeance on their heels, but he wasn't going to walk away from the only opportunity he might ever have to see her one last time. "Can I send her a message, Captain?"

Ching Shih eyed him with suspicion. "Whatever for?"

"Let me say my piece, and I won't bother you again. I can be tenacious when I want to be."

"I've heard what you can do with a rock," she said, tapping the ash from her cigar into a pirate-ship shaped ashtray. "You served?"

"How do you know that?"

"You have that look about you, and you're far too courteous," she said. "And no one calls me ma'am." She stubbed out her cigar and sat back in her seat. "You can write a brief note." She pressed a button on her desk and two beefy pirates came in the room.

They removed his restraints but didn't leave the room. He stood slowly, stretching out his back until it popped. His headache had abated some, but he'd compliment anyone for a glass of water. Ching Shih opened a drawer and pulled out a synthetic piece of paper, a strip torn from a larger piece, letting him know just how much he could write, and a pen. He'd never seen a fountain pen in real life, and he made a mess of the ink on his first try, leaving splatters on the page. He wrote in Prax, a language composed of shapes that conveyed meaning through action instead of nouns. Ching Shih could easily translate the language, but its meaning would not be clear. He wrote his short note and handed it back to the captain.

"Could I bother you for a glass of water, Captain?" he asked, his voice hoarse.

"No, I've had quite enough of you and this business," she said and tossed him his sleeve. "You'll be escorted out."

"Yes, Captain," he said, giving her a smile, determined to win her over.

"For the love of Pete, here." She pulled a packet of water from a drawer and tossed it to him. He caught it and drank from the straw like a dying man.

"Thanks, I owe you one," he said.

"Give Sierra my regards."

He paused and appraised her. "Do you actually care for her?"

"I don't see how that's any of your business," she said with a hard stare. He was possibly making an enemy of a very dangerous person, but he cared about Sierra more than he feared Ching Shih.

"She is my partner in all ways but romantically. I will make it my business if you're jerking her around."

She studied him. "I do care for her, but I think she's capable of taking care of herself."

"Just because she can, doesn't mean she should have to all the time."

She waved him off. Recognizing a dismissal and not wanting to push his luck, he turned, put on his sleeve, and walked out the door. The two guards, who were as big as refrigerators, escorted him out. They barely glanced at him as one led the way and the other took up the rear.

"Where'd you serve?" Tovi asked, seeing if either would bite. They stayed silent. "I was with the Trans-Asteroid regiment, an Omnia subsidiary. Moved around a lot, kept me strung along six months after my service was up. I left them a little present when I finally got my discharge papers. Do you know how hard it is to get glitter out of a command council?"

He thought he heard the one behind him choke on a laugh. They'd walked him through a labyrinth of hallways—decorated with maps from Old Earth and paintings of ancient pirate ships on rough seas and new ones engaging in historic space battles—until they reached a nondescript door that opened to a busy street. He was pushed out and the door slammed shut behind him.

"Have a nice day," he yelled at the now solid wall. He was jostled by people in the street. It must be between shifts, based on the number of people walking like they had somewhere to be. Sentients were as varied as their outfits—suits, saris, dashikis, hijabs, casual chic, safety orange, and yellow hard hats. He moved to the side and activated his sleeve.

Tovi glanced back at the unassuming door, bereft of handles and squeezed between two convenience shops selling burner sleeves, magazines, and soft drinks. A shiver ran through him. Somewhere in that underground labyrinth, Patini and the rest of his conclave hid from the universe. The Vengeance was sniffing around at their heels, and for what? He shook his head, feeling defeated. He needed to get back to the ship; he could worry once he was home.

As he turned away, he couldn't help but feel a multitude of invisible eyes tracking his progress. He'd been on the asteroid for less than two cycles, and he'd managed to make enemies of nearly everyone he'd met. Had he entirely lost his touch?

Chapter 25

Contemplating Siblicide

Del

Looks like our plan worked. Your sister must be furious.

Ryan

Bombing a pirate station in her territory was a bit of genius. Teach those scum to blackmail me.

Del

Did your lover boy make it out unscathed?

Ryan

They haven't checked in yet. I should have heard from them by now.

Del

Do you care?

Ryan

I do rather like the Praxian, against my better judgment. I don't think I've ever met someone so genuinely sweet.

Del

It was wasted on you.

Ryan

Rude.

Del

What about the Alcat?

Ryan

I tracked down the source. Seems we have a problem there. As far as I can tell, Tovi has the cat.

Del

You'll have to work your magic on him, assuming you didn't blow him up.

Ryan

Perish the thought, though if the cat was with him, that would solve the problem.

Chapter 26

Breaking Bread, Breaking Heads

What are you doing? Lulu asked, her voice in Tovi's head interrupting his train of thought, which resembled a downward spiral.

"I'm working on the shield for the mech," he said, searching for the black furball. Tovi was standing next to the mech's left arm, fine-tuning the release mechanism on its forearm, and he couldn't see where she'd gotten to, fearing she'd managed to get stuck somewhere. She jumped up from the other side of the arm, overshot the distance, and would have fallen into the arm mechanism if Tovi hadn't caught her. "Be careful, you could hurt yourself," he said, holding her in front of his face to give her a stern look.

She scrabbled for his arm and sat on his shoulder. *I'm getting better. Will you take me with you next time you go out? Pixie says there are explosions, and I'd very much like to see one of those.*

Tovi shuddered at the memory. He'd do anything to forget about the explosion, and all the ones that came before. Flashes of past percussive events warred for screen time in his head. There had been the oxygen tank explosion at the independent hospital on the tiny asteroid of Fafall. The hospital had served sentients needing medical attention they couldn't receive or afford elsewhere. Omnia had claimed the hospital was operated by a pirate group, and Omnia had sabotaged their oxygen shipments. The tanks had exploded when they'd been installed into the life-support system.

Tovi had been in his environment suit, canvassing the hospital at the time of the explosion, doing the more logical thing: sweeping the place for combatants. Instead, he'd seen the dismembered bodies of sentients in the ICU and the frozen expression of fear on their faces, caught in the wrong place when the vacuum of space replaced the void left by the explosion. By having their own people inside at the time, it gave Omnia plausible deniability. *The oxygen explosion was an error on the hospital's part, nothing to do with them. They lost their own people who'd been too near the blast, you see?*

"How about we take you to see the fireworks instead? They have them every five cycles," Tovi said.

That would be acceptable, Lulu said, rubbing her soft little face against his and melting his heart. Without realizing it, the resolve he didn't know he was holding on to broke and he let out a sob, tears bursting forth without warning.

Sentient, you are leaking. I'm most concerned, Lulu said, making Tovi laugh through his broken sobs.

"It's okay, Lulu. Sentients do that sometimes." He wiped his tears away, feeling better after a good cry.

Most disturbing. You will need an oil change. Lulu hopped down from his shoulder, stumbling a bit but mostly landing on all four feet—maybe she was getting better. She eyed a shiny piece of ribbon, probably left over from one of Iz's projects, and she hunched low, butt in the air, did a little wiggle, then attacked the ribbon, missing by a good few inches and rolling on her back, mouth open as if to attack but meeting only air. Maybe her coordination needed some work, but it made him laugh when he wanted to cry, and he was thankful for that.

The crew had set up a time to meet with Ching Shih, none of them trusting the net for a private conversation. It would be the third time he saw her since they'd arrived.

Sierra was doing better after a long sleep. She stared into space occasionally, the concussion lingering, and she kept her right arm in a sling, strapped tight to her side. She was messing about in the cockpit of the mech, putzing around, as far as he could tell. The cut on her cheek had been deep and was a pink puffy line as it healed.

Tovi felt strung tight, like a taut spring ready to burst in any direction. Not a damn thing was going right, and he'd done precious little to turn things around. Had he been back on Octto, he'd have more contacts and options available to him, but here, he was flying blind. Given time, he could form a network and make friends, more people to watch his back. Ching Shih was someone he could work with and get closer to. She had a wide network, one he couldn't personally tap into. He resolved to dig deeper with Ching Shih and see what came of it.

They met Ching Shih at a restaurant, not far from the husk of the warehouse, that served Nhethian cuisine, much to Cecil's delight. They were led to the back of the restaurant, down a short hallway to a beat-up door with the word "Utilities" painted on it by a sloppy hand. Inside was a smaller version of the same restaurant with a heavily guarded back exit. Ching Shih's crew sat at half a dozen tables, eating or eyeing them warily. Ching Shih sat in a corner with sight lines to both doors, her back to the wall. Tovi could appreciate her paranoia, especially with both her legs in medical wraps and her hip in a cast.

She waved for them to sit at the table that could comfortably sit six, or four humans and a bear.

"Cecil might cry if he can't order some food. Mind if we join you?" Sierra said.

"Please, we can at least share a meal together and cement our truce with beet root soup," she said, waving for them to sit. "I'm sure we can put past matters behind us."

They placed their orders with the eager young waiter waiting at Ching Shih's elbow and then eyed each other suspiciously until Ching Shih broke the silence. "You wanted to speak to me, if I recall," she said.

"We've been considering your job. We can lure Ryan here and deliver him to you, but we have one condition. We need to make everyone think the AIcat is destroyed."

"And what does that have to do with me?"

"We need a believable bust up that ends with a decoy being destroyed."

"Okay?"

"I can speak to Vandover and get him on board. There wouldn't be any actual fighting, more like a play. We'll record it and leak it on the net. Also, Ryan will see it, so if he talks to anyone, he'll think it was destroyed too," Sierra said.

"And you believe that will work?" She sounded skeptical.

"It's worth a shot," Sierra said, with a shrug as she perused the menu. Tovi noticed she was avoiding eye contact with Ching Shih, and wasn't that interesting.

"Why don't you just give the AIcat back?"

"She's family," Sierra said.

Ching Shih regarded her intently. The hardness in Ching Shih's eyes seemed to soften when she focused on Sierra, and Tovi thought she might really care for Sierra, in her own way. Ching Shih nodded. "I can appreciate that, as long as I get Ryan. No one gets away with killing my crew. We will make an example of him." She punctuated this sentiment by snapping a breadstick.

"It's interesting you're loyal to your crew when you didn't bat an eye killing hundreds of people on the *Hope of Trappist*," Sierra said, defiance lacing her words. Most people would be too terrified of the captain to offer such a public criticism.

Ching Shih bit into her bread and chewed thoughtfully, her eyes boring into Sierra's.

"About that," she said. "The ship was dead in the water when we arrived. We were commissioned to rough it up and extract all the hardware. Ryan never said everyone on board was unplugged. When we found out he set us up to take the fall, I decided to ransom all the evidence. He must think we're incredibly stupid, and I take offense to that."

"What happened to the ship?" Iz asked, sneaking a breadstick from the basket.

"The ship was intact, so I assume there was a malfunction," Ching Shih said. "Ryan was trying to cover it up, and make everyone think it was pirates."

"I wonder if that was why Lulu didn't self-destruct," Iz said. "If the ship's AI malfunctioned, cutting all power, then it would keep trying to reboot. Perhaps it was finally successful after you'd made off with the goods."

"We were told to bring the skins of ten cats, which we did, but turns out one was a compdroid and not an AIcat," Ching Shih said. "I wasn't there personally; I believe in the delegation of duties, but then these things happen. Though I have to say, it has heralded an interesting turn of events." She directed this comment at Sierra before her face grew serious. "However, I would prefer to have my crew back. I have a responsibility to them and their families."

"We're saying this was gross negligence on the part of Omnia?" Cecil asked. "The ship malfunctioned, and instead of doing the right thing and taking responsibility, they pinned it on pirates. I suspect because the insurance is more generous and to save face. Those ships are astronomically expensive, and if colonists lose confidence, that would have far-reaching impacts," Cecil said, and grumbled, like something else was on his mind.

"What is it?" Tovi asked.

"I left Omnia for many reasons, but I had come to believe there was something else going on. Omnia heavily subsidizes world-builders precisely because they are prohibitively expensive. In exchange for the subsidies, colonizers are essentially employees of Omnia, and Omnia owns all the intellectual property. As part of that arrangement, Omnia has the right to declare martial law on the colony and take command of operations. This is a deal-breaker for some colonists, but many agree, believing it to be an unlikely scenario. I didn't think much of it, until I found schematics for 3-D printed weapons, some of them large enough to take down ships. Finding them was a fluke, and they were quickly scrubbed from the servers."

"While concerning, what does that have to do with this?" Iz asked.

"That kind of information would be stored inside the AI."

"Oh," they said. "You're telling us they're highly incentivized to destroy Lulu."

Cecil nodded and scratched his cheek.

Their conversation was interrupted by the arrival of divine-smelling food they hadn't ordered—steaming plates of thickly cubed beef covered in a dark gravy, mixed berries in a sweet sauce, and root vegetables in a thick stew. Cecil tucked in with relish, momentarily distracted.

"That just leaves luring Ryan here and reaching out to Vandover. Who wants to do the honors?" Cecil asked.

Sierra and Tovi exchanged glances, knowing he was talking to the two of them.

"We should confirm with Vandover first and pick an advantageous place to meet. There's also the station security investigation. They've booted the ship. At present, we are perfect suspects since the bomb came in on our ship," Tovi said

"You didn't check for explosives?" Ching Shih asked.

"We did, as it happens," Iz said. "Just as the guns he provided were new tech, so was the cloaking on the explosive."

"Stands to reason," Ching Shih said, skewering some beef with her fork before popping it into her mouth. "There's always risk."

"I want to ask about my family," Tovi said. "Have you seen the Praxian again?"

"They are leaving. Looks like the Praxian government has hunted them down," Ching Shih said.

"I don't understand what their issue is with your family," Iz said, cutting up a carrot and dipping it into a plum sauce.

"They're labeled a rebel faction by the Praxian government because of their support of the human homebound movement," Tovi said.

"I still don't understand. Why are they so invested in humans?"

"I never fully understood the premise, but that's the nature of cults. They don't make much sense. There's one Praxian who really drove our conclave to extremes. His name's Tian. I think his obsession with human history and culture led him down conspiracy theory rabbit holes on the net. He believes there's a fountain of knowledge and life the Consortium is hiding on Earth, that they purged humans to keep it for themselves. The conclave is dedicated to returning to Earth with a faction of zealot humans."

"Which would be my family," Sierra said. "The zealot humans, I mean. They're running around the universe garnering support for their ludicrous ideas." She waved her fork with a pierced potato in the air. It slid off the end and landed in her lap. "Damn, these are my stain-free pants."

"There's a surprisingly large number of sentients who oppose the Consortium's interference in what they consider to be planetary autonomy. Some believe stronger sentients have a right—even a duty—to subjugate weaker sentients. They'd probably object to them being referred to as sentients. Others believe we were lied to and humans weren't as terrible and power hungry as the official history depicts," Cecil said, and Tovi saw Sierra shift in her seat while Iz listened intently.

It was a touchy subject. Nhethians had a deep suspicion of humans. Tovi knew other Nhethians judged Cecil's involvement with two humans. While he'd never spoken of it, Sierra was far too empathetic to miss the signs, even subconsciously, and had brought Tovi's attention to the situation. Since then, he'd tried to leave space for Cecil to talk about the ostracizing he no doubt experienced, but Cecil never did.

"That's silly. We have innumerable accounts, including video evidence from Earth and then the Nhethians. They think it's all been fabricated?" Iz asked.

"Xenophobia knows no bounds," Sierra said.

"You're talking about humanists, or my favorite, homoists," Iz said, laughing into their water.

"Yes, humanists," Cecil said, giving Iz the side-eye.

"I didn't realize they thought it was a conspiracy," Iz said.

"Some do. Some don't and think it's the natural order of things," he said with a sarcastic grunt.

"So you think Prax doesn't want the embarrassment and is trying to... kill them or arrest them? What can they really do about it? Praxian law doesn't extend off planet and every planet has their weirdos," Iz said.

"I don't pretend to understand Prax or their motives, but they're here, hunting down my conclave. I've never heard of someone actually seeing the Vengeance, so it must be something important," Tovi said.

"You'll want to watch your back, then," Ching Shih said.

"That's all we're doing," Sierra said.

"I have eyes on everyone coming and going from the asteroid," she said.

"You have those kinds of resources?" Sierra asked.

"I'm not the only one upset about the explosion. My crew had family and friends in other houses. An attack on the station is an attack on all of us. The houses are like siblings. Only we can terrorize our own. We can't have people like Ryan threaten our livelihoods and treat us like a joke. It devalues us all."

"Well, that's one thing to worry slightly less about," Sierra said. "Just a pissed-off Praxian."

Cecil picked up his stew and drank from the bowl, then set it back down. "At least a Praxian is easy to spot, and smell."

"What do you mean, Cecil?" Tovi asked, resisting the urge to smell himself and feeling slightly offended. "Are you saying I smell bad?"

"Not bad. I think it's the oils from your skin. Smells like sand and some kind of berry, something sweet."

"Huh, I can live with that. Ching Shih, can you ask Patini to see me one more time?"

"Why?" she asked. She wasn't being cruel; her tone and expression were curious. "Why do you want to see someone who's repeatedly turned you down?"

"It's personal," he said, and it was. Trying to explain something he could hardly understand himself to a room full of intently listening strangers wasn't something he was eager to do. "Just tell Patini I would like to see her before they go. This might be our only chance—our last chance," Tovi said.

"Last chance for what?" Ching Shih asked, clearly not taking the hint. She had the benefit of access to Patini and might know the reason she was turning him down, and if that reason confirmed all of Tovi's greatest fears—that Patini hated him and never wanted to see him again—he just had to know if it was true. Had to know if his first family couldn't stand the sight of him. It should have been enough that she hadn't wanted to see him. Why couldn't he stop hoping? Why couldn't he let it go? Sierra would have. She'd not gone searching for her parents or her brother. She'd let them go.

"I just have to know, Ching Shih. I just have to know..." He couldn't get the words out. He wanted to, but he knew how pathetic it sounded. How pathetic he was.

"I understand. I'll ask. That's all I can promise."

He saw pity in Ching Shih's eyes, and he hated it. He felt weak. Sierra placed a comforting hand on his leg under the table. Tovi gave her a small smile. She retracted the hand so she could keep eating. With her dominate hand in a sling, her usual discoordination with eating was twice as bad. A piece of beef toppled off her fork and landed in her lap. "Shit, stupid arm."

"Why are we pretending like that wouldn't have happened any-way?" Tovi asked.

"Shut up, you. I am beauty. I am grace," she protested, pointing her fork at him.

"Do you need help?" Ching Shih asked. "My legs might be busted, but my hands work just fine. I could give you a demonstration."

Sierra's face heated and Tovi saw her eyebrows knit together and her gaze harden, never a good sign.

"We should probably be going as it is," Sierra said and stood, the chair legs scraping against the floor. She made to walk past Ching Shih to the exit when Ching Shih grasped her wrist, halting her retreat. Everyone tensed, including Ching Shih's crew, who stopped what they were doing to zero in on the two.

"I think the two of us should speak privately," Ching Shih said, her tone deadly serious. "Don't run away from me again," she said, soft and pleading.

Sierra glared at her, then switched her attention to the crew, who were staring back at her wide-eyed, and she jerked her head to the door. They got the hint and evacuated, despite Cecil gazing longingly at the remaining food. Tovi was reluctant to leave her without backup, but he knew when it was best to retreat.

Chapter 27

Hitting it Off on the Wrong Foot

Sierra was suddenly and outrageously angry. She didn't have romantic or amorous feelings often. To be made fun of on the one occasion she felt this way—and by Ching Shih herself—was a gut punch. Ching Shih had always enjoyed riling her up; Sierra suspected that was half the appeal and why she had never taken Ching Shih seriously, despite liking her quite a lot.

Sierra considered her options. She could continue to storm out, or she could have a flaming row with the woman. The flaming row won over. She needed to blow off some steam, and this had been festering for long enough. Sierra slowly sat back down across from Ching Shih, like she was facing a lion and didn't dare make a sudden move.

"I honestly didn't expect to see you again," Ching Shih said. "When you left, I was angry. I didn't know what I'd done to scare you off."

"You only cozied up to me to get information on a rival house. I didn't realize at first. I thought you genuinely liked spending time with me. You can't believe how stupid I felt when I saw you doing the same thing to others," Sierra said, accusation in her tone.

"You are grossly mistaken if you think I was looking at anyone else the way I look at you," Ching Shih said, her intense brown eyes staring straight into Sierra's with a determined heat that made her insides go all squishy. It was the kind of gaze that promised a firm manhandling against the nearest hard surface, and Sierra warmed to the vision. "I admit that's why I approached you in the first place, but it's not why I kept turning up. Teasing you was fun; you made it so easy. It wasn't right, though, and I didn't understand until much later that you might think I was only teasing you for a reaction. And when you came back, I fell back into it, mostly because I'm no good at being sincere."

Sierra hadn't been expecting a serious conversation and was thrown off. She was ready for a knock-down, drag-out test of wills, not a frank discussion about feelings. "What are you saying?"

Ching Shih sighed. "I like you, at least I did back then. It's been ten years and much has changed. I'm no longer the second-in-command, always trying to prove myself."

"And I'm not a debtor. I don't owe anything to anyone, except my crew. Well, also the debt we owe Hazel, so I guess that's not entirely true." Sierra released her own sigh, dropping her head in defeat, then she processed the rest of what Ching Shih said and peered at her through her eyelashes. "Did you say you liked me?"

"Trust you to miss the important part. Yes, I like you. Assuming you haven't changed irrevocably in the last ten years, but from what I've seen, you're still a tornado of tightly packed emotion loosely held together by your neurosis."

"That does not sound like a compliment, but it's very astute."

"I was hoping we could start over, as friends first. Then, if we like each other, we could go on a date."

Sierra didn't know what exactly she liked about Ching Shih, and why she made Sierra feel some kind of way. Maybe it was Ching Shih's intense loyalty and the way she studied Sierra like she was trying to pull back the layers and see what made her tick. Few people had ever cared to look that closely. She knew she had a polarizing personality, a love it or hate it relationship with everyone she met, and most people opted out. So when someone came along who leaned in, she immediately clammed up.

"What I mean to say is, you're still the fiery, determined person who would risk everything for the people you love, and I find that very endearing," Ching Shih said, apparently willing to calmly wait her out. "And you don't defer to me just because I could make you disappear with a hand wave."

"You know, I don't really do this. That's why I get so flustered."

"I've come to realize that. To be honest, I did some snooping on the net when I saw you were our contact, and when I found zero reports about your dating life, it finally clicked. I'm sorry I made you uncomfortable."

"I don't know how long we'll be here," Sierra said. She was two parts elated and one part terrified. The terrified part was telling her to make a run for it through any open door or blast a hole in the wall and fling herself through. Though, with her luck, the door would be a pull and not a push door, and she'd run right into it.

"We don't need to rush things or think about the future. I just want the chance to get to know you again. Also, can I tease you in private, now that you know I'm not just poking fun at you? I do so enjoy watching you blush."

Sierra couldn't stop her smile. "I'll think about it," she said. "Would you mind if I took the leftovers to go? I can't risk losing the good favor of my business manager. He's a real bear."

Ching Shih snorted a laugh. "That was terrible, but yes, of course." She gestured to the waiter, who procured takeout containers, and much to Sierra's relief, filled them for her.

"Promise me one thing," Ching Shih said as Sierra stood. "Don't run away again. Distance is a matter of perspective. Even if you aren't here, there's no reason to cut me off."

Sierra nodded, unable to verbally make a promise she wasn't sure she could keep. The light dimmed in Ching Shih's eyes, and she waved a dismissive hand before pushing away her plate of half-eaten food. Sierra's stomach dropped. She wanted to make Ching Shih smile again, and look at Sierra like she was a present to be unwrapped. Instead, Sierra retreated outside to her curious crew, and she handed the precariously stacked boxes to Cecil, who cracked a rare smile.

"What happened?" Iz asked, their curiosity beyond containment.

"We had a heart-to-heart," Sierra said, striding away from the restaurant, and her crew followed. Around her heart, guilt played ring-around-the-rosy.

"And?" Tovi said. At least he was trying to mask his interest, but he failed utterly.

She flushed once again and shook her head.

"Awwww," Iz cooed. "That's so cute, and you'd make a very handsome couple."

Sierra thought her face was going to melt like a wax manikin from the heat, and she searched her brain for anything to change the subject. As they strolled through a tourist area, her silent plea was answered when Tovi stepped in front of her, and she bumped into him.

"Wha—" She stopped when she peered around Tovi's torso and saw Vandover, who was shadowed by four of his crew. There were probably more positioned at a distance, if she knew Vandover. She grinned at him and hung her good arm off Tovi's shoulder.

"Vandover, what a pleasant surprise. Did you come with *get well soon* balloons?" she asked. "I don't think my crew has had the pleasure. This is Vandover, head of House Kibaya."

Vandover wore a practiced smile that was polite but didn't reach his eyes and a vest jacket cut in a casual style that whispered money instead of shouting it.

"I heard about your little mishap. Bad for trade, you know," he said, appearing unbothered.

"You say that like I tried to blow myself up," Sierra said.

"I'm aware of your death wish, and it had your usual flair for the dramatics, but that's not why I'm here. I came to see for myself how you're faring."

Sierra lifted an incredulous eyebrow. "You're here to see if I'm fit to fight."

"And are you?" There was an unspoken tension in the air, a threat left on mute.

"And if I said no?" Sierra asked. She just had to stomp on the mute button with the glee of small child.

"You signed a contract. I could call it in."

"I believe there are escape clauses in case of injury."

"You don't seem very injured," he said, his gaze clinically dissecting her body.

"My arm is in a sling, and I have a concussion. I'm sure you have a leg to stand on, but it would have to go through arbitration, and what a waste of time and money that would be."

Vandover's lips pressed together. "Is that your answer?"

"I was wondering if you'd do a little deal?"

"What kind of deal?" he asked slowly, like he was walking into a trap.

"We need help solving a problem, of the exploding variety. If I fight, will you help us out? We need some backup on a job. More of a security detail than anything else. Only a few hours of your time."

He considered this. "If you forfeit your player bonus, I'll consider it an even trade."

"I could choose not to fight at all. I am quite injured," Sierra said.

Vandover stared at her the way he always did when he was reading her mind. "I'm glad you never got into gambling; you'd be in worse shape than you are now."

"It's her face," Tovi said unhelpfully.

"Hey! Okay, a measly compound fracture and possible hematoma isn't going to keep me down."

"You're kidding, right?" Iz asked. "How are you supposed to work a mech in a sling?"

"It comes off tomorrow, and that's what the sleeves are for. I don't need to move my arms to fight."

"And the concussion?" Tovi asked.

"I'm feeling much better, thank you," she said, placing her good hand on her hip.

"Excuse us one moment," Tovi said, pulling Sierra aside, far enough away to not be heard. Iz and Cecil followed. Cecil sat between them and Vandover, blocking his view.

"What the hell?" Tovi said. "You're not fit to run a mech right now, and we haven't had a chance to practice. We'll be at a major disadvantage."

"I don't have to win. We only need to make smart bets. Even if I give up the play bonus in exchange for his help, we'll make some credits. There's no reason not to do it. We'll make money even if we lose. Which we won't because we're the Snaketamers," Sierra said with a wild grin. She held out her fist to Tovi, and he couldn't help but comply with their signature handshake they'd made up seventeen years before, when they'd been two dirty kids picking fights in the junkyards. "That's what I'm talking about!"

Her joy was infectious, and Tovi returned her grin. She saw Iz's and Cecil's tense shoulders relax a bit, knowing they couldn't crush her joy, not when there was so little to be found. "Hands in if you're with me!" she said, sticking out her hand between them. Tovi joined her, and so did Iz, if reluctantly.

"I think this is a bad idea," Iz said.

Cecil huffed and rolled his eyes, extending his paw, covering all their hands.

"Goooo team!" Sierra said, then raised her hand into the air with a triumphant whoop. "Thanks for your support. I won't let you down."

They turned back to Vandover, who appeared excessively bored.

"Half," Cecil interjected before she could accept the deal. "We'll give up half her player bonus in exchange for a few hours of your time."

"That's acceptable," Vandover said. "I take it we're a go, then?" he asked.

"Yes, sir," she said with a terrible mock salute that would have made Tovi's superiors weep.

"Good," he said and snapped his fingers. On the wall behind him, a holographic image of Sierra facing Demi sprang to life with the words "Watch Veteran Mech Stars Go Head-to-Head in the Fight of the Century" scrolling on repeat. Sierra was surprised to learn she'd be fighting someone she knew. She had fought and won against Demi many years before. They'd had a contentious relationship. Demi was someone who'd immediately disliked her personality, and they'd brawled outside of bars a few times when her snarky remarks had rubbed him the wrong way.

"Veteran? That makes me sound washed up."

"It's a young person's game," Vandover said, and the small tug at his lips belied the joy he took in crafting those words for Sierra's benefit.

"Cheeky bastard," Sierra said.

"We'll see you soon, then," Vandover said before turning down the street he'd come from, followed by his crew.

"Is it just me, or is everyone a little on edge?" Cecil asked.

"I was thinking the same thing," Tovi said. "That was a lot of backup for a public meeting."

"Maybe it's our reputation?" Sierra said, then turned serious. "I imagine everyone's growing suspicious after one of their own was attacked from outside. The pirates here have their own rules for their own game, but when threatened by an outside influence, they'll rally together."

"That's kind of heartwarming," Iz said as they continued their journey back to the *Who Wants to Know.*

Do Humans Dream of Electric Mechs?

Sierra tried to focus on the task at hand—preparing Archy for the fight. Instead, images of her standing in the ring with their very own mech kept floating up to the frothy top of her consciousness. The crowd would be in an uproar, and she'd have the best fight of her life, trading blow for blow, with Tovi feeding her tactics over her comm.

Everyone would be blown away, and Sierra and Tovi would be offered a PR deal, with miniature versions of their mech printed and sold at corner stores and to passing tourists. She imagined a tour deal, traveling the asteroid circuit, maybe even a syndicated cartoon show, with their mech as the main character. If she started now, she could come up with a 3D printed design of the mech and they could sell them at the door. Did she have enough time? She checked her sleeve. Maybe? She could make a start.

"No, dammit," she said, banging her fist on the mech's metal thigh. "Shit, sorry." She petted the mech, checking she didn't leave any marks. "Focus, Sierra, focus."

The mech needed to be ready. If she got into the fight and made a fool of herself, she could kiss her miniature mechs goodbye. "Work, work, work, work, work," she said to herself, walking over to the mech and debating what she could realistically get done before the next cycle. Weapons, she needed to get her weapons sorted. She'd spent most of her time fixing the bloody thing, so she hadn't had time to fully arm it for combat, and the shield needed to be tested. It had initially been constructed for a southpaw mech. She'd modified it, but it could use some work and reinforcement.

Adding greater shielding would increase the weight and reduce her response time, but it was integral to protecting the body of the mech. She'd been working on a spring-loaded release that would hopefully turn it into a useful projectile. She set to work, trying to rein in her overactive imagination. Despite the distraction of busy hands, Ching Shih's plea echoed through her head, engaging in hand-to-hand combat with her attempts to focus on the upcoming fight. She shook her head and punched at her sleeve to turn on the overhead speakers and cue up a playlist of synch rock with a heavy bass.

After a while, she found a groove and was startled when she felt a large paw on her back. Sierra swiveled around to see Cecil gesturing wildly. Sierra punched at her sleeve, turning down the music.

"How can you think with the music so loud? You know you can play it through your implant and spare us all the headache?"

"It's not the same. I like to feel the bass in my feet. You know, when you feel those real deep beats in your chest, like your heart could almost stop from the weight of it?"

"That sounds unhealthy."

Sierra shrugged. "Can't all be paragons of health. What can I do you for, Cecil? Unless you came to argue; I'm happy to oblige." It wouldn't be the first time. Sometimes Cecil enjoyed a good banter and would seek her out to start a jovial fight about nothing at all. She was normally game. Tovi and Iz were too sensitive for a healthy argument; she could see them tense up whenever they started up. Arguing over nothing at all was cathartic for her, making imaginary points for each zinger and leading them down the most absurd paths. She and Cecil had once argued over who made a better grilled cheese sandwich, in which she argued that bread should be the color of cooled lava and harder than an igneous rock. Sierra insisted to this day she won that argument.

"Not today. I have something for you," he said. His porkpie hat had a red-and-blue ribbon wrapped around the brim and sat back on his head. An ear flicked as a blue feather arching from the ribbon tickled his ear.

"A present? For me?" she said, only partially overacting. Cecil was an excellent gift giver, though he liked to pretend otherwise.

He huffed and walked on all fours over to a shallow square case near the bank of lockers. "I did some business earlier with an acquaintance. They had a piece of equipment they'd picked up from an R&D facility. Guess they couldn't get it to work the way they wanted. I talked to Iz, and they assured me they could get it up and running before the fight."

Sierra clapped her hands together, a grin spreading across her face as she assessed the unassuming box.

"Go on, then," he said. She reached down and released the latch on the case. The inside was padded with yellow foam cradling a half disk with a hole on the flat side. The half disk was two feet across, with a sharp blade on the outside curve like a half-moon. The flat end was a bar with a handhold, the right size for a mech hand.

"Holy shit," she whispered.

"The handle is magnetic. Even if you lose your grip, you won't lose the weapon. It can also be programmed to return to your mech and is perfectly balanced to throw."

"I can throw it at my opponent and have it return to me, like one of those boomerang things?"

"Exactly. Well, hypothetically. That was one of the things that wasn't working exactly right and why they abandoned the project for more conventional weapons. It didn't have much use on a battlefield."

"This is so great," she said, wrapping her arms around Cecil's thick neck and burying her face in his scruff.

"Yeah, yeah," he said, but he didn't pull away. "Just be sure to win. I have a lot of credits on the line."

"Thanks, Cecil. I won't let you down."

"It needs fixing up. When Iz gets back, they're going to put some time into it."

She released his neck and gave his ear a scratch. "I'll win just for you," she said.

"Get back to work, you're making me itchy."

She laughed as he used his massive back claws to scratch at his offending ear, causing his hat to tilt at a precarious angle.

How was she supposed to work now that her imagination had a retractable discus to play with? Thoughts of beheading her opponents bounced around her noggin as she went back to working on the shield.

Chapter 29

Practice Makes Imperfect

Sierra pivoted to preparing for the fight. Tovi was right; they didn't have enough time to practice. Not that they could afford to rent a practice area anyway. Instead, they decided to watch Demi's most recent fights and work on strategy. They could practice their communication and strategizing on the fly.

After some research, they learned Demi had been out of the ring for the last seven years and was just as out of practice as Sierra and Tovi. He'd been managing other fighters while taking care of his elderly mother. With her passing, he'd decided to rejoin the circuit. Their fight was his comeback match, making them fairly evenly matched.

"He favors shifting his weight on the back right foot, making him easy to topple to the left and behind if you catch him off guard with enough force," Tovi said, pointing to the screen where he'd paused the match mid-swing. They'd found a recording of his last fight against a tall, thin mech wielding a circular saw for an arm.

"He's definitely a more aggressive, offensive fighter," Sierra said. "He likes to set the tone for the fight. I think that's what makes him a hero figure—copious amounts of machismo," Sierra said, feeling not at all like a child mocking a playground enemy out of jealousy.

"His blade is helpful too. Every good hero has a sword," Tovi said.

"I think it's an uninspiring choice," Sierra said. "*Every* hero has had a sword. I don't know, I just think it lacks imagination, but Demi in general lacks imagination. It doesn't mean he's not a threat or not good at what he does. He's a very good mech operator; he's just very... What's the word I'm searching for?"

"By the book," Tovi said.

"Boring, I guess that's the same thing," she said. "He fights like someone who was trained to fight with their fists."

"He fights like a boxer," Tovi said, nodding in agreement. "He has all the rules memorized. He has a strategy in his head and that's what he sticks to. Your great advantage is that you don't have a strategy," Tovi said.

"Why does that sound like an insult instead of a compliment?" Sierra asked.

"It's true," Tovi said. "And it is a strategy, keeping people off guard, making choices on the fly."

"Versus having thought it all the way through," Cecil interjected.

Tovi shrugged. "Yeah, I guess so," he said.

"This isn't really helping my ego here, people," Sierra said. "I've never been taught how to fight, only how to flee. I don't have any of those prejudices. Yes, that makes me reactionary and yes, that's gotten me into some bad situations, but it makes me unpredictable. He can know I'm unpredictable and be on the lookout, but that's all."

"And that's what we're relying on," Tovi said. "Especially since we haven't had any time to think this through. And it's been so long since you and I have worked together like this." They glanced at each other, both brimming with excitement and a bit of trepidation. Even if they lost, it didn't really matter. They just wanted to fight, to dip their toes in and feel like they were making moves in their lives instead of stagnating.

It felt like something new. Even if it ended badly, there was something beautiful about change, something captivating about watching newness unfold in front of you, even if it was rotten on the inside. Sierra knew that made her weird to other people. And that was why she was here, with these people, because even though they probably also thought she was weird, it didn't bother them. They maybe even liked it. She could be weird with them, and that was what she cared about. She didn't have to hide herself.

"Okay, so our secret weapon for round three is what?" Sierra asked.

"We don't really have one, to be honest," Iz said. "We're going to be pulling out the discus in round two after the hand-to-hand round, but I haven't had time to imbue it with any special properties. I was thinking we could modify it to shoot fire, or increase the magnetic strength to steal their weapon, or turn it into a drone, or electrify it eventually, but we don't have time now."

"Round one: fist fight. Round two: disc blade. Round three: fly by the seat of our pants," Sierra said.

"Yes, exactly," Tovi said, and Sierra nodded.

"I sharpened one side so when it goes slinging at him, maybe it'll take off his head," Sierra said with a smirk.

"It's disturbing how much you enjoy this," Cecil said.

"Oh, come off it," Sierra said. "You enjoy it just as much as I do. Don't pretend like you're not excited."

Cecil just huffed.

They watched a few more videos, going through strategy; it wouldn't make much difference at this point. They went through drills with Tovi giving her direction, going through shorthand and emergency cues, doing as much as they could. But in the end, they knew this wasn't practice. Practice was something done over and over again; once did not constitute the term.

Sierra knew she should be trying to sleep. Instead, she sat on the edge of her bed picking at a hangnail, then stood and rifled through her toiletries and grunted at the pile of junk that tumbled out of the small cabinet. She picked through cotton swabs, rusty tweezers, and a pack of unicorn stickers until she found her one bottle of black nail polish and a nail file.

On her sleeve, she pulled up a reel of Demi's fights, assembled by an overzealous fan she'd found on one of his many fan pages. She'd been surprised to find she had her own small following on the net. She smoothed the jagged edges of her nails and applied the black polish, half watching the videos as she tried, and mostly failed, to paint within the lines of her nails. She shook her hands to dry the polish. Her arm twinged at the movement, and she blew on her nails instead.

You didn't sspeak to the man, Rupert said, gliding along her shoulders.

"The man? You mean Vandover? I did speak to him."

You talked without sspeaking.

"It wasn't really the right time or place to have a serious conversation." She'd hoped Vandover's concern earlier wasn't only about the fight. A small, juvenile part of her hoped he wanted to see for himself that she was safe. Her parents hadn't checked on her since the day they'd walked out of her life at sixteen, and this need to be cared for clawed at her chest.

When will be the right time?

"I don't know, Rupert. Hopefully soon. Are you looking forward to the fight?"

I am very much looking forward to it. We will vanquissh our ene-mies!

"When we start making some money, I can get you an upgrade that will let you interface with the mech."

I can control the weapons?

"When you say things like that, I get concerned."

I will use appropriate discretion.

"I believe you. Hopefully, it'll happen soon."

Rupert circled her neck and retreated into her hair.

She let the reels play in the background as she lay down, feeling like sleep would evade her, but it didn't take long for her heavy eyes to shut.

Chapter 30

Demi Dearest

When she woke, Sierra had a pep in her step. She was ready to take on whatever Demi would throw at her. She picked her outfit carefully. The jester persona needed to be immediately visible to the crowd, especially with Demi as the hero figure. It would play off long-standing tropes and get the people hyped. She unwrapped the healing brace and checked the damage. There was a faint scar and the skin blossomed purple and red with bruises. She flexed her hand experimentally. It was sore. An uncomfortable tension tugged at her shoulder and ran down her arm. Good thing she didn't have to fight for real. She could lift the arm, but a punch was out of the question. Luckily, her hand motions were all she needed to move the mech.

She struggled into a pair of blood-red pants, covered in straps and belts and buckles, and donned a black crop-top with a big white X on the front under a leather jacket resplendent in zippers. Sierra topped it off with a pair of ass-kicking black boots. Her mech gloves were nearly the same color as her pants. She didn't have to wear them until the fight, but she felt it completed the outfit. She selected a mélange of mismatching, overlapping necklaces and a black stud for her nose ring.

She left her hair down for now, mostly because it was Rupert's preference. It was easier for him to hide in her hair when it wasn't up in a bun. Plus, the wild, untamed mass only added to the jester persona she was cultivating. So she left it as it was: blue, curly, and sticking out at all different angles.

She checked her little following on the net. They were speculating about what she would do and how she would do it, arguing with other fans about how she was a superior fighter, and she let it warm her heart.

Humanss are sstrange, Rupert hissed in her ear. *You are the ssuperior fighter. You will take no prissonerss. There iss no debate.*

"Aw, thanks, Rupert." She ran her hand along his scaly back. She checked her reflection and tucked a loose hair behind her ear. She was as ready as she'd ever be.

They showed up as a team to the press event. Tovi wore matching colors in opposite: black, form-fitting pants, black shoes, and a maroon collared shirt. Gold detailing laced his cuffs and the seams of his pants. Iz and Cecil also showed up in solidarity, clad in black and maroon. Cecil's lovely vest—black with maroon detailing—matched his porkpie hat.

Iz wore a jumpsuit in about a thousand shades of red that had been stitched in with other patterns. Sierra could see leopard prints and polka dots and stripes and herringbone patterns. Individually, they would be overwhelming, but in small sections all put together, the garment had a very striking appearance and was more cohesive than she'd expected.

The press conference was held inside the stadium. They'd set up a table in the middle of the ring. The ropes had been removed and seats added for the press. Sierra came through the front entrance, and people cheered from the stands. As she jogged down the steps, people stood and high-fived her or booed in her face. She was surprised so many people were here for the press conference. The barrier was lifted so each operator could make a grand entrance through the stands. The clear partition served two purposes during the fight: it was kept up for the crowd's safety, but it also allowed Vandover to sell exorbitantly expensive tickets for seats inside the glass section. A few fat cats sat in seats nearby just off the ring, cheering or booing in their turn.

At the bottom of the steps, Sierra hopped up on the platform in the middle of the ring. Suffused with excited energy, she squared up with Demi in front of the table set up for the press conference. Demi was once again dressed all in black, with a gold crown that Sierra thought was tacky, but it'd been one of his go-to character traits since she'd first fought him. A king of a lost kingdom out to avenge his people—the imagery worked rather well and made for a good show. His narrative of revenge for his people had the unfortunate side effect of endearing humanists to his fights.

Sierra hadn't understood why Demi had chosen that particular back story when he was Diné and not remotely European. She'd asked him about it once. He'd shrugged and said he wasn't going to exploit his people's traditions in the ring. It was easier to stylize himself as a European king of a made-up empire and keep his history sacred.

Tovi mooned over the sparkly crown, and Demi gave him the once-over, his expression unreadable when he was in character. Behind every buff or blustering mech operator was a nerdy theater kid.

Sierra stepped up to face off with Demi for photos and streaming on the net, as per usual. They would throw insults back and forth for the benefit of the press and the crowd. Vandover would take any excuse to sell tickets, but this time, the audience would get their money's worth.

Sierra even spotted some of Ching Shih's crew in the crowd keeping an eye on things. Demi and Sierra entered the ring, staring each other down. Demi's intense jaw clenched, and Sierra wore a big grin on her face.

"Hello, Demi dearest," Sierra said. "It's a great pleasure to see you again."

A muscle in Demi's jaw ticked at the nickname. "I relish the chance to redeem my good name and assert the superiority of Demi the Demagogue in the ring," he said, his voice booming.

God, she wished she could do that. She always thought she sounded like a tiny mouse taunting a big cat. She chuckled away her nerves.

"The only thing you're going to prove is how pathetic you are. I'm going to run circles around you, and you'll wish you hadn't embarrassed yourself so thoroughly," Sierra said with a confidence she didn't particularly feel.

Demi gritted his teeth through a grin. "I have some surprises in store, but we'll just have to wait and see, won't we? At the helm of the Demagogue, I'm unbeatable. Honestly, you should just give up now."

"Someone has to teach you a lesson, and who better than the Snaketamer?" Sierra said.

She held out her hand for a handshake, which Demi took, squeezing hard. She took the opportunity to tickle his hand with her fingers, and he snatched his hand back.

"What? Problem?" Sierra asked, and Demi just snorted. Sierra then turned to wave at the crowd and take interview questions, all of which were asinine dend boring. Sierra answered in her most jovial manner. She knew it was grating and obnoxious for most people, except for people who were also grating and obnoxious—they probably enjoyed it.

Public opinion was just as important as performance. If people didn't like the fighters, the crowd would thin, reducing the betting pool and erasing demand for matches. Her pay would be greater the more people they brought in. She leaned on that as hard as she could.

Vandover led Tovi and Sierra up a circular staircase to the strategist box. It hung above the ring right in the center but set back, giving the strategist a good view of the mechs and the audience a good view of the strategist.

The box was partitioned in two with a clear separator, allowing for verbal altercations between the two strategists without derailing the match with a fist fight in the strategist box. The partition gave a semblance of privacy; however, loud talking would certainly be heard by the opponent and give up the strategy. Sierra had seen more than her fair share of fights between strategists from banging on the separator, lewd remarks, middle fingers, and threats of violence—it was quite entertaining in and of itself.

Vandover handed them both an earpiece. "This is encrypted, so no one but us can listen in. We will be monitoring the line to make sure you're not fed any information on the bets and to confirm no cheating has occurred. Once you're done, you will return the earpieces to me. We do not tolerate cheating, as Sierra well knows. We will not hesitate to throw you out of an airlock if we find that it has occurred," Vandover said matter-of-factly.

It was not an empty threat. Sierra had seen it happen once or twice.

"You will need to be suited up within the hour," Vandover said, and then he left them.

Tovi took a shuddering breath. "It's going to be good. It's going to be fine."

Sierra felt as nervous as he sounded. "Yeah, for sure. Super good."

"Absolutely, we got this."

"No problem."

"Totally. We can totally do this," Tovi said, hopping from foot to foot like he was about to enter the boxing ring himself.

Sierra clapped him on the shoulder. "Don't worry, rain or shine, we did the thing. That's what matters. I mean, what could possibly go wrong? We've already been blown up."

"That is hardly reassuring," Tovi said. "You're going to jinx it. Speaking of, you should probably check the mech to make sure it hasn't been lined with explosives."

"Cecil hasn't left the Snaketamer on its own. He's keeping it heavily guarded."

"It's a good thing someone's thinking about these things," Tovi said.

Sierra gave him a big hug, her arms wrapped around his torso. Tovi returned it with enthusiasm.

"It's going to be great," she said with smile.

Then she left and found her way back to the Snaketamer, which was sitting in the storage facility behind the ring. The facility housed mechs and Vandover's supplies. A giant door opened into space, allowing mechs and other goods to be delivered directly into Vandover's warehouse. The Snaketamer stood proud and predominantly rust free. She wished she'd had time to give it a paint job, but some things just had to wait.

Cecil stood in front of the mech on all fours, watching over things.

"Where's Iz?" Sierra asked.

"They went to get some refreshments," he said.

He growled at the security wolves that kept circling past. Now that Sierra noticed it, there were quite a few wolves wandering around their mech.

"What's the deal?" Sierra asked Cecil, whose eyes never left Kaylo, who was pacing ten feet away.

"We have a sordid history, the two of us," Cecil said. "Some things live in your genetics, and wolves and bears aren't known to get along. They've become territorial since I arrived."

"I take pleasure in knowing Kaylo's not enjoying herself. She did once try to bite my head off, literally."

Cecil grumbled low in his chest. "I'm very happy to be here, then. That is an event that will not be repeated."

"Thanks, Cecil," she said with a pat on his shoulder. "She's got a bum back leg, just in case that comes in handy," Sierra said. It was the only reason Sierra had managed to survive their last encounter. She'd kicked her right in a sore spot, and Kaylo had loosened her jaw around her shoulder. Sierra rubbed her right shoulder and let out a little gasp, forgetting she was already sore from the bruises.

She held her arm very gingerly against her body. She didn't want to give up any weakness, but she wasn't able to fully extend it or let it relax. She checked the mech's shield, making sure it was secured on the left forearm, then opened the mech's chest with a flick of her fingers, climbed inside, and secured the door.

Sierra went through the motions of her diagnostic check, making sure everything was running smoothly. She felt herself calm as she went through the familiar motions, like a choreography, slowing her heartbeat, helping her reach a sense of order and peace. Being in a mech was one of the few times she ever felt like she was in control of the situation. She took a few steps forward, moving every joint, then skips, jumping up and down, probing for any signs of issues. Getting into the body of the mech as if it was her own.

Iz stood next to Cecil, holding a gigantic bucket of popcorn, smiling up at Sierra like a kid at a candy store. They waved, bouncing on their toes, their smile wide enough to hurt. They were her number one fan, if there was such a thing. She knew Iz lived for this too. While not a fighter themselves, they loved watching the game and crafting the mech to perfection. They loved being an integral part of the process.

Sierra wanted to make them proud, to make Cecil and Tovi proud, and to make Vandover proud. Let them know it was all worth it. All of this had to be worth something. They'd finally get to do what they really loved. Iz cheered and waved as Sierra passed, and Sierra moved the Snaketamer's arm to wave back.

Sierra stopped the mech at the big doors leading into the ring, and Demi came up behind her. They waited for the doors to open and for Sierra's name to be announced. Over the intercom, she could hear Vandover and his booming voice.

"In the blue corner is the veteran mech, back and ready to sow chaos—Sierra and the Snaketamer." Sierra walked out, hands wide open, taking in the boos and the cheers in their turn. She light-footed it up the few stairs to the ring and did a twirl and a bow to the audience, holding her hands out again as the crowd grew louder.

Then Vandover announced Demi and the Demagogue. Demi came out, hands on hips, then swung a fist in the air, stomping up the steps, before opening his arms above his head to the echoing cheers. They turned and faced each other as Vandover spoke into the microphone

In that moment, Sierra was ready. She was more ready than she imagined she could be. She wasn't going to waste one second of this.

She was going to win.

Chapter 31

We Can Mech it if We Try

Tovi scanned the crowd going bananas as the two mechs faced off. The Demagogue was giant and shiny black, a sword angled over one shoulder, yellow stripes running down its body along its sides, flames at its back.

Its golden, glowing eyes and two horns that pointed out the back were all for show. But the Demagogue's head, where the 360 camera was housed, was always a fantastic target to sever, and Tovi would be on the lookout for a way to make it happen.

In comparison, Archy—or the Snaketamer when competing—was smaller and a bit wider. They hadn't had the time or the money to give it a new coat of paint, so it was a riot of colors from all the parts they'd fitted together, edged with the rainbow gleam of fresh welds. In some areas, the paint was flaking, while others were as brilliant as the day it was powder-coated. One arm was bright red, the other exposed steel. The color scheme lent itself to Sierra's jester image for sure, but Tovi was embarrassed by the unprofessional appearance.

The two mechs stared each other down as Vandover expounded on their many accolades, hyping up the crowd for the fight. The announcer box was clear on all sides, giving the disconcerting feeling Vandover was floating in midair. The strategist next to Tovi, a Distellan with spiky brown horns and clawed hands, was speaking softly, and Tovi couldn't hear any of the words. The ropes descended from the ceiling, dropping into place in the ring and encircling the two fighters, signaling the show was about to start.

Tovi could see Cecil and Iz in the crowd up near the front. Cecil was yelling or growling, lifting his paws. Iz was doing the same, jumping up and down, throwing their fist in the air. Popcorn flew all over the place, only some of it making it into Iz's mouth.

The two opponents bowed with one arm crossed over their chests, then moved back into their respective corners.

"Let the fight begin!" Vandover yelled into the mic.

Sierra turned to the crowd, waving, seemingly ignoring her opponent. Her outside hand lifted, asking the crowd for more, while her inside hand stretched to Demi, giving him a mocking wave at the wrist.

"Taunting?" Tovi asked through the comm.

Just playing to the crowd, Sierra said.

"He's ready to charge. You know how to get under his skin."

Demi was circling, then he took off at a run, aiming at Sierra's middle, probably trying to drop her fast. Tovi knew she was watching him—the benefit of a 360 camera—and didn't need him shouting in her ear.

She did a pirouette, rotating on one foot out of his grasp, to the cheers of the crowd.

"Careful of the ricochet," he whispered into the mic.

Demi bounced off the ropes, using his momentum to come at her with a raised fist. Sierra got the shield up just in time to block the blow, glancing it in front of the mech's body as she stepped back and Demi kept moving past her, hitting the ropes and bouncing back again, trying to land a solid blow with the force of his moving body.

Sierra stumbled fast enough to lose her balance and go wind-milling back, hitting the ropes and sagging against them. Demi's trajectory was off and he stopped himself against the ropes, losing the force he'd built up.

"Did you do that on purpose?" Tovi asked.

"*Wish I could say yes,*" Sierra said. "*I'm getting used to the mech.*" She straightened and ran forward, pressing her advantage while Demi was stationary.

"He's turning for a round house," Tovi said, seeing Demi pivot away from Sierra.

She adjusted her position, raising the shield higher as he turned and kicked for her head. With her left arm raised, taking the blow from Demi's kick, she tried to grab the leg and missed but avoided losing points to a direct kick.

Demi was feeling energized and motioned for Sierra to come at him. It wasn't Sierra's style to initiate, especially when she wasn't feeling confident.

"*I'm going for it,*" Sierra said, lunging at Demi with the shield held in front of her, catching him off guard. He'd clearly expected her to stay in a defensive position. The shield, with the weight of the Snaketamer behind it, crashed into Demi, and Sierra hit him once with her right fist as the shield pressed against his right shoulder, blocking his right arm. She managed a second hit to his torso before he wrapped his arms around her, bringing her into a clench so she couldn't get in another punch, then kneed her in the chest.

"Grab the knee and push forward," Tovi said, covering his mouth so no one could read his lips. "Push forward and to the right."

She did as he said, catching the next knee and twisting to the right and then pushing forward. The Demagogue was tall, making its center of gravity high, and with only one leg on the ground, she was able to topple him over and back. Demi crashed to the ground with a loud bang, and Sierra was on top of him. She let go of the knee and punched with both hands, right and then left, before Demi twisted his hips and pushed himself over, flipping positions and landing two punches of his own, the sound of metal impacting metal reverberating through the ring.

"Go for the head," Tovi said. He hadn't expected her to head-butt the Demagogue, but she did, denting in one side of his camera. Who knows how much damage she'd done to the Snaketamer, but it wasn't as much as she'd done to the Demagogue. Demi rolled away and stood, one hand attempting to reshape the camera body.

"Got the fucker," Sierra said over the line.

"Don't stop now; get in points while he's blind." Tovi didn't know if he was fully blind, but it was enough for Demi to pull back.

Sierra stood and charged at Demi, but as she got close, he kicked out, hitting her in the side and sending her bouncing off the ropes.

"He was feinting, that bastard," Sierra said. She was getting mad and that wasn't good.

"Don't let it get to you. Stay focused," he said.

She pushed off the ropes and they circled each other, each searching for an opening. Then a bullhorn blasted through the ring, signaling the end of the first round. Tovi unclenched the railing he hadn't realized he was strangling for dear life.

"Nice job," he said, watching as she backed into her corner. They'd have thirty seconds before round two. "How are you feeling?" he asked.

"Good, ready to keep kicking ass. Who do you figure won the round?" she asked.

"I don't know, could go either way. You both got in good shots. I might be biased, but I thought you got in more. What's the damage?"

"Camera's a little wonky, keeps cutting in and out on my left side. Some dents in the body, but no alarms," Sierra said.

"Good. I'll keep an eye on your left."

The bullhorn went off again, signaling the next round. This was when fights got tricky. The rounds were shorter, applying pressure to the fighters to inflict as much damage as possible in a limited time. Sierra reached behind the mech's back and grabbed the hilt of the discus, unsheathing it from the compartment they'd built. The crowd let out a breath of surprise. As far as Tovi knew, no one else used a similar weapon. The Demagogue reached behind its head and unsheathed its sword.

They circled each other; Tovi's eyes were trained on the sword. Demi held it with both hands, the blade angling over his right shoulder, ready to strike.

"He's going to slash from your left," Tovi said.

Sierra angled her body to compensate for her blurred vision and lifted her shield a little higher.

Demi rushed forward, swinging the blade down in a slashing motion. Sierra put her weight behind the shield, ready for the impact, and the blade glanced off the shield. Demi swung the blade around and over his head, aiming inside the shield.

"He's coming straight down," Tovi said. He expected Sierra to lift the shield high and block the blow, and he sucked in breath when she didn't, leaving herself exposed. Instead, her right arm came up with the disk, parrying the blow. Demi brought the blade back around his head and sliced down again. Sierra used the shield to block and, seeing an opening, swung the disk and released.

Tovi held his breath. Sierra had zero practice throwing the disk, and she wasn't known for her aim. She'd once nearly taken out Tovi's eye throwing him a screwdriver.

The disk hit the Demagogue in the left shoulder, cutting through the shielding and exposing sparking wires, but it wasn't enough to sever the arm's function. The disk flung away, lodging itself in the protective barrier of the ring with a loud *thunk*. The crowd gasped. A few people screamed, some instinctively ducking or hitting the ground. The barrier held, with the disk stuck ten feet off the ground.

Demi stumbled back a pace and Sierra reached out her arm to the disk to call it back.

"Fuck, it's not returning to me," Sierra said.

"It must be stuck in the shield," Tovi said. That, or the retraction mechanism they'd cobbled together last minute wasn't working, but he didn't want to waste his breath. Either way, Sierra would have to finish the match without it or go get it. There were no rules about leaving the ring; anything within the confines of the shield was fair game.

"Dammit," Sierra said. Demi rushed at her, realizing she was without her weapon, but from Tovi's viewpoint, he saw that Demi couldn't lift the arm entirely—only as far as the shoulder.

"He's going low. I don't think he can raise the arm." With any luck, Demi wasn't ambidextrous either.

Demi swung at her torso and Sierra easily blocked, but the blows dented the shield inwards. He swiped again, this time going lower, cutting at her knees. Sierra jumped back and the sword hit against her thigh, cutting the metal but not slicing entirely through the leg. The hit sent Sierra careening to the side and she crashed to the ground.

The bullhorn went off, saving Sierra from Demi's next blow. Tovi could hear her breathing heavy on the comm as she slowly got to her feet and gingerly tested the stability of the knee.

"How's it holding up?" Tovi asked.

"It can take my weight, but it's throwing off my gait," she said.

"You need to get your weapon back if you can. There's no way you'll make it through the last round and win without it. There's no doubt we lost this round." What went unsaid was the fact they could have already lost entirely if she hadn't scored enough points in round one, but they wouldn't know for sure until the match was over.

There was silence on the line.

"Are you there?" he asked, worried he'd lost the connection.

"*Yes, I'm here,*" she snapped. "*Trying to figure out how to get it back if it won't retract.*"

"You could make a jump for it," he said. "Couldn't hurt to try."

"*Okay,*" she said, saluting him with the mech. "*Let's give it a go.*"

The bullhorn blew again, and Sierra wasted no time. The disk was behind Demi and to her right. She ran as fast as a clunky mech would allow, using the spring heels in the mech's feet—meant to assist in adding power to a run—to help give her some loft and propel her up. She'd just cleared the ropes with her front foot, her hands outstretched and grabbing for the disk, when her back foot caught on the rope. She managed to grasp the disk, but her foot was caught, her body suspended at an angle in the gap between the ring and barrier.

Demi was momentarily stunned, then he pulled his sword and flames burst forth from the sides of the blade.

"His sword is on fire, and he's headed your way," Tovi said in warning. He tried to disguise the panic in his voice.

She scrambled her foot free and tugged with her weight to try and get the disk to come loose.

Demi stalked toward her. When the disk wouldn't budge, Sierra walked the mech's feet up the barrier into a horizontal crouch and pulled. The disk gave way, and she fell to the ground with a loud thud as Demi swung the fiery blade, just missing Sierra as the blade fell.

"He's coming out for you; you need to move fast. Roll to your left," Tovi said, his heart hammering in his chest. He twisted his own body like he could make the mech move through force of will.

Demi slid between the ropes and jumped down, his blade pointed downward to stab into the Snaketamer's head. Sierra rolled the mech away from Demi and onto her feet, the flames licking the side of the Snaketamer's head. She threw the disk, this time only two feet away, and it lodged into the crook of the Demagogue's neck, tearing the metal and sending sparks in arches from the cut.

"Nice shot," Tovi yelled into the comm, anxiety and relief flooding through him.

"My cameras were burned. I can't see shit," Sierra said, panic in her voice. She backed the mech up, bumping into the barrier.

"I think he's flying blind too. Follow the barrier around behind you. He's swinging wildly," Tovi said. He wasn't exaggerating. Demi was parrying the sword like a flyswatter in search of a fly.

Sierra stumbled back, crashing into the barrier and then sliding around its curved surface, turning the mech's body at an odd angle.

The bullhorn sounded and Sierra collapsed, arms and legs spread wide in what was a signature ending move for her.

Tovi whooped into the comm. "Heck yeah! That was awesome," he said.

"Holy shit. I can't believe it's over," Sierra said, breathing hard through the comm. *"What's Demi doing?"*

"He's just stopped. I think you'll both have to exit your mechs. It's not like you can feel your way back to the ring."

Tovi watched as Sierra opened the hatch on the Snaketamer and awkwardly crawled out of its chest, holding her arm against her side. The Demagogue was upright, and after a minute, its chest opened and Demi stepped onto the platform, an arm raised to his fans and a smile that was a little too wide to be genuine gracing his face. He was striking though and played the part of the righteous avenger rather well. The light shone off his resplendent crown. Tovi would need to ask him if he could borrow it for a spell.

Sierra did a shaky bow to the audience. She was visibly off-kilter, stumbling and holding her still-injured arm to her chest.

"Are you okay?" Tovi asked, now concerned she'd done more damage to herself than he'd realized.

"I'm good," she said. *"Just have a headache."*

If she said she *just* had a headache, it was probably of the splitting variety. Coming off a concussion and getting tossed around in a mech wasn't a winning combination.

"You should sit down," he said as he turned and ran down the stairs. "I'm coming to you."

He saw her duck under the ropes on wobbly legs into the ring. It was normal for the strategists to join the operators when they announced the winner, and no one tried to stop him as his long legs ate up the ground to the ring. He slid under the ropes with practiced ease and popped up, closing the distance between himself and Sierra. She was worse up close, her skin pale and clammy. He wrapped his arm around her good side, holding her by the torso in a side hug, but he took on most of her weight.

"You look like death warmed over," he said into her ear.

"You say the nicest things," she said, pecking him on the cheek.

"Okay, let's get you out of here." His alarm grew with the glassiness of her eyes.

"Not until they announce the winner. I'm okay, really." She shook her head, like trying to dislodge an unwanted thought. "Oh look, there's Cecil and Iz."

He turned and saw them banging against the barrier and waving, all smiles and cheers. They both waved back and realized they were waving to the whole crowd as their image came up on the overhead display.

Vandover waltzed out and slipped between the ropes. Demi and his strategist were murmuring to each other a few feet away. Vandover gestured for them to come closer to the center of the ring. Tovi took on Sierra's weight and walked them next to Vandover. He realized the issue as he came up alongside Vandover. Sierra couldn't lift her right arm and they were on Vandover's left side. It was wishful thinking to hope he'd be lifting her arm in victory, but Tovi wasn't taking any chances.

Tovi gestured at Demi with his head and stared pointedly at Sierra's arm, held protectively against her stomach. He walked Sierra around to Vandover's right side, and Demi's eyes widened in under-standing. He switched sides without complaint, earning him some points in Tovi's estimation. Vandover, for his part, ignored their shift-ing and jostling as he spoke to the crowd.

"An exciting and unprecedented match between the Demagogue and the Snaketamer. It was a close match, but our referees have tallied up the points."

Tovi stepped back to give Vandover room to grasp Sierra's wrist, but he kept a steadying hand on her back.

The crowd had turned into a loud hum of background noise. The excited faces of the sentients behind the screen were like mimes, fists punching the air, hands cupped to mouths to extend their screams.

Demi stood tall and wide, face stoic like the ideal hero. Secure in his identity even if he lost. And Sierra's face, whether she'd wanted it to or not, was the face of the jester. She held a lopsided grin that was just this side of maniacal. Something that might appear cocky from far away, but Tovi knew she was in her own head, replaying her favorite parts and luxuriating in the game. She was probably also loopy from the concussion and no doubt possibly sustained another one in the Snaketamer—though he very much hoped not. The long-term repercussions weren't great even with the technologies at hand.

Sierra was in her own world, laughing and smiling, cocky on the outside and content within because, to her, she'd already won. It didn't matter what happened next; she'd beaten so many odds to be here. She was just happy, and Tovi tamped down his concern to relish in the moment with her.

Vandover took his time drawing it out before saying, "And the winner is... Sierra the Snaketamer!" Vandover's voice echoed through the room as he lifted Sierra's left arm.

Her eyes came more into focus, her smile widening even farther. She might have whooped and hollered and run around if she were capable of doing so. Instead, she turned to Vandover, shocked as he smiled at her with affection. Then, with unshed tears glistening in her eyes, she turned to Tovi and fell against him like a sheet in the wind, wrapping herself around him.

"We did it," she said with a sigh, like something had released inside of her, like an arrow drawn taut had finally been loosed.

He knew she was swimming in an ocean of guilt for how things had gone down on Zhital. Not only for what happened but in the disparity in their punishments. He'd be lying if he said he wasn't re- sentful, but not of her; it hadn't been her fault. This was redemption, and he felt it too.

He hugged her back, picking her up and swinging her in a circle, allowing his worry to retreat momentarily and joy to overtake him. They had spent years building to this; he could have his moment in the sun. He set her down and they smiled at the crowd and waved.

He pointed out Iz and Cecil, who were jumping up and down and screaming, and waved. Sierra smiled impossibly wider, waving to them specifically before she fairly collapsed into Tovi's arms.

He gave a jovial wave to the crowd, his arm once again wrapped around her torso, holding her up like a doll. Demi's face was like a sour lemon, eyes hard—the disappointed hero, but gracious—bowing to his fans and waving. But as he turned to Sierra, Tovi could have sworn he saw his eyes soften a bit. Maybe some concern flitted across his face, or maybe that was just what Tovi wanted to see. Tovi wanted to believe that someone here had cared for her in all the years she'd spent among pirates, that deep down, Demi was a good dude who was more concerned about her than the match. Plus, he was cute.

Demi, like a good sport, shook her good hand, then leaned in and said something to her Tovi couldn't hear.

"I'll hold you to it," she said in return as they turned to wave to the crowd.

It had been a doozy of a match; everyone would benefit. Tovi couldn't remember the last time he'd seen two mechs blinded simultaneously in the ring. They'd be in the news for cycles, leading to more matches, more lineups, and more hype.

Tovi got Sierra out of the ring as quickly as he could manage, with everyone wanting photos and interviews. He begged off, saying she needed to rest and promising they would hold a press conference after she'd rested. The reporters ate up Sierra's current state: wobbly legs, vacant eyes, and a head that didn't know which way to turn. She was like trauma porn incarnate.

He led her back through the maze of hallways, trying to find somewhere to rest, when someone waved to them from a room down the hall and Sierra waved back.

"You did it, you incredible bitch," the stranger said as Tovi approached, slapping Sierra on the back a little too hard for Tovi's liking. He read the name plate on the door. "I'm Andy, by the way. You're haggard. You can use my room."

He was grateful and set Sierra down on the well-worn couch. "Sierra, are you okay?"

"We won," she said. "We actually did it, Tovi." She smiled at him, and it was like the sun. It was a genuine smile; not one of her half-cocked, brave-faced smiles, but a real one. And he wished she'd wear it more often, that it wasn't buried under layers of protective coats keeping her warm in the rain.

"Sierra, we need to get you checked for another concussion," he said.

"I'm okay," she said, straightening a little. "I'm fine, I'm just a bit shocked by the whole thing, is all."

Tovi gave her a hug. They stayed like that for a time, sitting side by side on the red and gold couch, until Cecil and Iz came bounding through the door, and she released him to wrap them in her own embrace.

Chapter 32

From Success to Arrest

Sierra knew she had suffered another concussion, or she hadn't quite recovered from the one she'd received earlier. Everything felt fuzzy and far away, but she didn't care. They'd won. They'd actually won. It had seemed so impossible when they'd begun, but here they were, winners of the day. And she couldn't be happier. All that fighting, all that hard work, hadn't been for nothing.

After the medic wrapped her neck and lower skull in healing patches and gave her some medicine, she felt more stable and less loopy. Her arm ached more than ever, the muscles tense and shooting pain to her neck, back, and head. The medicine helped, but it would take rest to get the inflammation to die down, and rest wasn't in her near future.

She went through the motions of giving interviews and participating in photoshoots with Tovi and Demi. Demi had given her a curious expression, and then, during their last photo op, Demi leaned in close and asked, "Are you okay?" Concern laced his voice.

"Just a little punch drunk," she said, unable to stop the giggle that escaped her. If anything, he was more concerned. "I'm good. Just need to sleep it off."

"Okay, you just seem very out of it."

"Thanks, Demi, I appreciate it, but I'll be alright. And don't worry, I'm sure we'll have another chance to settle the score," she said with a wry grin. He returned it and slapped her on the back, jarring her tight muscles and making her suck in a breath. Why was everyone doing that?

"Who's your strategist, by the way? You should introduce us," he said, sweeping an appreciative eye over Tovi, who was charming a reporter.

"That's Tovi, and I'm sure you'll introduce yourself," she said.

"Don't mind if I do," he said and sauntered over to the pair while Sierra huffed a laugh.

It took hours to get through the press calls. In the meantime, Cecil and Iz packed up Archy, securing it and its busted cameras for the trek back to the ship. As they coalesced to head home, the press still milling around, a cadre of station security rolled up, appearing serious and well armed.

Sistemsisa, along with half a dozen guards, stopped in front of their crew. Without preamble, she addressed the group. "You are hereby, by the power of station authority, under arrest for the attempted destruction of the station. Four counts of murder, seven counts of bodily harm, and malicious intent."

Sierra stared at her, stupefied and unable to even curry a reasonable objection. She had hoped they'd have Ryan in custody before station security came calling.

They were quickly surrounded by guards and roughly handcuffed. Sierra yelled when they tried to restrain her stiff, cramped arm behind her back. Cecil growled, baring his teeth, and the guard reluctantly cuffed her wrists in front of her body. There weren't restraints capable of fitting Cecil and restraining quadrupeds went against station policy, but four guards kept their weapons trained on him as they were led down the street to station security. Sierra and her crew walked in silence, exchanging worried glances. The press swarmed them, taking photos and video, shouting invasive questions in Sierra's face. Sierra kept her features schooled, only occasionally smiling and giving a little wave to the camera, pretending she wasn't scared shitless.

The main headquarters for station security was on the administrative floor of the asteroid, a place Sierra rarely had reason to visit. It was located one floor below the tourist and residential hubs. With no one to impress, the ceilings were far lower—just tall enough for single-story buildings built from floor to ceiling. The station security building was nondescript; its gray, regolith exterior was all business and looked like an alien landscape.

The front door slid open as Sistemsisa approached. She ushered them through a drab atrium with public service posters plastering the walls warning of the perils of drug overdoses and sentient trafficking. Vacated hard-back chairs lined the walls and were the only witnesses to their walk of shame into the cell block. They were pushed into a single cell with rough rock walls illuminated by dim lighting that threw shadows at rough angles across the two bunks on either wall and a small cubicle for a toilet. Sierra hoped Cecil didn't need to pee.

Their earlier victory deflated like a popped balloon.

"I think telling them the truth is our best course of action," Cecil said. "With the exception of Lulu. The less who know about her existence, the better."

"I've no doubt Ryan covered his tracks. There will be no evidence of his involvement with the shipment," Sierra grumbled.

"We'll have to be as convincing as possible, then," he said.

Do not worry. I shall avenge your deaths, Pixie said.

"Thanks, Pixie, that's a great comfort," Sierra said.

She didn't have long to wallow before she was taken in handcuffs to an interrogation room, just big enough to hold her and Sistemsisa. Sistemsisa stood, while Sierra sat in a rickety chair, her gaze sweeping across the rock walls, searching for a hidden camera and wondering who would be watching.

"We believe you intentionally brought explosives onto the station," Sistemsisa said.

"Why would we want to kill ourselves?" Sierra asked.

"I suspect you had no intention of killing yourself. But due to poor planning, and incompetence, you were in the way of the blast purely by accident. The rest of your crew managed to clear themselves away in time, but not you."

"That's ridiculous," Sierra said.

"Is it? I have evidence showing you falsified documents to get on board the station. There's no record of the company you claim hired you for the job."

"This is absurd," Sierra said, then tried to calm herself. If she didn't convince station security they were innocent, they were dead. "The thing you need to understand," Sierra said in a measured, even tone she hoped conveyed her sincerity, "is that we have been framed."

Sistemsisa wasn't capable of rolling her eyes, but Sierra got the feeling that was exactly what she wanted to do. "And who, might I ask, would want to frame you?"

Sierra related the entirety of her story. All the gritty details, all the information she might need, leaving nothing out except Lulu, knowing Cecil was right and this was their best chance to save their lives.

"You falsified your trade documents to bring illegal weapons onto the station?"

"We didn't know there were weapons inside, and we did check for explosives, but as I said, this is new technology that's able to cloak itself."

"It's too bad it was all destroyed in the blast."

"Explosives have that effect," Sierra said and cursed herself. She shouldn't antagonize the person who decided their fate. "Look, we have a plan to bring in the person who *is* responsible. Just ask Ching Shih."

"The evidence I have is overwhelming." And it went unsaid that it was much easier for station security to collect the low-hanging fruit that was her crew.

"Just think, if it is Omnia, then they've attacked your station, and if they get away with it, they'll do it again." Sierra could tell she'd run out of steam with the line she'd taken, so she pivoted. "I'm sure Ching Shih and Vandover can vouch for us as sentients who are stupid, but not so stupid as to try to blow ourselves up along with an entire station, unlike Ryan, who is also an idiot, but a power hungry one with the force of Omnia to back him up. You can check our financial records. We don't have the credits for the kind of explosive that gets by your security."

Sistemsisa seemed to think about this briefly. There were internal station politics to consider, and no doubt Ching Shih had vouched for them. Then there was Vandover. Sierra was something of a meal ticket—not that he needed a meal, but she was added zest to his dinner. Despite the way she'd left things, she hoped the affection she'd seen in his eyes meant he hadn't written her off entirely. He'd saved her once before; maybe he'd do it again.

Making an enemy of Ching Shih and Vandover could have lasting effects for Sistemsisa's house and anyone else at station security, as well as whatever internal politics and war games were going on. Sierra was flying blind in that respect, having no insight whatsoever into the power dynamics at play here, but it seemed to be enough to make Sistemsisa reconsider immediate expulsion from the asteroid.

Sierra stared at her squarely in the eyes. As much as she wanted to hate this sentient and take out her frustration on her, this was her home as much as it had been Sierra's at one point. "I lived here for seven years. I have no reason to kill anyone on Terrana."

"You spent seven years on this asteroid, paying off your debts. It would be no surprise if you wanted revenge for that," Sistemsisa said.

"I can see why you would think that. Some debt brokers abuse their power, but I can honestly say Vandover was a good, kind man who never hurt me and was never cruel. I have nothing but respect for him, and Ching Shih and I are... friendly. I have no vendetta against her or anyone else here. Am I mad that one silly mistake led me to seven years of debt repayment? Yeah, I'm mad about that, but I also didn't have it as bad as other sentients, not even close. Tovi has far more reason to be upset for the treatment they put him through. If we had wanted to attack anyone, it would be Omnia. It would be the people who put us here in the first place," Sierra said. She paused for a moment. "It would be ourselves. It would be me," she whispered.

She had been the one to convince Tovi to hold the unsanctioned fights, and he had suffered far more than she had. What she hadn't understood at the time was how xenophobic the system was. Omnia had bought their debt and the company was headed by humans, but they predominantly used other races to fight in their resource wars, believing them to be stronger and deep down not seeing them as equals. Omnia often sold their debt holdings for humans to other human-run companies for manufacturing and relatively safe jobs, if still demeaning and abusive.

Sierra would never be able to live that down or set it right. And here they were again, one of her harebrained schemes leading them to possible death. If it came down to it, she'd take all the blame.

"You want someone to blame, I get that. If I can't get you the real culprit, you don't need to take us all down. I'll go without a fight, with a signed confession, but leave my crew out of this."

Sistemsisa considered her for a moment. She was so damn hard to read. There must have been a tell in the shake of her tail feathers or the occasional flap of her head feathers, but Sierra could have been trying to read the stars for all she could interrupt. Just like those constellations, she was trying to ascribe meaning to chaos and failing.

Chapter 33

All is Lost Boss

They returned Sierra to the cell and the somber eyes of her crew, minus Cecil.

"How'd it go?" Tovi asked.

"I told them everything, the whole story, except Lulu. Where's Cecil?"

"They're interviewing him now. They already interviewed me and Iz," Tovi said.

Cecil appeared with a plethora of guards. They escorted him to the cell, locking the door behind him.

After a flurry of activity, they had more downtime than four people on death row needed or wanted. Sierra sat next to Tovi, brimming with a deluge of things she wanted to say. She'd never been able to fully express the depth of her guilt, and now he was losing his last opportunity to reconcile with his family on top of everything else. Some part of her hoped the conclave would change their minds about leaving, now that he was in mortal danger.

"Do you know when your conclave is leaving?" Sierra asked.

Tovi shook his head. "I have no idea."

"Do you think maybe now that we're in all this trouble, they might be interested in seeing you?"

Tovi shook his head again. "I thought maybe if I could apologize, if I could just talk to her and explain things, maybe she could find it in herself to forgive me. I know it's hard for you to understand," Tovi said.

"That's not true," Sierra said, but it was a half-hearted lie. She didn't understand, even if she tried to empathize. "I can understand wanting to be close to your family. I struggle to understand why you would want to have people in your life who abandoned you."

"I wasn't abandoned," Tovi said, snapping at her. "I was the one who left them. I left them with no one to watch out for them. No one but Tian, and he only ever cared about himself."

The guilt crushed her, filling her lungs to the point of drowning. "I'm sorry, Tovi. I really am. If I'd never convinced you to do those bot battles, this never would have happened," Sierra said.

"You have to stop," Tovi said, turning his full attention to her. "I am my own person. I make my own choices. It was my choice to do the bot battles, and I wanted it just as much as you did. You don't get to take my autonomy from me. This was not your fault. We made this choice together. Of course I was going to join you, because it was all I ever wanted. It was the only freedom I had and the only time I felt like I was doing something just for me. I have to carry that guilt and make amends. So please stop. Your guilt is crushing us both."

Sierra was taken aback. His version of events wasn't how it had stuck in her head all these years. To her, she had goaded him, prodded him, been the eternal instigator. All the words her parents and her brother had thrown at her before they'd left her alone on that rock rang in her ears—but he was right.

Sierra had to fight the urge to try and fix this somehow, to say some magic words or to chase someone down. She couldn't fix this.

She couldn't make it right for him, no matter how much she wanted to, so she sat with him, thinking about her sins.

"When we get out of here, we'll go together, one more time, to Ching Shih. See if we can get some kind of answer before they leave."

He nodded, sullen.

"It's hard for me to relate, it's true. Thinking of my parents makes me angry," she said with a rueful laugh. Seventeen years later and she was still mad about it. "I can only think 'fuck them,' but your situation isn't mine. Patini and the kids were real good to you."

"I want the chance to apologize in person," Tovi said. "Even if she doesn't accept it. I didn't know the last time I saw her would be the last time, you know? I didn't memorize her face. I didn't tell her how much I loved her. I didn't say goodbye to the kids."

Sierra's family had packed up and left before she'd hit seventeen, not bothering to take her with them. Family had never been what she'd been born into because that was just a hot mess. These four sentients had been her family for as long as they'd been together, which, in the grand scheme of things, wasn't particularly long, and it might end here, but she was grateful that at least she had this.

They stayed like that for a while, sitting side by side. In the opposite bunk, Cecil was letting Iz weave rows of French braids into his fur, and they were having their own conversation. Sierra hoped this wasn't how their time together would end.

A Ghost From Explosions Past

Hours later, one of the guards came to the door.

"Someone to see you," they said, and the door opened to their cell.

"Anyone good?" Iz asked.

Ching Shih came to the door. She was doing significantly better than she had the last time Tovi had seen her. A leg assist ran up her right hip, stabilizing her as she walked.

"How is it possible to get in this much trouble?" she asked.

"Good question," Cecil said. "I've never been this close to death so many times in my life."

"Look at what you're missing out on," Sierra said.

Ching Shih walked into the room and stared at them with a raised eyebrow. "Station security is giving you three cycles to prove your innocence, and you're being released into my custody. Don't do anything stupid."

Sierra smiled at Ching Shih and fluttered her lashes.

"Are you having a seizure?" Cecil asked.

"No! I'm being alluring."

"It could use some work," Tovi said.

"I don't know, it's working for me," Ching Shih said with a small smile.

You have very strange taste, Pixie said. *But there's someone for everyone.*

I'll sshow them sstrange, Rupert said, his tongue flicking out.

"Come on, we need to set up a meeting with Vandover and get things settled," Ching Shih said, waving at them to follow her.

She didn't need to ask twice. They walked with her out of the station security building. Sierra sent a message to Vandover, requesting a meeting at his earliest possible convenience, though not using exactly those words. It took some negotiation and planning to secure a meeting because Vandover would only meet them in the safety of his complex, a place Ching Shih wasn't enthusiastic about entering.

They were greeted by Kaylo, who stared at them with eerie blue eyes. Not the most promising of greetings.

"You will follow me," she said, turning and then leading them down the hallway past Andy's room and into a large office.

Vandover sat behind a delicate, chrome-framed desk with a blonde faux-wood top leaning back in his chair, his fingers steepled in front of his chest. The back wall depicted a shifting scene of views taken from terrestrial planets, an oddly comforting decor choice for a pirate. The two blue suede chairs facing his desk were left vacant. Ching Shih and her crew were outside talking in low tones, leaving the four of them standing in front of Vandover's desk. Sierra shifted nervously, their shared past hanging between them.

"You were dragged away before I could transfer your credits for the fight," Vandover said and typed on his sleeve, transferring the credit to her sleeve. She stared at her forearm and the credits blinking on the screen.

"This isn't the amount we agreed on, not that I'm complaining," she said.

"I gave you the full player amount and the winner's bonus, exactly what you deserve. What you fail to understand, Sierra, is that I would have agreed to help you without payment."

A lump formed in Sierra's throat. She tried to swallow around it as tears pressed against her eyes. One slipped down her face, and she hurriedly brushed it away. "Thank you," she whispered. Before she could say any more, Ching Shih came in the room with two of her crew, the rest waiting outside Vandover's office.

Sierra took in all the people who were here because they were as close to a family as a group of strays could get. Remembering the biological family that had left her behind, these castaways were so much more. Her fear of abandonment meant she always ran away in anticipation of the inevitable, turning her into the very thing she despised in others. She couldn't make any of them stay, and she didn't want to. They should stay because they wanted to be a part of this adventure.

She decided then to put her cards on the table, and before she could second-guess herself, she acted on her impulse.

"I offered to take the fall for the explosion if we can't bring Ryan in," she said and braced herself.

"What?" Tovi said.

"Come again?" Cecil said.

Iz stared at her. "The fuck?"

"It was stupid, I know. I panicked."

"Why am I not surprised?" Ching Shih said, and Sierra risked a glance in her direction. Instead of being angry, her expression was soft, affectionate, and had a warming effect on her brain.

Tovi stepped in front of Sierra, and she didn't dare stare up into his disappointed face. "Sierra, look at me." She sighed and tilted her head back to stare into his concerned brown eyes. "We made a deal, a long time ago. Do you remember?"

The lump was back in her throat, and more tears slipped out of the corners of her eyes. "We both go down together." Her voice came out as a raspy whisper. "Sometimes, existing is exhausting. It's too much. I thought, if it had to be anyone, it should be me."

He didn't say anything, just wrapped her in his arms, and she rested her head against his chest. She took a shuddering breath, trying to collect herself. After a few moments, she stepped away and wiped her face with the cuff of her shirt.

"I'm sorry, everyone," she said.

"That was incredibly stupid," Vandover said, blunt as ever.

"This is exactly why you can't be trusted to make decisions on your own. It's a goddamn miracle you survived before I met you. My money's on sheer luck. Why do I work with ridiculous humans?" Cecil ranted.

"I often ask myself the same question," Vandover said. They exchanged the knowing glance of the long suffering.

Iz removed their sparkly purple scarf and thwacked it against Sierra's shoulder—repeatedly. "What"—*thwack*—"were"—*thwack*—"you"—*thwack*—"thinking?" Hands on hips, chin thrust out, they glared at Sierra.

"I wasn't thinking clearly," Sierra said, holding her hands out in surrender.

"You owe me, big time. You're not getting off easy." Trust Iz to take their pound of flesh.

"Of course, but I won't be quiet about it."

"That would truly be a miracle," Cecil grumbled.

Iz's glare was undeterred, so Sierra did the only thing she could think of and gave them a hug. They relaxed eventually. "I'm still mad at you," they said, voice muffled against Sierra's shoulder.

"I know," Sierra said. She released Iz and placed her hands on their shoulders. "I'll spend the rest of our time together making it up to you."

"You better," they said, pouting.

Cecil appeared bearish enough to commit violence standing on his back legs, but behind his glower, she could see his concern. She walked into the wall of fur and wrapped her arms around him as best she could, like hugging the hull of a ship. He grabbed her by the sides and she yelped as he lifted her to face height. "You are ridiculous," he said. "You may hug me once we clear our name, together, as a crew."

Sierra placed her hands on either side of his head and kissed him on his cold, wet nose. "That's a bet."

He huffed, blowing her hair away from her face, and set her back down. "We have work to do, and you are always a distraction."

"Love you too, buddy," she said, then turned back to Vandover.

"It appears your friends here are invested in whatever harebrained scheme you've come up with. Mind enlightening me?"

"Right, yes. We need to trap Ryan or I—"

Tovi cleared his throat.

"I mean, *we* are going down for the explosion. On top of that, we need everyone to believe the AIcat we took from an Omnia ship is destroyed. The plan is to stage a fight while Ryan Randolf is here to collect the cat, then destroy a decoy, which we'll get on film, and arrest him. We'll then leak the film so Omnia thinks the cat is dead."

"Ryan Randolf, the district manager for Omnia?"

"You're familiar with him?" Tovi asked.

"I'm more familiar with his sister, who's the district manager for this system. We have a tenuous alliance with Aster Randolf. She benefits from the trade and tourism to the system. Many tourists visit the moon of Denetia, entirely owned and operated by Omnia, and it's Aster's home. Also, we are an easy vehicle to off-load goods and supplies Omnia can't sell on the open market."

"It's safe to say Ryan would take any opportunity to lower his sister's esteem in their father's eyes," Cecil said. "Stirring up conflict in the system only benefits him."

"We can't allow outsiders to attack us without retaliation. It makes us susceptible to future interference from outsiders. However, we don't want to risk our alliance with Aster. This does give us greater bargaining power with her. She will have to pay for his sins. We'll convene a meeting of the Houses once this matter is settled and we have all the facts. Bringing in Ryan *alive* is to our benefit." Vandover glanced at Ching Shih, who shrugged.

"I make no promises, but your concerns are noted," she said, and Vandover sighed.

"We can be ready whenever he arrives."

"Awesome. All that's left is setting up the meeting with Ryan," Sierra said.

Chapter 35

I Trust You to the Moon and Back, But Not with My Snacks

This is such a clusterfuck

What now? I saw net reports on the explosion at Terrana. Your sister must be piiiissed.

That was rather satisfying. She went down In the standings by ten points. Father doesn't want to start beef with the pirates, not when we're so close to securing the End Goal. I think he's hoping they'll ally with us in exchange for mineral rights and trade deals.

He keeps his plans close to his chest. He's rightly worried he'll be double-crossed.

Ryan

He didn't get where he is through charm. I have confirmation that Tovi and his crew have the Alcat. Aster's heard the rumors and is connecting the dots. She's breathing down my neck.

Del

What are you going to do?

Ryan

They've offered to return the Alcat for a price.

Del

Do you trust them?

Ryan

No, I can't assume they haven't learned what the AI knows. It's regrettable, but they'll have to be dealt with. I had hoped we could build an alliance with Tovi, and maybe I still can. I have leverage, and an ace up my sleeve.

Del

Do tell…

Ryan

I wouldn't want to ruin the surprise.

Del

Don't you trust me?

Ryan

Do you trust me?

Del

Point taken.

Chapter 36

Lulu's Lemon

Sierra pulled at a hangnail and chewed on her lip. She had a feeling they were missing something, but she couldn't think of what it was.

"That's very convincing," Sierra said, hovering over Iz's shoulder at their workbench. The room they were working in was Vandover's tinker shop, which was used for projects that were too small and fiddly for the mechanic shops and needed precision tools. The room was lined with workbenches and had tools hanging from the walls, all neatly organized. Iz had swooned at the sight of the well-stocked shop, and they might never leave.

"You're breathing down my neck, Sierra," Iz said, their voice tight.

"Sorry!" She backed up and paced behind their back. "Looks like the real thing, though."

Lulu's doppelganger was standing on the table blinking owlishly at the wall. "There's one problem. I'm concerned the robot is... well... robotic. Lulu, despite her stumbling, moves more fluidly. I don't have the time to make something more elaborate."

I can help.

Sierra jumped. Lulu had recently gotten more comfortable with the rest of the crew and was broadcasting widely. After they'd come up with a plan, Tovi had fetched her from the ship. She was standing in the doorway, her tail whipping around like it had a mind of its own. "How's that, Lu?" Sierra asked.

I can control the robot remotely. I know how a cat moves.

"You can do that?" Iz asked, eyes widening in interest.

I can do lots of things, but I have to be in visual range.

Sierra gave her a side-eye, not believing that for a minute. She knew how much Lulu wanted to be a part of the action. Sierra didn't object; it was Tovi who was scared. Sierra could appreciate Lulu's desire to get out and stretch her legs, so she didn't argue.

"I'm good with that," she said.

"Wait, wait, wait, I heard that," Tovi said, appearing in the doorway.

"You can't coddle her forever. Everyone else is likely to have their compdroids, so she won't stand out among the others," Sierra said. Most people with compdroids took them everywhere, especially into trouble because they could spell the difference between success and defeat.

"What if something happens?" Tovi said, two seconds away from wringing his hands and clutching at imaginary pearls.

"I can promise you that something will eventually happen, just like it does for everyone else," Iz said, coming to her aid.

It's okay, Tovi, I want to help. I know I'm fresh, and you could have returned me to my maker to be destroyed, but you didn't. This is the least I can do for putting you in danger.

Sierra was getting the feeling Lulu was regaining her functionality and memory, though some of it was probably irrevocably damaged.

They'd have to ask her about Cecil's suspicions when they had the time to grapple with the implications.

Tovi's shoulders dropped, a sure sign he'd caved under the collective pressure. "Okay, but stick close by and don't do anything rash."

Lulu pranced around his feet before awkwardly launching herself at him. He'd grown adept at snatching her out of the air and grabbed her. Tovi held her up to his face, and she nuzzled his chin.

"Aw, that's so cute," Iz said.

Tovi grumbled under his breath, but he was failing to hide his smile.

"Do you need any alterations to control the robot?" Iz asked.

Only the receiving frequency. I can take it from there.

Iz sent her the details, and the legs of the robot cat softened at the joints, no longer stiff as rebar, and its body moved naturally, the head ducking to lick a paw, the tail swishing delicately.

Iz nodded in appreciation. "That's fantastic."

It's only marginally impressive, Pixie said, sulking above Iz's head.

"Aw, don't be jealous, Pixie." Iz grabbed Pixie and gave them a bracing hug, that Pixie soaked up by wrapping their pink tentacles around Iz's head.

Tovi was a proud parent and scooped Lulu in his arm like a baby, and she didn't protest, instead purring loudly into his chest. Sierra smiled at them, happy he'd found his own compdroid. She absently stroked at Rupert's scales.

"Shouldn't you be getting ready?" Iz asked, turning in their chair with a pointed look at the door.

Iz wants you to leave. You are being very annoying and distracting, Pixie said, wiggling their tentacles at the door.

Sierra ushered Tovi out the door, not wanting to incur Iz's wrath any more than she already had. "Yes, of course. Leaving now."

The crew was holed up in Vandover's labyrinthine compound that included the amphitheater and mech battle ring, along with a spidering system of hallways, warehouses, workrooms, and who knows what else he had stashed away.

She checked the time on her sleeve and had to concede that, yes, they really should be getting ready. At this rate, she'd surely get lost if she kept wandering the halls. They found their way back to Andy's ready room to get dressed for the rendezvous with Ryan. The only people who knew about Lulu were their crew, Ching Shih, and Vandover, and they wanted to keep it that way. They also wanted as many people as possible to see the decoy AIcat and then see it destroyed to corroborate their story and convince Omnia the cat was no longer a problem.

Sierra knocked at the open door to Andy's room and peeked in. Andy was suiting up in tactical gear, zipping up a black jacket over a white tank top. As far as Sierra knew, she'd never had formal training, but they all had their secret pasts.

"Come on in," Andy said. She sat to put on heavy black boots, tucking in her cinched ankle-length gray cargo pants.

"Hiya, thanks for letting us use your room," Sierra said, entering with Tovi on her heels. Lulu trotted behind him and Tovi held the decoy, setting it down in the middle of the room, where it sniffed around the floor.

"How did you get your hands on an AIcat?" Andy asked, crouching down and holding out her hand for the cat to sniff.

"Found it in a salvage operation. We've become rather attached to him."

"What's his name?" Andy scratched under the decoy's chin and it emitted a metallic purring sound, nowhere near as realistic as Lulu's, but Sierra hoped no one would notice the difference.

Sierra panicked, trying to come up with a name on the fly. "Um... we call him... Sandy," she said. Tovi choked on a laugh and coughed behind her.

"He's cute. I've never been this close to one."

"Fantastic technology," Tovi said as he walked over to a pile of clothes sitting on the couch, and Sierra followed. Cecil had the garment printer make them some basic clothes for the operation. "Did he have to pick all black? It does nothing for my complexion," he said, holding up a black tank top and black cargo pants.

"You forget, he's actually colorblind," Sierra said. "Black was probably the safest choice."

She had a matching outfit, which was fine with her; she was sharp in all black. Cargo pants weren't her first choice, but the pockets were useful. They changed behind the curtain while Andy petted the cat. Lulu was sniffing around the edge of the room, making herself inconspicuous.

Vandover appeared in the door. "We're tracking Ryan. He'll be landing in the hangar within the hour. Best get into place."

Sierra nodded. "Be there in a minute."

Vandover left, and Sierra tested the communication channel they'd set up on a secure line.

"Testing, Cecil and Iz, do you read?"

"Roger, Cecil here. Coming in loud and clear."

"Iz here, confirmed on my end."

"You getting all this, Tovi?"

"Coming in clear," he said.

"Let's do this," Sierra said, then turned to Andy. "Thanks for helping us out. You don't have to do all this. It could be dangerous."

Andy grinned at her. "And pass up the opportunity to whoop Omnia's ass? Not on your life."

"I didn't realize you had dealings with them."

"Who doesn't? They hold a contract on my parents, who are working in a mining operation. It would give me endless pleasure to hit them where it hurts." She cracked her knuckles and shot Sierra a conspiratorial smile.

Sierra felt like a heel; she hadn't known about Andy's situation, though she'd never been particularly forthcoming with her personal life, and Sierra didn't like to pry. "I'm happy to provide this opportunity." She smiled, and Andy grinned back.

Demi materialized in the doorway. "We doing this?" he asked. He was in his usual all-black clothing, with a stunner tucked into a holster; he left the crown behind. Unlike Andy, Sierra wasn't surprised when Demi jumped at the opportunity to flex his boxing skills in a real fight.

Cecil was waiting outside the room. His burly frame was covered in his tactical vest. Sierra thought it was overkill, but Cecil was a planner and didn't like surprises unless he was the one doing the surprising. Between him and Iz, they'd added a number of interesting additions to the vest. When she'd asked about it, they'd been cagey, and she thought it best to leave them to their plotting since they seemed to enjoy it so much. "Iz will be monitoring the situation from a drone and overseeing the operation. They'll be our eyes," Cecil said.

"Awesome, let's do this," Sierra said, anticipation making her antsy. She left the room with determination, Tovi, Cecil, and Andy following behind.

"Wait, we have to walk in slow motion with intense battle music playing, like in the movies," Tovi said. Cecil rolled his eyes when Tovi played a high energy song on his sleeve. Sierra was in front, and she slowed her speed, forcing Cecil and Andy to slow their pace as well. Sierra shot a smirk to Tovi, who'd assumed the role, decoy cat tucked under his arm, and they moved in dramatic slow motion. Lulu, tagging along behind, joined in; she seemed delighted. Demi walked at a turtle's pace with exaggerated arm motions, lifting a hand for a slow-motion high-five with Tovi.

A drone the size of Lulu sped past overhead, camera pointed in their direction.

"You look ridiculous," Iz said on their shared line. *"I love it. And now we have it in the databanks."*

Tovi waved at the camera, breaking the spell. Sierra laughed and went back to walking at a regular pace. She was glad for the mood booster. The reprieve didn't last long as they walked into the cargo bay and past the point of no return. Her heart was racing and her overstimulated brain was running through all the scenarios.

The hangar was as big as the docking bay they'd parked in. It was the same place they'd stored Archy after the fight, and the mech was stored on the back wall since they hadn't had a chance to return it to the ship after their arrest. Vandover had acquired more hangar space since she'd been here last, nearly doubling his storage capacity. The hangar was fifty meters long and ten meters wide before the platform dropped off into space. A few ships were docked off the end of the platform, framed by thick metal doors to keep the air inside the station. When the doors opened, a plasma barrier would take over the job of keeping them from the vacuum of space.

Vandover was standing near the end of the platform in the loading zone, a clear area big enough for a class 3 ship to land, then load and unload. Four of his crew positioned themselves nonchalantly around their captain. Sierra walked up next to him, arms folded across her chest, her hair pulled out of her face, and Rupert wound around her neck.

"I like the upgrades," Sierra said.

"It's turned into a damn parking lot, but the income is good," he said and gestured to the rows of storage.

"I bet operators appreciate the efficiency of parking their rigs and mechs in the same facility," Sierra said, noting the two stories of storage behind her followed by a line of mechs secured and covered in tarps against the back wall. Archy was near the access doors, tarp off and a little worse for wear. She winced, knowing they had a lot of work ahead of them if they made it through this.

"We offer lodging too."

"Even better. You've cornered the market. All the matches I've watched out of Terrana were from your arena." She wanted to say something more than banal small talk, tell him she was sorry, but now wasn't the time.

The slamming of the giant access doors leading out to the prep area and arena felt like the jail door closing on them. Ching Shih and her crew were waiting outside those doors for the verbal cue to break in and arrest Ryan, "accidentally" destroying the cat decoy in the process.

Vandover's crew was relaxed, but they were armed to the teeth and there was no denying their sharp gaze was also assessing her crew. More of his people were strategically placed around the room. Vandover's wolf pack was pacing, and various compdroids milled around, though most stayed near if not on their companions. A stereotypical parrot squawked on one man's shoulder, throwing obscene language at a monkey sitting at a woman's feet.

Vandover checked his sleeve. "He's nearly here. Open the doors," he said to a woman at his elbow wearing grey fatigues. She nodded and punched some buttons on her sleeve. A sheen of plasma flickered on and the doors slid open. In the distance, Sierra saw a speck of a ship headed their way.

"He brought the Jag 356," Tovi said. Sierra couldn't make out the ship, but Tovi had keen eyesight.

"Is that a problem?" Vandover asked.

"It's a pleasure model, not equipped for major fire power. It's a mech that doubles as a small vessel. If he brought backup, it won't be in the ship's small bridge."

"That's good news," Vandover said.

Sierra resisted the urge to pace like the wolves—something she very much wanted to do—or chew her nails, or mumble to herself. The ship crept closer, slowing as it approached the asteroid. She hadn't seen this new model in action like Tovi had, but she'd seen the PR videos and read up about it on the Mech Today forums. Ryan was a vain creature; it wasn't a surprise he'd want to flex his wealth.

Tovi had the decoy in his arms and Lulu was skulking around the edges of the room. Cecil stood off to one side, standing on his back legs and sniffing the air.

Can I bite him? Rupert asked, head lifted in interest at the incoming ship as it passed incrementally through the plasma barrier.

"I won't say no," Sierra said. "But I'd prefer you stick with me, as your bite isn't venomous."

I'm once again requessting to have that overssight remediated.

Sierra had considered that option, but seeing as he often threatened to bite the crew several times a day, she'd vetoed the decision.

"Hush now, he's landing."

The ship, gleaming white in the harsh overhead lights, was streamlined, if a bit bulky in the center. Transmorphing ships had to sacrifice some style for practicality, but this new iteration was surprisingly compact, much to her chagrin. She didn't like handing anything to Ryan, and certainly not Omnia, but what could she do when the company employed the best engineers to create their designs?

The ship landed on the platform, five meters from Sierra, landing gear clunking on the metal surface. Everyone was tense. Sierra reminded herself to breathe or risk passing out. A painfully loud hiss echoed through the cavernous space as the ship's door opened. It folded out and down, providing a sleek set of stairs. In the doorway, Sierra saw the outline of Ryan—dramatically framed by light pouring out from the ship's interior—before he descended the stairs.

Chapter 37

Tian One On

Tovi didn't know how he should feel seeing Ryan again. Anger was an appropriate emotion, but mostly he felt sad at what could have been and how things had turned out. He thought that somewhere inside the man was a decent human being twisted into something vainglorious by his upbringing and situation in life. Despite everything, Tovi didn't wish the man harm, only justice, and if Ryan could be convinced to leave Omnia and their bonkers infighting, he could be a different person.

Framed in light, Ryan was as handsome as the day Tovi had met him, but knowing him for who he really was had lowered Ryan in his estimation. Tovi held the decoy cat, its puffy ears tickling his exposed arms. He felt bad delivering the poor creature to its fate, even though it had no consciousness; it was a pitiable waste nonetheless.

He tried his hardest not to search for Lulu, who had thought it best to make herself scarce. They'd gone over the plan and now was the time to execute. Ryan paused in the door—for dramatic effect, no doubt—then sauntered down the short flight of stairs and stood taking in his reception committee.

"I hadn't expected such a hostile welcome," he said, eyes roaming over the dozen people clustered together in front of him.

"After you tried to blow us up, we thought it best to take precautions," Sierra said.

"I had nothing to do with such an unfortunate incident, but I hope you've learned it's important to be prompt."

Sierra scoffed. "You're ridiculous. It doesn't matter. We're open to letting bygones be bygones. We have the cat you wanted. Once we have our credits in hand, our business together will be finished. And speaking of being timely, I'd be quick about it. News travels fast around here, and Ching Shih is the sort to hold a grudge."

Sierra was going off script. That hadn't been part of their plan, but applying pressure wasn't a bad thing.

Ryan turned up his nose at her, and his gaze fixed on Tovi and the cat. He walked forward, stopping a foot in front of him, and Tovi had to fight the urge to step back. Ryan leaned forward and spoke in low tones.

"It is a pity. I had hoped we could renew our *friendship*. We had such fun together."

"You don't have to keep doing this," Tovi said. "Working for your father and covering up the company's mistakes. Don't you want more, or at least something different? You don't have to play the game."

Ryan's self-satisfied smirk dipped at his words. "Nothing is that easy."

"It could be," Tovi said with as much earnest sincerity as he could muster, and Ryan's expression took on a pitying expression. He raised a hand and placed it on the side of Tovi's face.

"I will miss your innocence. It's what keeps drawing me back to you. I want to live in the universe you seem to think is possible."

"But it is, it could be," Tovi pleaded, hoping he could make a connection with him and save him from himself.

"I'm so very sorry," he said, and Tovi could tell that he meant it.

"Sorry for what?"

A loud bang resounded through the bay and shrapnel went flying. Tovi ducked lost his balance, and sprawled on the ground, instinctively protecting the cat from the blast. Had Ching Shih forced through the doors early? They should have been waiting for the signal, one they hadn't been given yet.

By the time he gathered his wits, he saw a gaping hole in the ceiling and sentients dropping down the twenty feet on ropes. The next thing he registered was the cat being forcibly removed from his grip. He scrabbled to his feet to face Ryan, who was clutching the now flailing decoy in one arm and aiming a pistol at Tovi with the other.

"I told you I was sorry. For this, and for what comes next."

Gunfire was ricocheting around Tovi as Vandover's crew fought off their new assailants. Tovi tensed, expecting Ryan to shoot him dead on the spot. Instead, he backed away until his heels hit the steps of his ship, then turned and fled into it, the door shutting behind him with a soft hiss barely audible amongst the cacophony. Tovi was vaguely aware of the metal doors closing and trapping Ryan inside.

Tovi turned away to address the most pressing threat, pulling out his stunner guns and searching the chaos for who had dropped in on them unexpectedly. He froze when his gaze alighted on a dozen Praxians engaging in a heated battle with his crew and Vandover's—his Praxians. He spotted Tian immediately, a wild grin on his red face, guns firing off shots Tovi hoped to Hades were nonlethal. He was rooted to the spot, too shocked to move, until Tian's gaze fixed on his and he raised his guns.

Someone hurdled into Tovi, sending him tumbling, and the shot missed.

"Get your shit together, soldier," Ching Shih said in a no-nonsense voice, and just like that, his brain clicked into place and his body moved on autopilot. He rolled to the side, jumped to his feet, and ran directly at Tian, only ten feet away. All the hatred and anger he'd felt over the years coalesced in him and he threw himself at Tian, knocking him to the ground.

Tian had been expecting a firefight, not a wrestling match, and was unprepared for Tovi pummeling his fists into Tian's face.

"You motherfucking, ass-licking bag of dicks," Tovi screamed mindlessly. He might have beaten the Praxian to death with his bare hands had someone not come to Tian's aid. Another Praxian, one Tovi didn't recognize, hauled him off Tian. Tovi threw a wild fist and caught the Praxian in the gut, doubling him over. It was only then he noticed how young the Praxian was. They were all young, besides Tian, who was climbing to unsteady feet.

Tovi rushed him again, this time taking Tian by the throat. "You will tell me what the fuck you're doing here, protecting Omnia's interest and subjecting these children to violence."

Tian laughed and spat blood on Tovi's face. "It's as I always said. We will receive our reward on Earth—eternal life."

"Is that what that asshole promised you and you believed him?"

"You were always naïve. We aren't the only ones who covet Earth as it was."

A sharp pain sliced along Tovi's forearm and he dropped Tian. In his rage, he'd missed the knife Tian had sheathed on his person. Tian, like the coward he was, scurried away from the fight. He whistled high and long, and the other Praxians closed in, protecting their leader. Tovi searched for his crew. Cecil was rampaging through the group, his vest now armed with protruding spikes two inches long and taking bits of flesh as he barreled through the Praxians.

Sierra was back-to-back with Ching Shih as two Praxians circled them. Their stunners must have been out of juice because Sierra had her wicked new blade out, and Ching Shih, with blood oozing from her forehead, had a sword that must have been hidden in the walking stick she'd taken to using since the explosion.

While Praxians were naturally stronger and faster than humans, these Praxians weren't as well-trained as the pirate crew, making them evenly matched. All around Tovi, he saw his own conclave fighting his crew. He'd never had even the smallest inkling that they were capable of this. Looking closely, he realized he recognized some of them. They'd been children when he'd been taken away, and now they were pawns in other people's games. One ran at him, a knife held awkwardly in her hand.

He knew her too. "Teela, stop!" To his surprise, she stumbled to a stop, her face shocked at hearing her name. "It's me, Tovi. You remember?"

"You... You left us," she said, her voice laced with accusation.

"I didn't. I was taken away by Omnia. I would never have left you."

She shook her head, as if she was trying to clear out a bad memory. "No, Omnia is helping us. They promised us our share of the Earth."

"They told you what you wanted to hear. Omnia doesn't care about you, and neither does Tian."

She took a swipe at him with her knife, and he easily dodged. He wouldn't hurt her, he couldn't. "Liar!" she screamed.

She was full of rage, so much like his own at her age. He knew he wouldn't be able to reach her. He did the only thing he could and tried to plant a seed of doubt. "I know how you're feeling, and I'm sorry I wasn't there for you, I truly am. I've been searching the universe for you."

"I know the traps you tried to set to ensnare us. Tian told me." She swiped again, tearing his shirt and skimming his belly with the blade. She was stunned at her own capacity for violence and the blood coating his shirt.

He stumbled back. "No matter what you do, I won't hurt you. We are conclave; we are family. Ask Patini. I will always be here if you need me."

Teela backed away from him, the knife trembling in her hand. Behind her, Vandover pointed a gun at her back.

"No!" Tovi yelled, and Vandover jerked, the shot going wide. "Let her go. Don't hurt her."

Her eyes were wild, the knife held out in front of her and swinging erratically. She backed up into the larger group fighting the pirates. He turned to run after them when Iz's voice came through the shared line. *"Shit, Ryan's transformed the ship into a mech."*

Tovi whirled around to see Ryan's ship, now the same sleek and beautiful mech he'd strode out of all those months ago. Tovi no longer thought of it as a pleasure craft as it strode forward, kicking at Vandover's crew, who scrambled out of the way or were tossed across the room, crashing into the stacks.

Chapter 38

When One Door Closes

"I very much regret covering for that Praxian bastard," Ching Shih said at Sierra's back.

"I bet," she said. The Praxians circling them had more confidence than skill, which Sierra had to admit was her usual approach. Sierra really wanted to have her mech at this moment, but lucky for her, Ching Shih made up for her lack of skill in spades. She wielded the sword with grace and kept their attackers at bay.

"They're stalling," Ching Shih said.

Sierra brandished her knife as a Praxian lunged at her, then skittered out of range. "Probably to give Ryan time to transform."

"It's working," Ching Shih said.

Sierra saw Cecil bowl over two Praxians who still had their stunners, which weren't turned up high enough to take down the bear. Iz was sitting on his back, wielding a large stun gun. Cecil charged toward Sierra, scattering the two who'd been circling them, Iz hitting them with their stunner.

This was Sierra's chance to get away. She could operate Archy to intercept Ryan and give everyone a chance to run away and regroup. With the optics damaged, she'd have to operate the mech with the hatch open, leaving her without chest protection, exposing her fully and pretty much guaranteeing she'd be injured or killed. Sierra turned toward Archy, then back at the chaos.

She took in all the sentients fighting for the memory of the ones they'd lost, for the ones they loved, and to protect their community. Some were even fighting for her. Vandover was restraining an unconscious Praxian while yelling to his crew, who were pushing the larger group of Praxians back the way they came, climbing the ropes into the ceiling. She'd left these people behind in uncertainty, too afraid to face the truth—that they cared for her—and she'd left to avoid the very thing she'd done to them.

Instead of running for the mech and certain death, something she'd have done without question mere days before, she let out a loud whistle, calling for everyone to fall back and regroup. Ryan's goal was to escape. With the doors closed, he was trapped inside for the time being. Everyone moved to the back of the warehouse, the wolves snapping at the Praxians.

Cecil came sliding to a halt, Iz hanging on for dear life. Tovi backed up into the group, firing his stunner at anyone in his line of sight. Vandover, Ching Shih, Demi, and Andy joined the group.

"He's going to go for the doors. It's the only way out of the base," Vandover said, blood oozing down his left arm from a nasty gash.

"The Jag has a laser gun, but only in the mech form. It is truly a luxury ship. Most of the tech is for protection, not offensive action while in ship mode. He'll be able to breach the hull, and once he's outside, he'll transform back into a ship and be out of here."

"I'm raising the plasma barrier, in case he shoots through the doors," Vandover said.

It was a good thing, because Ryan raised the arm of the mech and pointed it at the doors and fired a shot. Sierra winced, but the doors held, denting outward but not destroyed.

"The doors weren't built to keep people in, but they will withstand cannon fire from a class I Interceptor."

"Really?" Iz said.

"It would be a sad day if a single mech could compromise the entire station."

"He's a fox in a hen house," Ching Shih said. "He'll figure that out soon."

"We have to move this outside to reduce the casualties," Sierra said.

"But you'll lose any advantage. If he has the time to transform back into a ship, he'll leave, and station security will convict you of his crimes," Andy said.

Sierra's instinct was to take on the responsibility, martyr herself to the outcome, but it wasn't her decision alone.

Sierra turned to Tovi, his expression hard, tinged with sadness and an aura of despair, and he nodded. His conclave was suffering the greatest casualties; she didn't doubt he wanted Ryan as far away from them as possible. Iz was sitting on Cecil's shoulders, just behind the fluffed hair around his head. Their expression was grave, and Cecil's eyes were piercing as he panted from the exertion. They both nodded to her.

"We're willing to take that chance," Sierra said.

"Station security is en route as well," Vandover said. "We just need to keep him occupied long enough for them to take control of the situation."

"What mechs are operational in here?" Tovi asked. "Archy is blind."

Andy raised her hand. "Mine is good to go. It's also fitted with guns."

Sierra quirked an eyebrow at that.

"I do protection jobs when I'm not fighting," she explained with a shrug.

"Good to know," Iz said.

"I fixed the optics on mine. It can fight, but it has some damage," Demi said.

"That's all we have at the moment," Vandover said.

"It will have to do," Sierra said. "When we open the doors, Demi and Andy will follow Ryan and keep him engaged until backup arrives."

"Let's get moving," Tovi said, his anxiety pouring off him in waves as stunner and ballistic fire echoed off the walls.

Andy ran for her mech, restrained against the back wall, but Demi lagged behind, and for a moment, Sierra thought he was going to run back into the station to safety, and she wouldn't have blamed him. Instead, he turned to Sierra and her crew. "Take my mech," he said, and Sierra was startled. No one let an outsider pilot their mech.

"Are you sure?" Sierra asked.

"I don't have experience piloting a mech in zero-g, and this is your quarry. You should have the honors."

She realized then that he didn't see her as an outsider, but family. A complicated family she'd run away from, only to end up back where she started with a chance to do things right this time around.

"Thank you," she said and held out her hand. He took it and shook with a firm grip and then left to ready his mech.

"Tovi, you've worked mechs in zero-g," Sierra said. "I think you should pilot the mech."

Tovi nodded. There was an irony that Sierra didn't want to overly agonize over. His space walks had all been at the behest of Omnia, and now he would use that skill against them. It felt right.

Tovi followed Demi to get ready for the fight ahead.

"I'm going to see if Vandover has a ship we can borrow," Cecil said. "I want to keep an eye on events outside and communicate with station security." Vandover was ten paces away, talking to his crew.

"Good idea," Iz said. "We can be Tovi's strategist."

Cecil headed to Vandover, and Sierra was going to join them when she saw Ching Shih standing to her right. She was far enough away to give them space to talk in private but close enough to show her interest.

"I'll be right there," she said to Cecil's furry butt, and Iz waved in acknowledgment, along for the ride until they decided to disembark.

Ching Shih stood near the back wall, sword resting on her shoulder, every ounce the pirate—her hair sticking to the sweat on her face and a jaunty tilt to her hip—but her expression was uncertain.

Sierra was more certain than she'd ever been, and before Ching Shih could say a word, Sierra backed her up against the wall, making her drop the sword so it pointed to the ground. Sierra looked into Ching Shih's eyes as she caressed either side of her face, their lips close enough to share each other's breath. When Ching Shih whispered a soft "Please," Sierra kissed her. Ching Shih raised her free hand and cupped the back of Sierra's neck to deepen the kiss.

She tasted of salt, like a glimmering ocean, and smelled like fresh turned earth and grass. Sierra broke away, her smile flirtatious, enjoying being the one to make Ching Shih flush for once.

"I won't run away this time," Sierra said, taking in Ching Shih's shocked expression and reddened cheeks.

"I'll hold you to it," Ching Shih said softly.

Sierra wiped her moist lips with the back of her hand, and Ching Shih followed the movement with her eyes. "See you soon."

Chapter 39

Giving it All Before the Fall

Tovi's body was taut, vibrating with every blast and shot fired, knowing his conclave was being whittled down by an absolute maniac and he couldn't stop the bloodshed.

Demi was busy prepping his mech. Tovi needed to focus on the fight to come, not the one raging in the warehouse between his Praxians and the highly trained crews from Vandover's and Ching Shih's camps.

It seemed to take an inordinate amount of time to ready the mech, and Tovi was about to explode into a million frustrated pieces. He felt pressure against his leg and glanced down at Lulu. Tovi could kick himself for losing track of her in the fray. He picked her up and checked her for injuries.

I'm intact, do not worry, Lulu said. *There are many alternate versions of you, and they aren't playing nice.*

"No, they aren't. I'm glad you're okay."

He didn't notice Ching Shih until he nearly jumped out of his skin when she placed a hand on his shoulder. Lulu jumped out of his arms and circled the two of them.

"Christ on a cracker, you scared me," he said.

"Apologies. You were bouncing around like a pinball," Ching Shih said. "I wanted to ask you, those Praxians, they're just babies, right?" Her question surprised Tovi.

"You can tell that? Most people think we all look alike."

"I won't admit to being less prejudiced. Their body language gives them away: nervous, trigger happy, wasting charges on their firearm. It's like someone handed them a gun and said shoot."

"I'm fairly certain that's exactly what happened."

Ching Shih grimaced. "Was this reunion everything you imagined?"

"And more," he deadpanned, then dropped his head into his hands. "How did it come to this? If I'd just been there, I could have stopped him."

"Are you serious?" she said, eyebrow cocked. "You think someone like that would have let you hang around? Sentients who can brainwash that many kids would have seen you as a threat and gotten rid of you."

Tovi paused and thought back to his time on Zhital. There had been a handful of times Tian had tried to get him jobs off world or far enough away to require lodging, and he had always refused. When he and Sierra had started the fire, the police drones had arrived within minutes. Too fast for a part of town no one cared about and wasn't constantly monitored. He'd taken Tian's camera that day. Had the bastard framed them? Now that he saw it with some distance, from Ching Shih's perspective, it was obvious. Tian was always going to find a way to remove Tovi's influence from the conclave. It was probably why all his attempts at communication had been thwarted, why no one came to see him when he'd been arrested.

All the anger he'd directed at himself found a new home in Tian.

"If you're lucky, we'll have some of them in custody and away from his influence," she said.

"Then they'll be arrested. I'm not sure that's much better on a pirate asteroid."

"They will be returned to their home planet. That's the protocol for nonhuman sentients considered minors by their home world."

"That's very… considerate actually."

"Some bridges are built on the bones of our enemies, and others float on a stream of goodwill. It's a balancing act. Anyway, you and I both know the Praxian government is sniffing around. Based on what this group is up to in the present situation, Prax is rightly concerned."

"It's gone way beyond a harmless, eccentric cult," Tovi said, nodding.

"Evidently. I'll leave you to it. Happy maiming."

Tovi turned to her. "I now fully comprehend why Sierra likes you."

Ching Shih shot him a grin, and was she blushing?

Demi slid down the rails of the ladder built into the side of the mech.

"He's all yours. Goes by Thelonious, Theo for short."

The kid living in his brain wanted to jump up and down and ask if Demi had an interest in Earth's antiquity, but now was not the time.

"Thank you. I don't know how to repay you."

"Bring Ryan in, that's how you can thank me. There's some damage to the leg, but that shouldn't matter much once you're in space. Here you go." Demi handed him a pair of black sparkly gloves. Tovi grinned and slid them up his arms.

"Take good care of him. I'll see you shortly," Demi said, then jogged away to join Vandover and his crew.

Tovi climbed up the mech and jumped into the cabin, moving his hands to command the hatch closed. Before it closed, Lulu jumped in.

"Lulu! What are you doing?"

I have to be near the robot cat to control it. Once it's outside, I'll lose connection. Ryan could send a communication alerting Omnia that he has the wrong cat. Also, I can interface with the mech.

Why did she have to be so convincing? She'd proven herself capable, and he'd take any help he could get at this stage.

"Okay, we'll do this together."

Tovi commanded the mech away from its parked position as Lulu settled on his lap. Every mech had its idiosyncrasies and variations. Thelonious had an upgraded swinging chair Tovi had long coveted and a minifridge under the console he'd love to rummage through, but that was for another time. He directed the mech to walk forward, taking the limited time he had to adjust to the mech.

Through the external mic, Tovi heard Ryan speaking, and he turned up the volume.

"I will kill everyone in here, then make my way through the station, mowing everyone down, if you don't let me out."

He couldn't see Ryan from where he stood behind the stacks, which loomed higher than the mechs, so he moved around the outskirts until he came to the end of the stack. If he moved forward, Ryan would have a clear view of Theo.

Tovi ducked the mech down so he could see through the openings in the stack. Between piles of mech parts and shipping crates, Tovi saw Ryan had the Jag facing his audience, arm—and therefore guns—pointed at a group of terrified and shocked Praxians.

"I'm in place. Correction, Theo is in place," Tovi said.

Ryan sent out a wild shot, felling two Praxians and sending the rest running. Tian was nowhere to be found.

Tovi had to fight the urge to run at the Jag. Theo wasn't armed. He'd be throwing himself and the mech away for nothing but rage.

"Okay." Vandover's resonating voice filled the warehouse. "We're opening the doors. The platform will extend to the plasma wall."

There was a *thunk*, then whirring as the platform in front of Tovi slid out to meet the plasma wall. The Jag could have flown the distance, but Theo didn't have that kind of propulsion; this ruse was for him.

"Andy is in place," Sierra said over their dedicated line. *"Vandover is letting us borrow one of his freighters so we can keep an eye on everything and send you any important information."*

"Don't do anything stupid in an unarmed ship," Tovi said.

"No promises," Iz replied.

The doors whirred open, like the yawning of a mouth. Ryan wasted no time, taking two steps then jumping out into space through the plasma barrier. Tovi was fast behind him. He ran at an angle to gain momentum and get him closer to Ryan. He jumped off the platform and pressed his arms to his sides to turn Theo into a missile, throttling at the Jag.

He impacted the Jag, jarring it and hopefully Ryan, then wrapped his arms around the Jag, trapping one arm.

Tovi didn't see Andy, but he felt when Ryan fired his guns. He switched through varying visual modes until he had a better view. Andy was flying toward them. Her mech had powerful propulsion in the feet and was spiraling to avoid missiles Ryan fired. She had more space warfare technique than Tovi expected, and that gave him a surge of confidence. They might get through this alive.

What he was mostly worried about was the AIassist in Ryan's mech. He didn't need to be a good pilot—the mech would do much of the work for him.

Ryan's mech pulled at his trapped arm, and when it wouldn't give, the boosters in the Jag's feet fired, hurdling the both of them away from Andy. The Jag spun, and the centrifugal force was pulling Tovi away and making him dizzy.

"Andy is on your tail," Sierra said.

Tovi held on for dear life. As long as Ryan couldn't transform, they stood a chance.

He didn't know how Ryan had hooked up with Tian. He didn't know if it was Ryan's or Tian's idea to exploit the vulnerable young Praxians who needed something or someone to hold on to, or to hold on to them. Some part of himself that sounded like Sierra asked him why it mattered. They were both bastards, but Tovi didn't believe that. There had been something good left in Ryan that was eroding in front of him in real time.

The Ryan he'd met months ago wouldn't have believed himself capable of shooting his own team, teenagers at that. He'd been pushed here by outside forces and his own ambition. Tovi held on tight because he believed Ryan was worth saving. Ryan should be forced to reconcile with his decisions and those he harmed.

Tovi's vision tunneled and he felt his grip slacking.

"Tovi, Andy is right on you. Let go in ten seconds to give her a clean shot," Sierra said.

"Don't kill him. Tell her we need him alive," Tovi said, voice strained.

"I'll tell her," Sierra said.

I have calculated the optimal timing. I will signal when to let go, Lulu said.

He tried not to rush out of sheer desperation, waiting for Lulu's cue.

Now, she said.

He released his grip. He went careening to the side and into space. He directed the mech to right itself, and ion engines around its body activated to steady the mech. He was upside down to the action when the world stopped spinning. Andy's mech was firing on Ryan's, and the mech was taking the hits with a shield it must have unfolded from its arm.

Tovi engaged the ion engines and pulled the blade from Theo's back. He restrained his speed, needing accuracy. While Ryan was blocking the rocket-powered grenades that were swiftly eating through his shield, Tovi came up from behind. The AIassist capability would see Tovi coming and warn Ryan, so he had to move quick but with precision. He directed the mech to speed him forward. He lifted the sword overhead and swung down, aiming for the mech's right shoulder. It struck true, the blade hitting at the joint. It sliced halfway through the armature before the oppositional force halted the blade's progress.

Theo reverberated with the hit. A more jarring hit followed from a slurry of armor-piercing rounds released by Ryan's operational left arm.

"Station security is nearly here," Sierra said, voice steady as a rock.

Tovi didn't know what they would do when they arrived, and he made a last-ditch attempt. He hailed Ryan on an open frequency, and after a tense moment, his connection was accepted.

"Ryan, station security is moments away. You aren't going to make it out of here. You need to give yourself up."

"I am not a coward," Ryan said.

"No one is saying you are," Tovi responded.

"I can fix this."

"You can; just turn yourself in."

Their connection stuttered and was severed.

"Lulu, is there anything you can do with the decoy?"

The decoy is very basic. The most I could do is distract him. Incoming ballistics. Get out of range.

"What? From where?" He wouldn't be able to get out of the way in time. Lulu gave him the trajectory and he did the only thing he could. Tovi fired the engines to move Theo behind the Jag.

Chapter 40

Lost Loves, Found Families

There's no noise in space. The enduring silence is a mocking reminder that the universe is inured to suffering. In moments of sheer rage, we raise our voices in defiance, only for them to be siphoned from our lungs. Behind the Jag, Tovi watched the Jag jerk from the impact of a ballistic shot to the shoulder, throwing its arm back and shrapnel fountaining into space. It jerked again and again and again, spraying gleaming white pieces of casing away from the Jag.

"Stop!" Tovi screamed into the public line. He could only watch as the mech turned into a rag doll.

When the mech stopped moving erratically and was dead in the water, Tovi tentatively reached out an arm and latched on to the loose housing of the Jag's shoulder. He tugged it toward him so he could see the damage to the front of the mech.

The chest cavity, meant to hold the pilot, was obliterated. Tovi turned away. If he looked too closely, he knew what he would find—pieces of Ryan, frozen like shattered china.

"Tovi, are you okay?" Sierra asked.

Tovi couldn't respond at first. Lulu jumped on his lap and bumped her head on his chest. He placed a trembling hand on her back.

"Tovi, please respond," Sierra said, desperation edging her voice.

"I'm here, we're fine. Who fired on him?"

"It was Andy."

"Why? He was losing. We could have captured him."

"He was firing on you."

Tovi shook his head, but she was right. Ryan had been ready to do whatever it took to get out of the situation, including killing him and his conclave. He'd done what he could, and while it hadn't ended the way he'd wanted, it had to be enough.

"What's Ryan's status?" Sierra asked.

"The chest cavity is destroyed. There's no way he lived." What went unsaid was the decoy also wouldn't have survived the onslaught.

"Roger, come back to the station. Station security needs to do an investigation and retrieve the body."

The body. There was something jarring about going from a person with a name, and therefore an identity, to just a body. Nothing left but the component parts of what made a sentient.

Tovi took his time. While the space outside the mech was a vacuum, he focused on what he could hear inside: Lulu's purring rumble, the low hum of the equipment, the slight creak of the rotating chair, the scuffing of his shoes on the floor of the cab.

Once he was out of the mech, there would be only chaos. Questions, concerns, allegations. Without Ryan to take responsibility for the bombing, they were still in hot water. There was a mountain of evidence for his attack on Vandover's warehouse, but would that be enough?

On autopilot, Tovi moved the mech through the air barrier. The full weight of the mech and his body regained gravity, and he felt every inch of himself being brought back to reality. Station security was swarming through the warehouse, restraining Praxians or giving aid to the injured. A stretcher covered in a white sheet, like a ghostly mountain range in the shape of a body, sat motionless, a dusky red hand peeking out of the sheet. Had Tovi, years ago, given this body a piggyback ride or pulled them along the slick wood floors on a magic carpet ride?

He couldn't face it. All he wanted to know was if Tian was among the captured.

He stopped the mech when station security ordered him out of it, and he complied. They checked him and the mech before moving on. Sierra, Cecil, and Iz came running over.

Sierra saw his face and slowed as she reached him.

"Tian?" he asked.

Sierra shook her head. "No sign of him. When Ryan left, some of the Praxians retreated the way they'd come. Station security is running them down." She put her hand on Tovi's forearm. "I'm not going to ask if you're okay. I know you're not. What do you need?"

Tovi let out a breath. "It's okay. I did what I could." He took in the scene. His people arrested or dead, pirates injured or killed, prowling Nhethians pacing the stacks, licking bloodied muzzles and paws, and station security, all in white, cleaning up the mess. "Ryan chose his own fate. Tian is responsible for their deaths," he said, his gaze taking in the carnage. At the back of the warehouse, by the wide-open doors, a hooded figure walked toward them, limping and crouched.

Fear lanced through Tovi. Was Tian back to finish the job, or was it some other zealot? Tovi broke away from the group, walking swiftly across the space, not wanting to alarm anyone into an unnecessary firefight.

As he approached, he could see the sentient couldn't put their full weight on their left leg and their head was bowed. They made no move to attack as Tovi slowed and grasped their shoulders. The black hood fell back and he was confronted with a face he hadn't seen in nearly two decades.

"Patini," he whispered like a prayer.

Her face was the same, with the addition of deeper lines around her eyes and forehead. The burn mark was there, bracketing her stormy gray eyes. A nasty bruise was forming on her cheek and swelling.

She stared up at him and her gaze softened as she raised a shaky hand to his cheek.

"Tovi," she said with a tight but warm smile before dropping her hand. "I have come to make amends. It was in my power to stop this madness, and I didn't. I wish to do what I can now."

Within seconds, they were swarmed by station security.

"Stay away from her," Tovi said, holding her waning body against him protectively, wanting more than anything to offer her the comfort he craved for himself. She smelled like he remembered, like warm bread from the oven, and his heart convulsed for her.

She laid a hand on his shoulder. "It's okay, Tovi. I'm ready. I should have done something back when it would have made a difference for you. I can't turn back time, but I can do this."

Tovi reluctantly let station security pull her from his arms. "She needs medical attention," he said. He watched, helpless, as she was placed in an emergency vehicle, her face a blur as she was whisked away.

Sierra took him by the hand and led him—in a daze—back to their ship.

In the aftermath of the attack, they were questioned again by station security, who seemed content to blame the whole business on

Ryan and Omnia, thanks to the testimony of Vandover and Ching Shih. The trial was highly publicized. It took place in an auditorium, the judge gleaming from the neck down in a crisp suit that would shatter if bent. Reporters and interested spectators filled the auditorium, murmuring, swapping gossip, and betting on anything they could.

The crew was called to give testimony. It had been intimidating to sit in the middle of the semicircle, the eyes of some of the most powerful sentients in the system staring gravely in his direction. Tovi's voice shook as he retold his version of events, leaving out the real Lulu. After they'd all testified, Tovi stayed as the trial dragged on, wanting to be there when Patini gave evidence. Andy was short and to the point, recounting the battle from her perspective—her decision to fire on the badly wounded Jag when it targeted Theo with ballistic rounds.

It was painful to relive that moment.

Tovi sat and listened to everything, wanting to understand and find some kind of peace. His crew joined him in the crowded seats.

Patini was led in, hands restrained in front of her. She was walking better than before. As he listened to her testimony, he learned that she'd jumped from a second-story window after being locked inside their rented rooms. She'd injured her leg and hit her face on a step, then struggled her way to the warehouse, hoping to stop the impending violence, but she'd been too late. The judge decided to have Patini and the captured Praxians remanded to the Praxian authorities. They would be tried on their home planet under Praxian law. The Praxian Tovi had fought in the alley was there to take them into custody. Teela wasn't among the dead or the captured.

As they walked Patini down the aisle, her head bent in shame, Tovi stood and pushed his way through the row to meet her. The guards tensed, ready for a fight. He held his hands up to show he meant no violence.

"I just want to walk with her," Tovi said. He recognized one of the guards with a jaw like unforgiving stone—he was one of Ching Shih's crew. He scanned Tovi up and down, then nodded. Tovi walked in step with her, slow and measured.

Patini grabbed his hand with one of her own. Bony fingers that haunted his dreams held him tight. "I let you down all those years ago. Tian told me you'd run away. One day, I found the video, the one you'd recorded of Sierra on the day you disappeared. I confronted him. He said he'd turned you in because you were trying to break up the conclave. By then, I was concerned about the children. I couldn't leave them to his sole influence. I wasn't strong enough to save them. I should have left long ago, when the love was gone and you were in danger."

"It's okay," Tovi said. "I understand. You did what you had to."

"And so did you," she said with a sad smile that carried the weight of her guilt.

They walked out of the auditorium and were escorted to the cells. As they approached the clear cubicle, Patini stopped to place a hand on his cheek. He took in this moment, the closest he would ever get to having her in his life again. It could never be like it had been, when he was a defiant teenager and she a lonely caregiver, demoted in Tian's hierarchy of importance. That time was gone.

The warmth suffusing from her rough hand to the matching roughness of his face was like bathing in the sun after years of rain. He would treasure it forever.

Chapter 41

Making Amends

Sierra left Tovi to have his moment with Patini. The session decided on a short break, and Sierra tracked down Vandover, who'd left the auditorium out of a side door. Sierra followed him into a room that said it was a temporary office for visiting legal counsel. Vandover sat in a simple high-backed chair behind a utilitarian gunmetal desk. Vandover set his tablet down when Sierra entered the office and closed the door behind her. She stayed standing, leaning against the closed door.

"Are you here to berate me?" Vandover asked.

"For what?" Sierra asked, taken aback.

"I don't know, Sierra, but you seem to hold me responsible for something that displeases you."

"That's not it," Sierra said. She took a moment to compose herself. She wanted nothing more than to rely on sarcasm and deflection, but she knew she couldn't take the easy way out now. Not if she hoped to get what she needed.

I'm here with you, Rupert said, moving along her shoulders, and she held her hand up to him so he could twist between her fingers, something she found comforting. She took one of the chairs in front of the desk, the stress making her nauseous.

"I'm sorry," she said with more force than she intended, like a waterfall escaping her mouth.

"You're sorry," he said, clearly not believing her.

"Yes, I'm sorry for leaving the way I did and never thanking you for what you did for me. You were kind to me when no one else was. I am thankful you helped me pay off my debt, and you protected me, and I repaid you by leaving without a word." She hung her head in shame.

"Why *did* you do that?"

She bit her lip and let herself be honest with him and herself. "I was afraid that I wouldn't be able to leave. That I'd see you and all you'd done for me, and I would feel compelled to stay. I would always be paying you a debt; we would never be standing on the same ground. So, I just left, like a coward. I want you to know that it wasn't anything you did, and I am grateful."

He took it all in, his hands steepled in front of his face. Sierra told herself she didn't care, she'd said what she needed to say, and he could take it or leave it. The part of her that was a child desperately seeking his approval felt different, and it curled inside her, bracing for impact.

"I can't say I wasn't disappointed when you left, and that I didn't miss you. I am glad you found your own life. I'd always known there was no way to contain you, and I didn't want to. It was why I took on your contract. Targon saw you expanding and wanted to suppress you, stamp out your energy. I couldn't let that happen."

"Why didn't you tell me this before?" she asked, her chest aching and tears pressing against her eyes. She'd always felt like a rogue wave, crashing through everything and everyone. She'd never suspected anyone saw her as an asset, except her crew, and even then, she hadn't always been certain.

He spread his hands wide, in a searching gesture. "You left, and I'm not the best at articulating my thoughts. You never got in touch, and I figured you would suspect some ulterior motive if I contacted you out of the blue."

He was right; she would have assumed the worst of him. She slumped back in the chair. "I thought for sure you wouldn't want to see me."

"You were wrong," he said, a small smile softening the blow. "I didn't take you on just because you were the best mechanic on the asteroid, though that was a nice bonus. You probably don't know that I'd been in your situation once. That's how I ended up here."

Sierra blinked and shook her head. She'd had no idea.

"I'd been caught doing some unscrupulous work and accumulated a considerable debt. The man I call my father took me on, groomed me for his position. He wasn't a kind man, but I stayed on because I wanted to make this house more than it was."

Something tickled at the back of Sierra's mind, a nagging itch of a memory. "Your father, he died in a shuttle accident, didn't he?"

Vandover drummed his fingers on the desk. "According to the official records," he said.

Sierra smiled. "You old so and so, mad props to you."

A smile plowed through his stoic demeanor, and a shared conspiratorial moment passed between them. Everything made more sense now, like a window thrown open in a darkened room.

"I'd appreciate it if you'd keep this between us. I have a reputation to maintain," he said.

"Of course," she said, holding out a hand, and he clasped it, his long, warm fingers wrapping around her smaller hand. She relished the moment, feeling like she'd taken off several heavy, burdensome coats.

He came around the desk and leaned against it, folding his arms.

Sierra saw the warmth in his eyes, and she felt a thousand feet tall. She matched his stance. She leaned into his side until he wrapped an arm around her shoulder in a half hug, and her heart grew soft and pliable.

Sierra returned to the atrium, where Tovi was conversing in a loose circle with Iz and Cecil.

"What a day," she said.

"You're telling me," Tovi said with a tired smile. She pulled him into a hug.

Sierra stepped away and gazed up into his kind brown eyes. "I want to say, if you feel like you need to be with them or if you want to go back to Prax, I won't keep you here."

He quirked an eyebrow at her. "Sierra, if that's what I wanted, that's what I'd be doing. I'm not going anywhere."

Sierra felt a weight lift off her chest. She looked to Cecil and Iz. Iz smiled at her and Cecil nodded.

"With Ching Shih paying off our debt, we have to decide what to do next. At some point, I need to collect my things from Lana's apartment," Iz said.

Sierra, feeling especially affectionate, pulled them into a hug. "You okay, Glitter in Chief?"

"Umph, I can't breathe," they said. "I'm okay. I'll be okay anyway."

Sierra let them go. "Did you want to head back to Octto Station?"

"We don't need to leave immediately. Plus, I've been checking out the job listings, and there's some good opportunities on Terrana," Cecil said.

"Really?" Sierra said. She'd been torn about what to do with Ching Shih. They'd had their moments, and she wanted more of them, but she didn't want to uproot everyone so she could see where all this would lead.

Cecil's gaze focused on something behind her and nodded. Sierra turned and saw Ching Shih leaning against the wall, arms crossed and a mischievous smile warming her face.

Sierra glanced back to Cecil, then stepped forward to wrap her arms around his neck. "Thanks, buddy," she said. He huffed in her ear, and she laughed before letting him go. She turned to Ching Shih and mirrored her stance against the wall, inches in front of her.

"Funny meeting you here," Ching Shih said. "Are you leaving?" Sierra saw the tension in the lines between her eyes. Sierra lifted her hand and smoothed her fingers against the crease.

"We've decided to stick around. I told you, I'm not running away."

Ching Shih took her hand in her own and interlaced their fingers. Her hand was warm and dry, sending a chill up Sierra's arm. She smiled a silly grin she couldn't hide, and Ching Shih mirrored her.

Chapter 42

Salvaging the Wreck

In darkness, space expanded around her. Sierra floated in the nothingness inside Archy, newly repaired and out on their first job since the utter chaos of the last few weeks. Station security commissioned them to salvage the wreck of Ryan's Jag. They had a particular reason to want the job.

She took a deep breath before getting back to the salvage. Luckily, station security had removed Ryan's body and returned it to his family, or Sierra would have passed on the job. She volunteered for the spacewalk to secure the largest pieces of the Jag for tow.

The rest of the crew was in the *Who Wants to Know*, using the drones to siphon the small pieces of the mechs and munitions before the debris damaged ships coming and going from the asteroid.

"We're all clear," Sierra said over the comm, signaling to the crew that she'd found no evidence of the decoy large enough to bring suspicion on the crew. The net and news stations had repeatedly played the now infamous video of Ryan taking the decoy cat from Tovi and retreating to the Jag, which was now fanned out in a thousand pieces.

Anon-1

> **Mission complete**

Del

> God he was such an idiot, but I'll miss him. It was like watching a shipwreck in slow motion. Was it fast?

Anon-1

> Yes, I did not make him suffer.

Del

> Good, it is a small mercy. You have a new directive: shadow the crew of the *Who Wants to Know*.

"What are you looking at?" Tovi asked.

Andy hit a button to close the screen. "Checking my messages."

"Anything good?" he asked.

"Nothing of note."

Acknowledgements

I want to thank my husband. This book has been a long time coming, and you supported me through years of anxiety and the endless hours of writing and editing. Your belief in me carried me when I couldn't carry myself. To my parents, who always asked about my stories, and bought me books on craft, thank you for being my biggest fans. I couldn't have asked for more supportive, loving parents. To my brother: You're the worst, stay classy.

Bishop, we have discussed the joy of found families, and how every black cat needs their golden retriever. Thanks for being my golden retriever, or sea lion, or whatever, to my black cat. I want to thank my Italian tutor and friend, Lulu, whose name I stole. Piper, you'll never read this, because you're a dog, but I love you.

Without my writing partner, Mari, none of this would have been possible. Thank you for coming on this journey with me and continuing to see it through. To Angela, you showed me how to slow down and enjoy the ride. Our trips together make me feel human when I'm burnt out with little left to give. A big thank you to my mentor and friend Michael La Ronn for your encouragement and advice. Our friendship has enriched my life.

Ava and Clif, thanks for being the best book club and getting me through the pandemic.

To Jese, you were my first friend in Colorado and you taught me things I can't unlearn, like it was Flavor Aid and not Kool-Aid consumed by the doomed Jonestown members. More importantly, I learned about queer culture and history, and you were there for me during some of my hardest moments—I'm not crying, you're crying.

Finding a cover artist to bring my idea to life took some time, but it was worth all the digging when I found Sonata. We exchanged enough emails to throw a wrench in the servers. Thank you for your patience and beautiful artistry. Find her incredible work @sonatacreates on all the socials.

A number of editors helped with this project, and I'm incredibly grateful. Thank you to Chris Barcellona for his developmental edits that led to a complete overhaul of the pacing and order of events, but whose enthusiasm for my characters gave me hope that others would love them as much as I do. A big thank you to Samantha Kassé for being a fantastic sensitivity reader and making my book all the better. And to Beth at BZ Hercules, thanks for the line edits and proofing, and for putting up with me.

Broadly, I want to thank the teachers who encouraged my writing no matter how insufferable I was in high-school. Don't worry, I'm still insufferable. This one is for all the teachers out there; you do make a difference.

To all the queer kids who grew up isolated, look at you killing it out here. Take a twirl, eat a cookie. You deserve it.

About the author

Rae Ryan writes science fiction that lets readers escape into stories where people are still the worst, but they aren't discriminated against based on their identity. Life has enough of that, thank you. When she's not walking her silly dog, Piper, on the Colorado Front Range, she's collecting more hobbies than is strictly necessary, drinking an unadvisable amount of coffee, and making dad jokes.

Find more stories by Rae Ryan and follow her on her socials for free giveaways and book deals!
https://linktr.ee/backaswords